TIED UP IN Riches

Author's Note

This story was never supposed to be written, and yet, it's found its way into your hands–for that, I'll forever be grateful.

It wasn't a thought in my mind when I created Marcus as a side character in book one of the Finding Home series. I had no idea that when I wrote Brooke into the end of the same book she'd become the love of Marcus' life.

But here we are, at the beginning of their love story that's somewhat unconventional. The basics are the same–attraction, secret feelings, waking up one day and realizing you don't know how you lived so many days without them. Along the journey, there is light use of blindfolds and restraints—think of it like vanilla with sprinkles. This is *not* a dom/sub story, there is no torture or degradation, and everything is consensual. The kink is simply character preference and a tool used to guide an arc centered on feelings around control.

All of that said, *Tied Up In Riches* is the fourth and final book of the *Finding Home* series. For the best experience (and to avoid spoilers), the series should be read in order. However, this book can be read as a standalone.

I hope you fall in love with these two the way I have, and above all else, I hope this story reminds you to constantly find your own glimmers while romanticizing everyday life.

Keep your eyes on the stars,
Tisa

To the guy whose friends
always get the girl.

Chapter One
Marcus

"Why does my coffee look like art?" My worn black mug with the "MC" logo from my first business venture warms my hands, steam seeping through an intricate leaf design in the foam as I hide a smirk.

"Because." Maci, my best friend's fiancée's smile lights her face like a kid who washed a classic car with dish soap, thinking they were being helpful.

"What did you do?" I raise an eyebrow over the edge of my mug, taking a sip. Goddamn, that's good. She would rather drink bacon grease than choke this down, but somehow she knows how to make the best damn cup. It also helps that I only drink Global Delights.

"Nothing. I made your coffee like I do every morning." She turns away from where my hip leans against the kitchen counter to rinse out the French press. She's not wrong. Every day since she moved into my house with Dean, my coffee is religiously ready at 6 a.m. sharp, unless I'm away on business. It's like she thinks I'd kick her out if it wasn't. They are welcome to stay as long as they'd like. I'll be bummed when they move out eventually and not because I'll be responsible for my own caffeine intake.

Becoming a millionaire was a result of my hard work and diligence. The fact that I keep it a secret is my choice, but my mentor instilled the belief that it's better that way. There's so much more to having money than how you make and spend your income. Money makes people deranged–lie, cheat, steal, manipulate, create misconceptions. They're less likely to do those things when they don't know about your wealth. Though, when you only trust a handful of people and don't have time for more than a coffee date here or there, it can get lonely. Dean and Maci keep my house feeling like a home.

I mentally toggle through the items on my to-do list. I have five minutes to spare, and it won't take Maci that long to crack and give me the real reason my usual jet fuel looks more like art.

Taking a slow slip of my latte, Maci senses my patience. She spins on her heel, reaching for the black towel looped around the oven handle beside me. Wearing one of Dean's T-shirts and sleep shorts–an addition compared to the first time she spent the night here–she scans my outfit. It's only six a.m., but I've already worked out and am ready for the day. Thank fuck I don't have an investment meeting. One of my favorite parts of being my own boss is that I set the dress code, so gray jeans and black V-neck are appropriate for most days.

"Are you going to Jameson's today?" she asks.

She knows I go to the bar almost every day that I'm home. I cock an eyebrow at her.

"What?" She scrunches her nose with a mocking smile. "Maybe you have big plans. Maybe a date?" Her voice raises with hopefulness at her last question.

I stare blankly.

"Or maybe you were planning to take the day off for once!"

"Maci."

"Fiiiiine," she fake whines. "You know my friend Brooke who lives in Thailand?"

Of course I do. I've listened to every story about Maci's solo travel trip a hundred times. I give her a pointed look, leaning back against the counter and taking another sip of the magic liquid that will get me through the hours of paperwork that I'm not looking forward to today.

"She's visiting in a few weeks, the beginning of May." Maci bites the corner of her lip.

I chuckle. "This is your house too. You don't have to ask if your friends can stay."

"I know . . . It's just . . . Since you and Dean converted the guest room into a gym, there's no place for her. So, she'll have to sleep on the couch. Or Dean and I can take the couch. It's not a big deal. I just want to make sure you're good with it."

"It's fine. She can have my room. I'll sleep on the couch in my office."

"Are you sure? I don't want to mess up your routi–"

"Positive." There are very few people I would do anything for, and somewhere along the way, my best friend's future wife became one of them.

"I'll do all the dishes. And your laundry."

With a slight shake of my head, I take a bigger gulp of my coffee now that it's cooled. "You already do that." Since she and Dean returned from Spain, where they worked for six months, they are taking some time to figure out what they want to do next. In the meantime, she's made it her full-time job to take care of my house, despite my insistence that it's unnecessary. Maci living here is like having the world's best roommate–unless that roommate was also a girlfriend.

Fuck, I miss sex.

"You'll love her. She's great."

"I'm sure she is."

Her eyes study me. "You know, it's unfair that when I tie my hair back in a bun I look like Miss Trunchbull, and you look like," she waves her hand toward my neatly tied back hair, "that."

I chuckle, my gaze shifting to the side as Dean joins us in only basketball shorts. His blond hair is messy and pushed to the side, sleepiness emanating from every part of him, including the smile he sends his fiancée. "The only similarity you have to Miss Trunchbull is the reliability of your car, and on a good day, your ability to restrain yourself around chocolate." He pulls Maci to him by his grip on the small of her back, her arms immediately falling to his chest.

"It's only to save room for all the tacos. OH. And the pizza. You know what we haven't had in forever?" Maci's eyes light up like she's talking about picking up an airline ticket for her next adventure instead of whatever simple food she's about to ask for.

"I'm not driving two and a half hours to get Dump City Dumplings." Dean chuckles, squeezing Maci closer. How the hell did he get dumplings from *that*? My chest tightens as I try to push away the jealousy of their connection. I'm starting to think I won't find it. It's getting more difficult to convince myself that I'll find someone I'm compatible with after each failed coffee date.

"But," Maci pouts.

"I have a long day," I cut in. "I won't be home until late, but if you don't mind doing the shopping, I'll send you a list and cook tonight."

Maci's eyes widen like an hour of my time and Asian food is equivalent to Chef Morimoto stopping by. I don't cook very often these days, and I know she and Dean tend to resort to tacos almost every night, but I still have to eat, and it would be a nice treat compared to my late night DoorDash orders. "Really?!"

"Yes." I chuckle.

She releases Dean, and I have just enough time to set my nearly empty coffee mug on the counter before she flings her arms around me. "Thanks, Marcus. Do you want to switch places with Dean? I could use someone to satisfy my cravings."

"Hey!" Dean chuckles. "I seem to recall a lot of satisfaction last night."

I lick my lips with a smirk as Maci pulls away to grin at her fiancé. "How about you just spread the word to all your single friends," I tell her.

"Trust me, I try. How you are still single is beyond me." She hums.

"Not many people can handle so much of a good thing," I tease, moving past them to put my mug in the sink. I'd probably have to let someone in longer, to see the extent of what I have to offer, to know if that were true. "Thanks for the coffee," I address Maci before turning to Dean. "Later, man." I slug his shoulder on my way to the front door.

Chapter Two
Brooke

"Hiiiiiii," I squeal, my backpack falling to the cement walkway outside of the baggage claim at Eugene airport. Throwing my arms around Maci's neck, I hug my friend, my blonde waves flying over her shoulder. It's been a year since we met on her trip to Thailand.

"I'm so happy you're here!" she says, squeezing me tight. Tears float along my waterline. Besides my dad and my childhood best friend, Cam, no one is ever unconditionally happy to see me. Shaking partly from excitement and partly from the chill of the early May weather in the Pacific Northwest, I cling to the warmth of her sweatshirt. *Or maybe just the warmth of her.*

Maci drops her arms, grabbing the handle of my suitcase containing everything I own as I reach for my backpack. Taking me in, she laughs. "Are you freezing?"

My favorite pair of loose tan shorts and white and navy striped ribbed tank were perfect for the 30°C it was when I left Phuket yesterday. "This is not exactly appropriate for the 15° it is in Oregon."

Maci searches the depth of her mind for a math equation. I guess I better get my brain back on track with America–the country that feels so superior that they calculate everything differently than the rest of the world. I try to calculate it for myself.

"I think it's like 60°F." She chuckles, reading my mind.

"Yeah, it's too cold." I laugh. "It's been a while since I've needed a jacket." Three years to be exact. Outside of a few instances, I haven't worn one since I left Connecticut and moved to Thailand. Maci pops the trunk of the Range Rover she picked me up in. This thing is huge. I slide my suitcase against the charcoal carpet of the tailgate, unzip it and pull out my plum zip-up hoodie–the only piece of clothing I kept from my life before Thailand.

Tugging my arms through the sleeves, I slide onto the passenger seat. "Did you upgrade your car?" I ask Maci as she flicks on the blinker and looks over her shoulder. This car doesn't seem like *her* at all.

She pulls out of the loading zone lane. "No. Dean dropped mine off to get new tires before he left on a boys' camping trip. They took his truck, so I borrowed Marcus' car. Plus, I thought it would be a nice change from Tuk Tuks." I already miss Thailand, despite my main mode of transportation being a motorized cart that is so small your head hits the ceiling and knees jam into your boobs.

"Did you forget to tell me Marcus is rich?"

She shoots me a look before paying attention to the road again. "No. Don't do that. I know where your head is going, and I can confirm he's not part of some fancy country club."

"Hmm."

She glances at me with a sly smile. "His mom was a bus driver and his dad was a crossing guard. I think that's how they met."

I need to find a way to stop prematurely jumping to conclusions. It's hard when I've been proven right about rich people so many times. "Sounds sweet. It's nice of him to let me stay at his house."

"He's great. He's easily my favorite friend of Dean's. They've known each other forever. He said you can have his room too."

"Oh, no. I don't want to take over his space."

"He'll be fine. He's not home a lot, and when he is, he doesn't sleep much anyway."

I don't bother fighting her. A bed sounds like . . . not an economy seat on a cheap airline for fifteen hours. "Thanks for letting me visit this week. I really need some time to reacclimate to the US before I have to deal with my mother." That will take enough adjustment. I also need to figure out what's next for me. The owner of the restaurant I worked at in Thailand for the past three years was selling his business. That was enough to convince me it was time for a new adventure, but I don't have a plan past that.

"You can stay as long as you want. I'm so happy you're here. I can't wait for you to meet the girls tonight." Since the guys are out of town for a camping trip, Maci invited her best friends over for a girls' night. Pizza Rolls, Cheez-Its and the three types of Girl Scout cookies I had Maci buy and freeze–all things that were nearly impossible to get overseas.

Twenty minutes later, we've pulled into a gravel driveway and Maci has given me a quick tour of the house before leaving me to settle in.

Flicking on the light, I scan my temporary room. I'm comfortable having strangers in my house. It happened so many times in Thailand. Most people were just passing through or stayed over after a night out on the town. Maci is the only one who stayed long enough at my apartment that she moved into a permanent place in my life. Although, I feel like she would have anyway.

But being in a stranger's house? After three years of living alone, it's far out of my comfort zone. This room is bigger than my entire studio. An unsettledness hollows my stomach like when I first arrived in Phuket and every street was unfamiliar. Though, I like how simple it is. There's a deep brown rustic bed frame with dark olive green bedding against the center of the back wall. To the right is a door that opens to a bathroom. To the left is a bookshelf that matches the bed frame. My fingers bump across the spines of the books sitting at eye level. They're all self-growth books. Success. Business. Mindset. A lot of books about mindset. I haven't read any, but that's not surprising considering I only read romance. I wonder if he's a one genre kind of person too or if he ever strays into fiction. Either way, a man who reads is hot. Reading and maturity are paired together at the top of my *qualities I want in a man* wish list.

There's one sleek black picture frame with a photo of a family at the lake. Picking up the frame, I take a closer look at the guy. Black swim shorts hang on his hips, showing off deeply ingrained abs and a massive tattoo of a koi fish swimming upstream from his waistline to the armpit of his lightly tanned skin. Damn, everything about his body is impressive. I wonder if that's a recent picture. I hope so because that man is hot. Excuse me while I sleep in his bed, naked in his sheets.

I let the fantasy play out in my head. Marcus comes home late at night, forgetting he has a house guest and climbs in bed with me, not disappointed at all by the surprise.

Damn, it's been so long since I've gotten laid that I'm imagining scenarios with a stranger who could be an asshole for all I know. Who am I kidding, though? I would never sleep with someone I don't have a connection with. Not anymore. I haven't focused much on sex in years. No reason to think about it now.

Still, my chest constricts, nerves pulling on my heartbeat until it's erratic. Why am I so on edge today? Maybe because I didn't sleep at all on the plane.

I unlock my phone. Oh. Probably the seventeen missed calls from my mother wanting to plan my trip back home to Connecticut. By plan, I mean her setting me up on dates with men she deems worthy–aka men with pockets deeper than their personalities.

Sighing, I fall backward onto my bed for the next week, my blonde hair splaying across the comforter. Wow. It could easily trap me like those foam pits I jumped into during gymnastics class as a kid. I might not even bother moving from this spot until it's time to go. Maybe then I'll feel rested enough to visit my mother. Although, I doubt it. Three years searching for peace in a different country wasn't enough. Thank god Dad will be there too. Seeing him is *almost* enough to balance out the negative.

Opening my meditation app, I set the timer for five minutes. Setting my phone on the mattress next to me, the sounds of a light breeze with ocean water lapping on a shore softly crackle out of the speaker. I close my eyes, instantly transported back to Thailand and overcome by a wave of longing. Taking a deep breath, I focus on my inhale. Hold for four seconds. Exhale slowly. Hold. Repeat. Repeat. Repeat.

I continue until a soft chime indicates the end of the timer, desperate to cling to *Thai Brooke*, to the me I love to be–not the one that exists physically or mentally near my mother.

Chapter Three
Brooke

"Samoas are superior. They are the perfect blend of sweet and savory," Avery says from where she sits on the floor in her matching cheetah pajama set. She sets her morning coffee on the living room table, and the plastic container crinkles as she pulls a cookie from it.

"But Shortbreads go with everything. And feel much more appropriate for breakfast. It's basically like having scones." I wish I had tea to go with these, but I'm uncomfortable digging around Marcus' house when I haven't even met him yet.

"No way. Thin Mints are hands down the best," Maci argues, tucking her hair behind her ear. "You can't beat a frozen Thin Mint or ones blended into ice cream." Her eyes light up as she shoves a whole chocolate cookie into her mouth.

"I bet that's Troy's favorite," Lexy contributes, her blonde messy bun flopping as she chuckles. "I mean, that man would eat mint chip ice cream for breakfast every day if I let him."

"I still can't believe you've never had Girl Scout cookies before." I shake my head in disbelief.

"That's what happens when you have a loser mom." She shrugs, unbothered as her hand hovers over the three boxes, deciding which flavor to eat next.

"Oh, hey! I have one of those too," Avery jokes, her straight brown hair nearly identical to Maci's.

"Also in that club." My phone skips across the glass coffee table as it lights up with a call. "Speak of the fucking devil." I groan.

I've been avoiding her long enough. I swear she'll somehow find out where I am and show up–although she never visited Thailand once in the past three years. "Ugh. I should take this." The three girls sitting around the table in their pajamas finish their cookies in silence as I pick up my phone. "Hello, Mother."

"You could sound a little more excited to speak with me."

I take a deep, calming breath, channeling *Thai Brooke* energy. "I'm sorry, Mom. I'm not fully awake yet. How are you?"

"Awake? It's nearly midnight there." Her snark implies many judgments she has about what that could possibly mean.

Shit. Oh well. Might as well get it over with. "I'm in Oregon. Visiting a friend."

"Excuse me?" She scoffs. "You haven't seen me in three years. Home should have been the priority."

"It hasn't been home in a long time," I mutter, more to myself.

"What did you say?"

"You could have visited me."

"With what money, Brooke? You think I absorbed richness from all the people I work for at the club?"

"I would have paid for your ticket if you wanted to make the trip." I sigh, pushing back the anger.

"This is why you should have married Beau. Money wouldn't have been an issue. Lack of it is the source of all arguments, Brooke–arguments that could be prevented if you had stuck with the plan."

"Beau is a dick."

"Watch your language, young lady. Beau is a nice man. A successful, wealthy, nice man. He would have taken care of you–of us."

My chances of winning this argument are next to nothing. Shy of moving back to Thailand again, the only solution I have is an attempt at a topic change. "How's work been?" It's the only thing she ever does, so it's really my only option.

"Don't change the subject. Beau just got out of a relationship." My body instantly itches like I'm wearing a wool sweater at the idea of getting back together with my ex. "Now is the perfect time to come home. It's fate. There's an event next weekend at the club. I'll get you an invite. He would love to see you."

I highly doubt that.

"I won't be there next weekend." I glance at Maci. I was only supposed to stay a week. I haven't gotten my ticket to Connecticut yet, but I intended to leave on Thursday. She doesn't seem bothered by my abrupt change in plans.

"Yes. You will. I told all the ladies at the club about your homecoming. Do not make me look like a liar. Beau's mother will be so disappointed in you."

"I don't care about Martha. She's as awful as her son," I spit.

"Take that back." The loud shriek of her voice pierces my inner ear. I yank my phone away from my face. "You will not speak with that tone or words of disrespect for the people who have done so much for you."

I want her to clarify what they've done for me, but my and my mother's definitions of positive and negative actions are not in alignment. It'll be a waste of breath for both of us. "I have to go, Mom. I'll let you know when I book my flight."

Without giving her the chance to respond, I hang up. My phone buzzes in my hand immediately. I stare down at the black screen, *Mom* lighting up in white.

"What did she say?" Maci's soft voice trickles into my awareness. I had forgotten where I was for a moment.

"I'm sorry. I don't have to stay here. I can find somewhere else to go. I just can't go home. I thought I was ready, but–" a sob cracks my voice. Maci wraps her arm around my shoulder, pulling me to her. "Money is more important than happiness to her," I mumble into her T-shirt. "I hate it."

"I know," she whispers. "You can stay here as long as you need."

"If Marcus says no for some reason, you can stay in our guest room," Lexy adds.

"Or mine. I have a baby who wakes up at 5 a.m. like his life depends on it, but you're more than welcome to crash with us."

All the offers only make me cry harder. I met two of these three girls less than twelve hours ago, and they already care about me more than my own mother.

"It'll be okay. Shhh," Maci hums against my hair.

A click comes from down the hallway, deep laughter filling the air. I sit, clearing the tears from my eyes to see two men enter the living room.

They halt in their tracks, taking in the scene, then awkwardly glancing at each other. I look back at Maci who seems to be having a silent conversation with Dean as she sits cross-legged on the living room floor next to me. I run the back of my thumbs under each eye again as I stand. "Hi. Sorry. Don't mind me. My mom is a mosquito. She sucks the life right out of me." I fake a smile, walking around the couch to introduce myself.

"Brooke. You must be Dean." I reach my hand out to the blond in front of me. He's wearing basketball shorts and a T-shirt, the sleeves tight around his biceps. Nice work, Maci. He leans in for a hug instead.

"Nice to finally meet you, Brooke," he says before pulling back. "Thanks for taking care of my girl." I knew she'd choose Dean before I ever met him. And the energy he gives off only helps confirm she made the right choice for her.

"She'd do the same for me." I glance back at my friend appreciatively before turning to Marcus.

"Marcus, I'm assuming?"

"That's me." He accepts my handshake, and I scan his body. His dark sweats cinch mid-calf. He *definitely* doesn't skip leg day. His white shirt perfectly highlights every muscle in his upper body. Looks like he takes advantage of the home gym Maci showed me on the tour yesterday. My gaze jumps from his stormy blue eyes to his dark hair, tied neatly into a messy bun at the back of his head. It should be a sin for any man to look that good, especially after spending two days in the woods.

"Thanks for letting me stay here. And for sharing your bed." Oh shit. Did that come out wrong? Or is it only wrong in my head because of where my mind just went?

"No problem. A friend of Maci's is a friend of mine." Thank God he can't sense my pulse quicken under my skin and his warm gaze. I think I'm sweating. Jesus, what has gotten into me? You'd think I'd been living in a convent with the way my body heats at the mere thought of sex.

"Well, we are going to unpack and shower," Dean says. "So, continue your," he glances around me to look at the table, "very important meal to start the day." He chuckles.

As quickly as they came, they leave. My gaze lingers on Marcus, and a weird pit in my stomach forms when he doesn't spare a glance back.

"Well, on that note, I think I need a cold shower and some yoga so the next time those two see me, they believe I'm not a complete psycho."

The other three stand, all making a similar statement about how I'm not a psycho, and pick up the now empty cookie boxes.

"I need to get home to Canaan anyway," Avery says.

"And I need to wake my fiancé up with sex. I have no idea how long I can milk this engagement high, but I plan to make the most of it." Lexy grins. She got engaged a few weeks ago, and it's evident that my experience was not the same as hers.

We finish our goodbyes, and Maci wanders away to find her own fiancé. Heading down the hallway, I wonder if Marcus will be in his room, but I enter anyway. Scanning the space, I don't see him, so I close the door behind me. Digging through my suitcase, I pull out my elephant pants. I shed my pajamas and slide on the baggy, light-weight purple fabric covered in elephants and cinched at my ankles, finding a sports bra and an oversized white T-shirt in my bag to pair with them.

Making my way to Marcus' home gym, I sit cross-legged on the empty mat space in the corner. I open my meditation app, tapping to play the self-guided music softly. My hands rest on my knees as I close my eyes and take a deep breath. In. One. Two. Three. Four. Out. One. Two. Three. Four.

At least ten minutes have passed because at some point I'm conscious of the fact that my music has stopped, but I continue with my breathing. With clearing my mind. With searching for the peace that will help me accept my mom might never love me the way I wish she would–the way that my dad does.

I miss Thailand. All of that seemed more accessible there.

The door creaks, and my eyes fly open, my head spinning toward the sound.

"Hey." I scramble to my feet. "I'm sorry, do you need to workout? I can leave."

Marcus chuckles. "You're good. I thought maybe you could use some hot tea."

I glance at the mug full of steaming liquid in his hand, torn. "Oh, umm. That's sweet. Thank you . . ."

"But?" he asks, still standing in the doorway.

"But, umm, I really can't stand tea from a bag anymore."

A smirk flashes across his face, but then he hides it. Taking a few steps toward me, he holds out the mug.

Feeling like an ass, I take it from him, letting it warm my hands and move to sit on the weight bench next to me. "Thank you," I whisper, taking a small sip. What the . . . Without pulling back all the way, I stare into the amber liquid. I look at Marcus. His hands are shoved into the pockets of his joggers as he observes me.

"Is it alright? I made it how I was taught."

"Taugh–This is Thai Tea. Like *real* Thai Tea."

"Yes." He leans against his leg press machine.

I take another sip, my eyelids fluttering closed as I take a deep inhale and let the perfectly spiced tea soothe my soul. It's exactly what I need right now. I return my gaze to his. "Have you been to Thailand?"

"Yes." He scans the bottom half of my body and quirks a brow. "Have you?"

Glancing down, I chuckle. "My pants?"

There's an amused glimmer in his eyes, but he doesn't respond.

"I know, I know. Elephant pants are only a tourist thing. But have you *tried* them? They are like sitting inside a cloud."

"I'll take your word for it."

"Don't tell the natives, okay?" I fight back a smile. "I won't be welcome back."

"Your secrets are safe with me. If you need any-thing else during your stay, let me know." His words, his stance–they're guarded and professional. I wonder what reveals the other side of him. I wonder what *Thai Marcus* is like.

"Thank you," I say as he turns to leave, wondering if he knows he handed me so much more than tea.

Chapter Four
Brooke

"The vibe in here is great, huh?" Maci asks as we simultaneously slide onto the black leather stools at the wooden bar top in leggings and T-shirts. Even though we ran two miles to get here, I'm hardly sweaty. The lack of humidity is a godsend. I retie my high ponytail as I swivel for a 360 view. An orange glow from the ceiling reflects off the alcohol bottles lining the shelves in front of us. I love the checkered wood flooring and the orange and yellow retro canvases on the wall in the billiards section of the bar off to the right.

"I love it. Have they made a lot of changes? Or is this what it looked like when they bought it?"

"Most of it is the same. Except for the flooring. You should have seen it before. It was this ugly green and brown carpet."

"Carpet? In a college bar?" I chuckle. "Sounds disgusting."

"Oh, it was." I look up to see a light brown ponytail bouncing with laughter as the bartender approaches us.

"Hey, Jess," Maci greets her.

"Hey, babe. Troy ordered that Sweet Cheeks wine you love. We just got it in."

"Oooh, yay!" Maci does a happy dance in her seat. I love seeing how much more vibrant she is now that she's confident about the direction of her life. "Are you good with wine? You'll love it." I nod. "Two glasses, please!"

It still feels early, but we're on a walking tour of downtown Eugene, so why not wine? Jess sets the glasses down in front of us before helping the only other customer. I know it's only 4 p.m., but it's dead here. "Do they do well?"

Maci chuckles. "Don't be fooled by the lack of crowd right now. I don't know the exact numbers, but Marcus and Troy definitely know what they're doing."

"Troy is Lexy's fiancé, right?" I take a sip of my wine. Damn, this rosé is good.

"Yeah." She grins. "Long story short . . . I went on a date with Troy senior year of college. Then he ghosted me and ended up running away to California. While I was living there, Lexy and I ran into him. A few months later, they connected and fell in love. You know, with a bunch of drama first, though." I join in on her chuckle. Always drama when you're in your early twenties. "Anyway, Troy's uncle owned this bar. He wanted to sell it and made Troy an offer. Troy knew he couldn't make it happen on his own, so he teamed up with Marcus. He and Lexy moved here shortly after I got back from Thailand, and here we are!" She takes a sip of her wine.

"At least I'm not the only one who likes to run away from my problems."

"There would be a shorter list of everyone *not* in that club." She laughs.

"Seems like it worked out, though."

"It really did. I'm so happy with everything."

Looking into my glass, I smile. "Such a difference from you crying on my couch, having no idea what to do with your life." Maci was on a self-discovery solo trip when we met at the hole-in-the-wall Thai restaurant where I worked. She ended up staying with me for a few weeks before flying back here for Avery's wedding and making the biggest decision of her life. "You're *Thai Maci* now."

She scrunches her nose over the rim of her wine glass.

"That's what I call it. For me, *Thai Brooke* is calm, aligned, happy, and at peace. It's the version of me where I feel safe to be myself–*proud* to be myself. I feel like that's how you are now–ironically, not how you were in Thailand."

Her hand lands on my arm with a laugh. "Thank God that phase of my life is over." She sighs. "Now we have to figure out yours."

"Ugh. Tell me about it. I don't know what to do. Part of me thinks I need to go 'home' since I haven't been in years, but I feel like it'll wash away all the progress I've created when it comes to choosing paths that make me happy."

"Maybe you could stay here for a while? I'm sure you could easily get a serving job with how much experience you have."

"Yeah, maybe. I don't mind it, but I don't think I want to do that anymore. I'd rather use my degree."

"I didn't know you went to school! What for?"

"Accounting. My mom all but forced me so I could be 'qualified' to work as an assistant at my ex's law firm."

"Did you like it?"

"Working for that asshole? No way. But as far as the actual job, I did. I'm good with numbers. And I didn't mind the secretary part of it. Besides the dry-cleaning. The man would make me get his underwear dry-cleaned. Who does that?"

Maci scrunches her nose. "No one I know."

"Exactly."

"Well, I bet we can find you something similar. This town feels small, but it's fairly big. There's a lot of businesses."

"Thanks, but I don't want to overstay my welcome. I doubt I'd make enough to afford my own place. And I feel like I have to go back to Connecticut eventually."

"Why do you feel like you have to go back?"

I consider her question. Why *do* I feel that way? I miss my dad. And my best friend, Cam. Outside of that, though? "Obligation, I guess? I think in my head, Thailand was always a temporary escape from reality."

"I get that, but I don't think 'reality' has to be the same as you knew it before. If there's anything I've learned from my journey, it's how much power we have in creating our reality. You heard the girls yesterday. They love you like I knew they would. It's not a problem for you to stay for a while and see if Oregon could be your new home." I know part of her statement is her own wishful thinking, but I believe she means it.

"Thanks, Maci. We'll see. I guess I'll just enjoy this week, then make a decision."

"That's a good plan. You can't know if a choice is right until you actually try living it. I'm here to help you regardless of the path you go down." She smiles and leans her head on my shoulder, her positive energy charging my mood a bit.

Chapter Five
Marcus

Troy pulls two chairs at my kitchen table out, sitting on one and kicking his sock-covered feet up on the other as he sets his motorcycle keys next to some papers I've laid out for the bar. We'd usually go over business in my home office, but I ordered Café Yumm since we'll be here a while. I've been in California for the past week, resolving software issues for one of the companies I invested in a few years ago. I leave again at the end of the week to consult on the creation of a new app for a startup in Seattle that's finally getting off the ground. So, we need to get things sorted. I have really overextended myself.

I take the seat across from him, my back facing the kitchen. "Alright. I have a few hours before my meeting." I slip a neatly aligned stack of papers from my labeled folder.

"Perfect. I have a cake tasting tonight."

"No luck with talking her into ice cream for the wedding?"

He chuckles. "Not yet. Hoping for an ice cream cake compromise."

"I didn't take Lexy for the type to get obsessed with all the details."

"Trust me. I was surprised too. The girl didn't have a single picture frame on her wall when I first met her. Not even a throw pillow. But she's all about making this day perfect. She also doesn't want to make any decision on her own, so I'm helping her with everything."

"You love it."

He chuckles. "Yeah. I do. I would even if she didn't reward me every time after." His grin slips into a smirk. "Oh, speaking of. I was going to book our honeymoon this week. I know it's still a ways out. You sure you're still good if we take three weeks?"

"Absolutely, man."

"Lexy's been bugging me for the past year about taking a break. It's all been a blur since we moved home, you know? Thought this might be a nice surprise."

"You've been working hard. You deserve however long you want to take. Both of you. Where did you decide to go?"

"A week in Italy and two in Greece. It'll be both our first time traveling out of the country so I thought we should go to a couple of places."

"That's perfect."

"I think she misses the beach from growing up in California too."

"Or you miss her in a bikini?"

He chucks the pen he was twirling in his fingers at me, but his smirk tells me I'm right.

I catch the pen where it hits my chest. "I got you covered." I toss it back to him. "We'll figure it out."

"Thanks. Now if only we could convince *you* to take a vacation."

I chuckle. "Yeah. I don't foresee that happening any-time soon."

Before Troy can respond, our heads spin toward the entrance to the kitchen from the hallway. Brooke is standing there frozen like she walked in on a drug deal, but I can't *not* take a moment to check her out. She's beautiful. I thought so when I met her, even with tears streaking her cheeks, but goddamn, she's gor-geous. Her spandex shorts barely peek out from under a zip-up hoodie that hangs off one shoulder. Her bare skin pulls my attention from wondering what color her eyes are, the purple fabric loosely hanging across her chest. It subtly highlights the soft curve of her breasts, and my hands ache to find out if they fit perfectly inside them.

"Oh. Hi. I'm sorry. I didn't mean to interrupt."

Her voice pulls me from my thoughts, and I grip my water glass tighter. Fucking hell. Get it together, man. Being attracted to Brooke is not on my to-do list. I don't have time for that. And even if I did, her time here is limited. Pulling my drink to my lips, I wash away all the inappropriate thoughts trying to sneak in and break my stare as I clear my throat.

Words get caught in my mouth, but thankfully Troy recovers for me. "Hey. I'm Troy."

She gives him a slight wave with a growing smile. "Oh. You're Lexy's fiancé! It's so nice to meet you. I'm Brooke." She smoothes her hair down, retying her ponytail, and the urge to tug it loose until her wild blonde waves fall down her back is strong enough that my dick twitches.

Troy sits up, moving his feet from the chair to the floor. "Tell me, Brooke. You worked in a tourist town, right? At a bar?"

She shrugs, leaning against the kitchen island. "It was more of a hole-in-the-wall restaurant for locals."

"Maci said something about you being responsible for keeping the place open?"

"I wouldn't go that far, but I helped, yes. Why?"

"We're brainstorming, thinking of ways to drive more business to the bar. Most of our clientele are college kids, but a lot of them go home over the summer."

"Oh. Hmm. What kind of ideas are you looking for?" She glances my way even though she's having the conversation with Troy, like she's expecting me to answer. But for the life of me, I can't make my voice work. What the fuck is wrong with me?

"An event maybe?" Troy's response pulls her attention back to him. It feels like a loss, and the way I miss her intense eyes on me has me questioning my sanity. "We have a few themed nights planned. Karaoke. Pool competition. That kind of thing."

"Are you open in the mornings as well?"

"No." There's my voice. Fucking finally. "We've never opened before three." Brooke's gaze catches on mine and holds it.

"Not as long as the place has been opened, as far as I know," Troy chimes in. She hesitates before glancing back at him.

"We're coming up on summer," I add, unsure why I feel she needs this information. "Over half the students at the University of Oregon are not residents and many go home for the break. Seeing as most of our customers are college kids, we're expecting a decrease in profits. I want to prevent that as much as possible. We're hoping to come up with some creative ideas and spearhead a few projects to keep people coming in–maybe even bring in others from the community who don't usually choose Jameson's." I'm fully aware I word-vomited everything Troy already said, and I'm not sure if it's because it took so long for my vocal cords to get their shit together or just to have her attention back on me.

"Okay. I'll see if I can come up with something to help. I'm just going to grab my tea, and I'll be out of here." I turn enough to see a pot of tea on the stove, barely able to make out the star anise spice floating on top of the amber liquid.

"There should be snacks in the pantry too. Help yourself to anything you see." I cut myself off before adding "What's mine is yours," because that's insane, right? What the hell is it about this girl? I feel like I know her–the way Maci has talked about her for a year–but I don't. Yet, despite my natural ability to feel calm, confident and in control, she's already under my skin.

"Thanks." I turn back to Troy at her word, the unzipping of her jacket and watching it fall off her shoulder out of the corner of my eye nearly derailing me.

"Alright, so," I start.

Troy looks like he's about to say something I'll want to smack him upside the head for, but the universe has my back, and his phone buzzes, jumping across the worn wooden table.

I catch our bartender's name flash on the screen before he picks it up.

"Hey, Jess. What's up?"

His eyes flick to mine as he pinches his phone between his ear and shoulder, readjusting to his previous position with his feet kicked up on the chair next to him.

"It's okay. We'll figure it out." Pause. "No, really. Get some rest. Feel better." Pause. "Of course." The call ends and he taps his phone lightly against the table in thought.

"What's up?"

"Jess is sick. She offered to come in anyway."

"Nah. Maybe I can push my meeting." Lexy is our only other bartender. Between the two of them and Troy stepping in if needed–me as a last resort–we've never needed anyone else. Those two girls can rock a crowded bar like I've never seen anywhere else.

"No. I know this one is important for you." It is. But this is the cost of juggling so many things at once, and it's not fair for Troy to suffer because of everything I'm piling on my plate. "I'm sure we can do the cake tasting another day. The wedding isn't for months."

A throat clears behind us, capturing both of our attention. "I know this isn't Thailand where the rules are all more like 'suggestions,' but I can help if you need it." Fucking hell. Her hoodie hangs on the crooks of her arms, and I can barely make out her nipples through the thin white fabric of her sports bra. What is she saying? "I can sign a waiver or something too."

I replay her words, catching up my brain. "You're on vacation. We aren't going to put you to work." I know Maci wants her to find a job, to stay, but I don't want to take advantage.

"I offered." She shrugs, bringing her mug of what I'm assuming is Thai tea to her lips, her eyes fluttering closed for a moment as she inhales the steam. When they open again, she locks them on me. "My only plans tonight were to babysit for Avery with Maci. I'm sure she can manage on her own."

"Thank you, but no," I say firmly. "It's not your responsibility."

"That would be great actually," Troy cuts in, then gives me a look. "You can't do everything yourself. Let her help," he insists.

"Whatever you guys want works for me, really. I totally understand either way." She looks to me for confirmation. Outside of my meeting, the time it took me to find the right vintage pinball and Pacman arcade machines to add to the billiards room earlier made me more cramped on time than usual. I don't have a better option on short notice. Conceding, all I manage is a short nod and a "thank you."

"Alright, well, I'm going to go shower then. Let me know when and where to be."

I watch her leave before turning back to Troy. When I do, he's leaned back in the chair, pen twirling in his fingers, a shit-eating grin on his face. "What?"

"What do you mean 'what?' You were practically undressing her with your eyes."

Fucking hell. I shake that exact thought from my head. "Do you think she noticed?" There's no point in denying it.

"Nah. But dude! Why didn't you tell me?"

"Tell you what?"

"That you're into Brooke. Obviously."

"I'm not." She's hot. That's it.

"Uh-huh. You keep telling yourself that."

I don't have time to be into some girl who doesn't even live here–not to mention one who is flighty enough to pick up her entire life and move it places she's never been. "I will."

I'm waiting by my car when Brooke comes out of the house. Her jeans are tight and I guarantee her tank top will ride up and show skin when she's reaching across the bar later. If I didn't drink for free, I'd probably go broke if she was my bartender because *goddamn*.

Getting out of my head in the nick of time, I half-jog to the passenger side of the car and open the door for her.

"Oh. Thanks," she says in a combination of surprise and shyness.

I give her a slight nod, making my way back to the driver's side and sliding in, pressing the push start and bringing my car to life with a quiet hum. Brooke buckles her seatbelt without a word, and fucking hell, it's like I forgot how to have a conversation with a woman.

Luckily, she did not forget basic adult skills. "So, what took you to Thailand?"

"Business."

I can feel her stare on me as I back down the gravel driveway like she's waiting for me to expand on my answer, but I won't. My mentor taught me that the less you say the better because the more you give people, the more they can take. Apparently that rule has translated to my personal life.

"Just business?" she presses.

"Mostly. Tried a lot of street food." Food is hands down the best part about traveling.

"Where else have you gone?"

"I do more business in the states, but I've been to Tokyo, Paris, and Dubai. Greece too." I think back to the trip to Athens that I took with my parents when I graduated high school. I have a feeling Brooke would love it there.

"Ooh. That's amazing. Where was your favorite?"

"Dubai. The architecture is insane. And there are so many things unique to that country."

"Like what?"

I scan my memory for which part of the city Brooke would like best–based on the very little information I know about her. "They have the biggest choreographed fountain show in the world."

"Bigger than the Bellagio in Vegas?"

"Yup. They were actually designed by the same engineering team. But in Dubai, you can go on a boardwalk on the lake or in a boat."

"Oh, wow. I would love to go there someday. I love nature, but the modern world is pretty incredible too."

"Yeah, it's inspiring. They also have ATMs that dispense gold." Not sure why that random "attraction" popped into my head. I glance over when I'm met with silence. Her nose is scrunched and it's cute enough it makes me want to laugh, but why does she seem so irritated by the innovation?

"Why would someone even need that?" Her voice drips with disgust.

"I'm not sure." I chuckle, uncomfortable. "Convenience, I guess." I've looked into gold investing, but it's not a route I've ever taken.

"Rich people," she mutters under her breath. Rich people? What the hell is wrong with rich people? They're not all great, but that's the case with everything.

"The UAE is very innovative and technologically advanced." Why I double down on a country I have no investment in past intrigue is beyond me.

She glances at me quickly but says nothing.

Hating the awkward silence more than usual, I shift gears. "Have you traveled internationally outside of Thailand?"

She hesitates another moment. "I traveled through Europe a bit with my ex's family the summer before college."

"Wow." That must have been a pretty serious relationship for her to be traveling the world with him. I'd pay a lot of money to have someone to travel with for pleasure instead of business–someone I actually connect with and not in a mail-order bride kind of way. "Sounds fun."

"Something like that," she mumbles, and fuck, it's awkward *again*. If I were winning money for hitting Brooke's trigger points, I'd become jackpot rich all over again. Who knew someone who meditates as much as she does would be so bothered by some light conversation?

We drive the next few minutes to the bar in silence, and I give her a quick tour when we arrive. Mostly it's me pointing out necessities, running her through the POS system and setting up her change drawer while she watches me.

"Well, I think that should do it." I have an urge to stay and just be around her, but we don't seem to be riding the same wavelength today. "Is there anything else you need?"

"I don't think so."

"Here." I reach next to the terminal to print a blank piece of receipt paper and scribble a number on it. "Troy's number. You can call him if there's an emergency."

"Oh. Shouldn't I have your number too?"

I'm about to tell her that she won't need it–I won't be able to answer while I'm in my meeting anyway–but my better judgment kicks in. "Yes." I write mine below Troy's.

"Thanks. I should be good, though." She pushes against my arm like she's shooing me out the door. "I got this. Good luck at your meeting."

"I'll be back when it's time to lock up."

"I'll make sure the firemen have put the fire out or their clothes back on by then." She grins, then turns on her heel and disappears behind the bar like she didn't bring sex to the forefront of my mind.

Seven hours later, I walk through the doorless divider to enter the bar area, stepping behind the bar. "Hey."

Brooke looks up from where she's dipping two glasses into the three-compartment sink behind the bar. "Hi."

Her hair is wild in a ponytail on top of her head, stray wispy hairs framing her face. She's hardly wearing any makeup–maybe mascara. She's finally close enough that I can see the hint of green in her hazel eyes.

The glow of the orange light above the bar highlights her tan. If the backdrop fell away and was replaced with a beach and shorts instead of the jeans she's wiping her wet hands on, she'd fit right in. She belongs somewhere as beautiful as she is.

"How did it go?" The whole interaction before her shift returns to thoughts, the tension of it making me want to smack myself even if I still have no idea what I said to get under her skin. It was the first time we have ever been alone together, and fuck do I hate small talk. I'm a *fake it until I make it* type of guy, BSing my way through a conversation without giving up any connection points until I deem you part of my very small inner circle. It's always been like that for me. I've never needed or wanted it to be any different. Or do I? The circle has been consistently growing as everyone brings in the person they want to settle down with. Maybe it's time for me to get more intentional about doing the same. Maybe I should work on my small talk skills *first.*

"Busy, but good. No problems except running out of that wine Maci loves. I may have recommended it to everyone."

I chuckle. "Not you too." I might as well buy the winery at this point with how obsessed Maci is with that damn wine. I wonder if that's a possibility. It would be a kick-ass wedding present for Dean and Maci. Nah. My other idea is still superior.

She smiles. "It's not such a big thing in Thailand. And way more expensive." The look in her eyes tells me she misses being there nonetheless. "I'm almost done here. Might just need help with how you like the money dealt with."

I nod. "I need to take care of something in the office." I briefly scan the bar. It looks great in here. If she didn't tell me otherwise, I would have assumed we were dead. "Everything looks good, so come back when you're finished with those glasses."

"Sounds good." She turns back to the dishes, and I walk away with the clear picture of her in front of me fading from my mind, urging me to stay near her. We threw her in a Devil's Snare pit, but I can tell by the look of this place and the security camera feed I pulled up earlier, she remained calm enough to survive it without a scratch.

I make my way to the office, sitting hard enough in the spinning desk chair that it slides along the concrete until the back hits the wall. I pull my phone from my pocket. I didn't have time to do a full check before the shift, but a quick Google search now tells me the basics of Brooke Fields. Where she graduated, the city where she grew up. It looks like her mom works at an elite country club, and her dad is a hotel manager. I easily found a gossip article about the lawyer she worked for.

"Hey." I glance up at Brooke's greeting to see her standing in the doorway, the cash part of the till resting against her hip and drawing attention to the sliver of skin showing between her jeans and tank top. I place my phone face down on the desk, reaching for the drawer. Our fingers graze in the transfer, and she pulls back quickly.

"Thank you. For helping tonight." I set it down, leaning back in the chair again and ignoring the ghost of our touch on my skin because Jesus fucking Christ. "Did you take your tips out already?"

"Yes. Was that okay?" She smooths her hands over the blonde hairs straying from her ponytail. "I'm willing to hand them over. For rent or whatever. I know I'm staying longer than you expected." She's been here almost two weeks now, but since I've been so consumed by work, I've only seen her a handful of times.

"No need. So, you're staying here?"

She shoves her hands into the back pockets of her jeans, looking at her Nike-covered feet. "I don't know," she mumbles. "I don't want to overstay my welcome."

I hate asking for help. I don't *need* help. But something is pulling me to keep her here. "Do you want a job?" I blurt, surprising the both of us. For fuck's sake, man. You were not supposed to offer her permanent employment.

"Don't take this the wrong way, but I don't want to be a bartender. There's nothing wrong with it. I've just been working in the industry for a while. I'm ready to go back."

A pang of something unfamiliar hits my chest. "Go back to Connecticut?"

"Not if I can help it. At least not yet. I meant go back to using my degree."

"Accounting?"

She scrunches her nose a bit like she's wondering how I know that. "Yeah."

The perfect out. I don't need an accountant, and I wouldn't want her to settle for a job she doesn't want. "How do you feel about helping me with something else?" Sure, man. Go your entire life never cashing in favors, then suddenly ask for back-to-back ones from a girl you hardly know.

"Sure. It's the least I can do." She rocks back and forth on her heels. Fucking hell, why does everything she does make me want to touch her?

"I have a meeting in a few days. I could use a woman to sit in with me."

"Why a woman?" she asks with genuine curiosity.

I decide which truth to tell her for now. "Because they tend to have the magic touch. Plus, it's a woman-run company. Just feel like your presence might help seal the deal."

She chews her lip, her eyes full of questions, but she doesn't ask any. "Okay. I'm in," she says with a slight raise of her shoulders like I asked her to simply order a pizza.

"I'd pay you, of course."

She looks like she wants to reject the offer, but something stops her. "Okay. Well, I'm done out there if you're ready to go home." I freeze in my processing, taking a moment to realize that right now, *home* is the same place for both of us.

"Yeah." I stand, swiping my phone from the desk. "After I take care of this money." I pull the cash bag from between the computer and the wall on the desk.

"Okay. I just need to grab my jacket." She disappears from the doorway, and I unlock my phone, drawn back to the article I was reading about the lawyer she worked for when something catches my eye. *Engaged to be married to his assistant, Brooke Fields.* My stomach jolts like a head-on collision, and I curse it as Brooke peeps her head back into the office, her zip-up hoodie draped over her arm. Shoving my phone in the front pocket of my jeans, I make a mental note to investigate that new piece of information when I get home.

Chapter Six
Marcus

Sliding into the driver's seat of my Portofino Blue Range Rover, I toss my briefcase onto the passenger seat. Heat warms my backside through the leather. I fucking love this car. I don't typically spend money on extravagant things, but I need to look professional when I show up to investment meetings. Plus, I deserve this–all I do is work. Although, I'd rather find *someone* I want to spend my time with rather than *something* to spend my money on. I shift into reverse, barely noticing my phone vibrating in the cupholder. I hope they aren't canceling. I stayed up until 3 a.m. making sure I was prepped for this meeting. I want this client. For multiple reasons. I've done everything within my reach to be the right fit for them.

Maci: *Did you forget something?*

I'm wearing my favorite suit. It's charcoal with a white shirt and a solid black tie. I know I put the papers I need into my briefcase. Oh. Fuck. Brooke.

Shifting back into park, I leave the car running and return inside. At the end of the hallway, both girls stand in the kitchen giggling.

"Sorry about that. I'm not used to having anyone with me. Are you ready?" I scan her outfit to make sure she's ready to go. Her Nikes and sandals–the only shoes

I've seen her wear–are nowhere in sight. Instead, she's wearing brown wedges that draw attention to the tight black jeans that show off her lean legs. Her loose-fitting white shirt and navy blazer cover more of her body than I've seen since she arrived, but goddamn, she looks good. Around her neck hangs a thin rope chain necklace with five different shell charms hanging just above her chest. It looks handmade, presumably from Thailand. Her blonde hair looks like it's been curled compared to her natural waves.

"Marcus?" She says my name like she's just said it and I didn't hear her. "Do I look okay? I wasn't sure what to wear, but I can change if you want me to."

I clear my throat. "What? No. You look perfect."

Maci chuckles under her breath, and it draws my attention toward her smirk. How fucking long was I staring? I shake my head, reaching for the cup in Maci's hand. She meets me halfway, handing over the coffee I also forgot.

"Thanks, babe." I wink.

"What would you do without my future wife?" Dean appears along with his voice.

"I'd forget all the important things." I look at Brooke in time for my breath to hitch as she takes a step toward me.

"Can't be late on my first day, boss. Let's go!"

I chuckle. "If I get this deal, do you guys want to go to dinner tonight?" A treat would be nice. I don't think I've been out with my friends since the last deal I closed a few months ago.

Maci grins. "Yes! You'll get it. I'll make a reservation. Izakaya?"

My favorite. I turn to Brooke who is halfway to the door. "Do you like Japanese?"

"I like everything. Thank you." I had a feeling she wasn't a picky eater.

"Izakaya it is then. Thanks, Maci. Invite Troy and Lexy too?"

"I will. Now go kick ass," Maci says, and Dean adds, "You got this, man," as we fist bump, and I head out the door. Making reservations at Izakaya has become a good luck routine, and I'm hoping it stays that way.

Setting my briefcase in the backseat, Brooke slides onto the now empty space. Her hand brushes mine when we both set our coffees in the cupholder to buckle our seatbelts. She's unaffected, clicking her belt in place, and reaches for her coffee again.

But me? Goddamn. I must be desperate to fuck someone. Or have a girlfriend. Or I don't know. But the image of those soft hands tied to my bedposts, giving me total control, sounds like the perfect vacation.

"You good?" Her distant voice pulls me back.

"Hmm? Yeah. I'm good." I clear my throat with the lie and flick on the seat warmers. "You ready?"

"Yes." She leans back against the seat, both of her hands wrapped around her coffee. I pull my stare from her to the driveway behind us as I back out. "This coffee is pretty good. It's not Thai tea, but it will do."

Shifting into drive, the gravel crunches under my tires as we pull onto the street. "Yeah, my friend Michael roasts it. Best coffee in town."

"That's really cool."

I quickly glance at her. The way she's holding her coffee to her lips should be a sin. "I ordered more Thai tea ingredients. They should be here tomorrow."

Checking her reaction, I manage to catch the way her eyes light up before they swarm with guilt like she's ashamed for being happy about something she shouldn't. "You didn't have to do that."

"It's not a big deal. I forgot how much I enjoy it."

"Well, thank you. So, umm. Can you turn down the heat on my seat, please? There's way too many buttons in this thing."

I chuckle, clicking off her warmer.

"Thanks. So, where are we going exactly?"

"An investor meeting." I haven't decided how much information I want to reveal yet–debating between only what's absolutely necessary and settling on even less than that. If this deal goes through, it'll be the third company I've invested in since taking over the bar with Troy. I'm an angel investor for eight other companies, but collecting investments isn't part of my plan anymore. While I do support the mission statements of the companies I'm currently investing in, they aren't ones I'm interested in working with hands-on. I've decided I'd rather be the seed that helps the smaller start-ups prosper. I want to focus on finding ones I believe in, with owners who deserve my help, and *together* we can make a difference.

She takes a sip of her coffee before bringing the cup back to rest on her thighs. "Something for the bar?"

"No. It's a company I'd like to partner with if we are in alignment."

"Okaaaaay." She wants more details, but she doesn't need them. This is just a one-time work favor, not the start of her employment. "What do you want me to do?"

"Your presence is enough."

I feel her stare as I merge onto the freeway.

"You'll see."

"Alright," she asks, and I wonder if she's patient enough to wait or if she's too hesitant to press further. "So, I came up with an idea."

My gaze shifts to hers for a split second before they're back on the road. "An idea for what?"

"For you and Troy. For the bar."

"You did?"

"Yeah. There are a few things I need to research a bit before I want to tell you, but trust me, it's a great idea."

"Cryptic."

"Like how you were a minute ago?"

I smirk. "I'm going out of town tomorrow morning. Finish your plan and we'll sit down with your proposal next week?"

"You got it, boss." Fucking hell, that word coming from her mouth sent a jolt straight to my cock. I try to push the feeling away, focusing on how her excitement has relaxed her. But pulling into the parking space at the business center, I can't help but wonder how long it would take her to be comfortable with me in any situation.

Chapter Seven
Brooke

Following Marcus to the conference room, I take advantage of my view. Damn, he has a nice ass. I'd take the sweats he wears at home or the jeans he wears to the bar over this suit, but I can't deny how handsome he looks. He pushes open the glass door, holding it with his arm for me to enter first.

I hope I'm not getting sick. Between the heated seats and the lack of air conditioning here, I can't seem to get control of my body temperature. Scanning the room, I see two women standing at the head of the glass table, their products laid in front of them. I can't quite tell from here, but they look like . . . mini pregnancy tests?

"Charlotte, Emma, it's good to see you." Marcus closes the distance between him and the women, shaking their hands.

"Thank you for meeting us," Charlotte says. "We're grateful for this opportunity."

"The pleasure is mine," he says, his voice deep in a way I'd love to hear in the dark. "This is my assistant, Brooke." Did he just introduce me? Beau never did that.

Mentally shaking away the shock, I join him at his side and reach my hand for theirs as well. "Hi. It's so nice to meet you."

"You as well," Emma agrees. "Should we get started?"

Marcus nods, pulling out a chair for me. Once I sit, he takes the seat next to me, and I command myself not to let his nearness be distracting.

"Before we talk numbers, do you mind sharing your business with Brooke? I thought you two could do it more justice."

"Yes, of course." Both the women smile, their eyes lighting up. Charlotte hands me a piece of plastic, no bigger than my finger. "What do you think this is?"

"Ummm."

She laughs. "It's okay, we know what it *looks* like. You can say it."

"It looks like a pregnancy test."

"Yeah. An outside investor could help us with that. If we can mass produce this, we'll be able to afford to change the design a bit to avoid confusion."

"So, it's not a pregnancy test?"

"Nope," Emma takes over. She reaches past Marcus and pulls the small clear cap off the end of the flat plastic. "Instead of peeing on this part to detect pregnancy, you stick it in your drink at the bar. Then–do you see that screen?" It looks nearly identical to where a pregnancy test would show one or two lines. I nod. "That tells you if your drink contains date rape drugs. It tests for GHB, Rohypnol and Valium–the most common."

My mouth falls open as Charlotte cuts in. "Unfortunately, we haven't found a way to make them reusable, but they are small enough that you can always carry a few with you."

"And tell her what makes them unique compared to others on the market," Marcus interjects.

"We've created a test strip that's far more affordable than anything that currently exists and is equally as effective." Both women grin.

"And your marketing plan?"

"We do plan to market toward women, but we don't think it should be fully their responsibility to avoid assholes. We want to focus on selling in bulk to bars."

"How are you going to convince them it should be *their* responsibility?" I can't help myself from asking. I glance at Marcus, hoping I'm not overstepping, but the corner of his lip twitches up into a smirk, reassuring me. This is new territory for me, not just with him, but with my opinion being requested and valued in a business setting.

"Great question. That is a risk, but we have a few ideas. We want to position it as a marketing tactic for bars to prove they care about the well-being of their guests and that they won't turn a blind eye to the crime. If they order enough at once, it should pay off more than it will hurt. It will only cost about three cents to manufacture, and we'll charge ten. But if women have the choice between a bar that provides a test with every drink and one that doesn't, we're confident the extra business will easily make up for the added costs. It will also be a tax write-off."

"Wow." This sounds . . . I glance at Marcus. He's leaned back in the black computer chair, his elbows on the armrests and his fingers pressed into each other across his lap. How much does it even cost to invest in something like this? How does he own a bar *and* have that kind of money? Maybe the bar is a loan? *Or maybe he's just rich, Brooke.* I banish the thought from my head, refusing to believe that's the case.

"Do you have any more questions?" Marcus asks me.

I shake my head. I don't know the first thing about investing, and I see why he said it would be good to have a woman with him. I just want to be the credibility he needs to show he's a good guy. "No. This sounds amazing."

He eyes me like he's questioning my honest opinion, then turns back to the women. "As you know, I would love to form a partnership with you. What is your proposal?"

The women look at each other, Emma nodding at Charlotte to speak. "Contingent on your ability to get us access to a factory to mass produce at the costs we are aiming for, we're asking for the upfront cost of 100,000 units to prevent the need for preorders and help creating and managing a system to track said orders. In return, we can offer ten percent of our company."

"Thank you, ladies. May I have a moment alone with my assistant, please?"

"Yes, of course." They exit the room.

Marcus only turns to me once the door has closed behind them. "What do you think?"

"About the deal?"

"Yes. Do you think we should accept?"

I can't help but wonder if he's asking out of courtesy, for appearance, or because he genuinely wants my opinion. I doubt it's the latter. He seems to know what he's doing, and he doesn't know me. "Umm. Well, I have a question."

He nods permission to ask.

"How many units have they sold so far? What are their profits?"

"They haven't sold a single one. And they are about twenty thousand in debt."

My eyes widen. "Well, from a business standpoint, accepting the deal would be a major risk. They are valuing their company at . . ." 100,000 units times three cents. $3,000 doesn't seem like a huge investment in the grand scheme of things, but that's not including the time it'll take to do the accounting. And for only ten percent of the company. "$30,000. That's hardly more than what they owe."

A smirk flashes across his face. Oh, he was testing me, to see if I knew that. "Do you think this business could be profitable?"

"There's no real proof, but my gut tells me yes." I'm definitely a *trust your gut* kind of girl.

"What's more important? The numbers or your gut?"

"Both. But if I have to choose, I'd say gut. As long as it's not clouded by poor judgment."

"Do *you* think this is a worthwhile investment?"

I want to say yes, but it's not my money on the line. I also am curious about one other thing . . .

He reads my mind. "What's your other question?"

"Why *this*?"

He just stares.

"You don't have to tell me. But there is *something*, right?"

Again, no reaction.

"If there is, I think the risk to possible reward is worth the chance."

Without another word, he motions through the glass for Charlotte and Emma to return to the room.

Chapter Eight
Marcus

"I want to hire you," I blurt as Brooke clicks her seatbelt into place. It was probably shitty of me to test her the way I did in the pitch meeting, but I had to know how her brain works. Forcing her into the deep end with my questions was a fast and easy solution. Her mindset was in total alignment with mine, and that makes her the perfect person to be my assistant.

Hiring a woman who I'm extremely attracted to, and one who is only here temporarily, seems like a bad business move, but it also makes sense. I *could* use an assistant. Troy is responsible for the front end of the bar, but my back-end work is piling up alongside everything else I have going on. I tend to find it easier and faster to do things myself–it ensures everything is done correctly. But the way Brooke handled herself in there . . . She didn't just prove her mind is beautiful, she made it clear she's capable of helping me.

This has nothing to do with me wanting to keep her here to get to know her more. Did I go out of my way to make her tea when she first arrived? Yes. But something told me she needed it, and a cup of it sounded good to me as well. Plus, I hate tears, especially when I don't know how to fix them or understand the situation. Did I also give her my bed? That's just good hosting etiquette. Every choice I make is simply the best option. Just like she's possibly my best option for help with work right now.

Brooke's attention shifts from her seatbelt to me. "What?"

"I'd like to hire you."

"I mean, technically I just did a job for you?" she confirms as she weaves her fingers through her hair, lifting it into a ponytail and securing the elastic.

"You're not ready to go home, right?"

"Right . . . but I also don't want to overstay my welcome or bartend. Again, no offense."

I'm flying by the seat of my pants. Something I never do. "None taken. I don't need a bartender."

"I also don't want a handout."

"Not a handout. Right place, right time."

"Ohh, okay. Well, I'm also not sure how long I'll be here."

I can't tell if she's trying to avoid my offer or if it's just pride standing in the way. "That's fine. I can work with that."

"What's the job?"

"I need an assistant." Troy has been nagging me about hiring someone for months. I've piled a tad too much on my plate this year, and I'm ready to accept it. Win-win. And besides the fact that I know Brooke marginally better now, I trust my instincts. And if she's working for me, I won't allow myself to get distracted by her in an unprofessional way. Plus, I highly doubt she'd be interested in what little I can offer with my schedule. Although, I can't help but wonder if she'd be interested in what I bring to the bedroom.

"For the bar?"

"Yes. Amongst other things." I shift in my seat to face her more. "What are your strengths?"

"Is this an interview for the job you just offered me?" She giggles, and it's damn cute.

"I am a businessman." I smirk. "Still have to do my due diligence."

There's no hesitation. "I'm good with numbers and finding places to improve business." She sits taller, and I'm impressed by the quick reply, already believing her without hard proof. "I helped the Thai restaurant I worked at increase profits significantly."

"What about the lawyer's office? What did you do for them?"

She hesitates this time, questions flickering across her face for only a moment. "Same. But not in a way I'm proud of."

Humming, I debate prying further. Her honesty makes me believe she'll tell me if I need to know. "What about your weaknesses?"

"I will throw a temper tantrum if you ask me to dry clean your underwear."

I arch a brow, leaning back in my seat.

"There would likely be kicking and screaming in-volved." I've never seen someone so serious about something I didn't realize was a thing.

"I can do my own dry cleaning. You would be my business assistant, not a personal one."

She scrunches her nose, and I have a sudden urge to kiss her. What the fuck. "So, you take your own under-wear to get dry cleaned?"

I replay her question in my mind, paying attention to it this time. "I do not." I'm curious about this as well, but I don't have time for it.

Her eyes don't scan me. She just locks hers on mine.

"I think you could be an asset when it comes to working with Emma and Charlotte. Figuring out a tracking and organization system for their launch will take time that I don't have on top of securing their production."

She pauses like she's debating it, but I know she wants to stay as much as I want her to. "Alright. I'll help."

"Great. We can discuss hours and pay."

"I can work whenever. It's not like I have any other obligations. And I don't need much. You can take some out for rent. Also, I can move to the couch, or find another place if you'd rather–"

"Are we friends?"

"Umm. Is this a trick question? No? Kind of? I don't know you well enough."

"I agree," I say in an attempt to keep this as professional as I can but meaning it in more than one way. "So, don't offer me a handout. This is business. Tell me what you think you're worth."

"Ummm. I'm not sure what's average pay . . ."

"I hardly think you're average."

"No . . . . I just–" She stutters her words, her cheeks turning pink.

I don't intend to make her feel bad, but after seeing her demeanor change with the mention of things she had to do for a previous boss–who was also apparently her fiancé–I have the urge to make her confident this arrangement will be different. I put her out of her misery. "Your life only becomes what you want when you set requirements rather than expectations. If someone can't meet those requirements, you don't lower your expectations. You leave."

She smooths her hands over her hair and pulls the elastic. Her ponytail falls, and she combs her fingers through the highlighted strands, the curls now resembling more of her natural waves. I wish she'd put it back up so I could pull it loose myself. Hands back in her lap, she takes a deep breath. "Alright. The first week I'd like my pay to be $20 an hour. Once I've completed all my assigned tasks to your satisfaction, going forward I'd like $30."

My thumb rubs against the leather of my steering wheel, my tongue swiping over my lip to hide a grin. "That's more like it."

She glances at me. "Yeah?"

"Tomorrow I have another meeting. You can go with me. We can discuss more details on the way."

"Yeah. Yes." She sits up straighter. "Absolutely."

"Do you have any questions?"

"I don't think so--oh. Where should I sleep?"

"You can stay in my bed."

"With you? Oh shit." Her eyes shift in panic. "I don't know why I said that. Just pretend that didn't happen."

I chuckle. "I'm good in my office."

"I thought you don't give handouts to people who aren't your friends?"

What I'd like to give her isn't appropriate for someone who isn't a friend either. What I'd like is to be in bed *with* her. Maybe not feel so fucking lonely for once. "Day after tomorrow I'll be away on business on and off for another week anyway."

"Okay, well, thank you. Your bed is really comfortable."

I smirk, wondering if she'd feel the same if she were tied to it.

Chapter Nine
Brooke

The four of us pile into Marcus' car, Maci and I sitting in the back seat, and make the short drive to the Japanese restaurant. We're meeting Troy there, but Lexy couldn't get out of work.

Closing the door behind me, I walk toward the restaurant. My head turns when I hear Marcus' voice call out to Maci. She stops, taking a few steps back to him by the car.

"Yeah?" I hear her say, but noticing how Dean hardly acknowledges it and continues toward the entrance, I follow him.

Standing outside the row of bike racks by the front door, I turn away from the cute white-paneled building toward Dean. My curiosity gets the best of me. "What's that about?"

"No idea." He shrugs.

"Marcus seems like a good guy."

"He is," he agrees without hesitation, shoving his hands in the pockets of his jeans, his maroon and black flannel shirt rolled just above his forearms.

"I'm really not intruding, right? I don't want to be an imposition just because he's too nice to say no."

"Trust me, Marcus doesn't agree to anything he doesn't want to. He's big on consent." Dean winks.

What the hell was that about? I'm about to ask, but movement draws my attention to where Maci and Marcus stand by his car. She practically falls into him, wrapping her arms around his waist. He embraces her hug, pulling her closer, his hand petting her hair like he's trying to soothe her.

Not a moment later, they break apart. The way Maci rubs her fingers under her eyes, I know she was crying. I look at Dean, sporting a half-smile and no concern, and I feel like there's a secret I'm not in on.

Marcus and Maci join us, Dean pulling his fiancée to him in a side hug and kissing her temple. "Let's keep him," she whispers through a few residual tears, and Dean laughs subtly.

"If you insist."

I check Marcus' reaction, wishing it could give me some indication of what's going on. He's checking something on his phone, not paying attention to any of us. I'm about to ask what happened when Troy bounds in front of us, blocking our path to open the door.

"Hey!" he greets. I slip through the doorway with Maci and Dean, catching Troy's hand slap Marcus' shoulder from the corner of my eye. "Congrats on your deal."

"Thanks, man." Marcus grins, sliding his phone into the front pocket of his dark gray jeans. His black V-neck strains slightly across his chest and biceps. What was I just thinking about?

Focusing forward, I catch up to Maci as she slides into the brown leather seat at the bar top. Sitting next to her, Dean takes the other side, Marcus next to him and Troy on the end. She wasn't able to get reservations last minute, but this section of the restaurant has such a good ambiance.

Behind the bar, there are six shelves of liquor, reaching so high there's also a sliding ladder like you'd see in a dream library. The lighting is a moody, deep brown over red oak counters and shelving.

Once we're settled, Troy orders everyone a round of green tea shots. "To Marcus," he says, holding his shot toward the rest of us. "The guy who helps make all our dreams come true. It's time for you to have your own."

"I'll cheers to that," Dean adds as he glances at Maci, catching her gaze. She gives him a soft smile, lifting her shot in the air as she leans her head on his shoulder. I want that.

"To my favorite person," Maci says, and Dean shakes his head slightly, chuckling. From what Maci told me, Marcus really grounded her in her decision with Dean and giving him a chance. I think he definitely played a role in their story.

A tingle of happiness flows through me as I lift my shot into the air, joining theirs. Witnessing the strength of a found family is one of my favorite things. But this one in particular gives me a strange feeling that I could become a part of it and that I might be on the receiving end of Marcus' magic too.

Halfway through dinner–all of us ordering authentic Japanese ramen–the bartender checks on us. "Everything is great, thanks," Troy tells her, but her gaze isn't on him.

Marcus looks up from his bowl like he can sense her stare.

"So, the waitress over there," she points, and we all follow the invisible line created from her finger, "wanted me to give you this." She slides him a piece of receipt paper with a name and number scrawled across it.

"Thank you," Marcus responds, but there's not enough infliction in his voice to determine how he feels about it.

As soon as the bartender leaves our line of sight, Troy slaps the back of his hand against Marcus' chest. "Dude. Everything good starts with a piece of receipt paper."

Maci grins. "That's only in bartender romances, Troy."

Troy waves her off with a flick of his wrist. "Come on. This could be *it* for him."

"You know nothing about her, man," Marcus chimes in.

"Well, you'll find out once you call her," Maci assures. "Did you ever go on that date with the girl Lexy set you up with?"

Marcus sighs. "Yeah. She was cool but not cool with how much I work."

"See!" Troy smacks his hand on the bar top. "I'm not the only one who thinks you need to take a vacation."

"Yeah, I don't think that would quite do the trick."

"You're never going to meet someone if you don't make the time," Dean adds.

"Make the time? I'm talking to two guys who knew the second they met their girl," Marcus says, reaching for his hot sake and taking a sip.

"Hey! Technically, it was the second time," Troy counters.

"Look, I'll make the time when I find someone who is worth it." Everyone else is amused, but the conversation seems to be putting Marcus on edge. I don't think it's the teasing, though. I wonder if he genuinely wishes he had a girlfriend. It's kind of hot that he seems to want to settle down.

"We just want you to be happy, Marcus," Maci says, her voice soft and sweet as she looks at him on the other side of Dean.

"Yeah." His single word attempts to end the discussion despite me wishing someone would share more insight.

"At least call her?" Maci presses, raising her own white ceramic sake shot glass to her lips.

Marcus nods, adding nothing as he adjusts his chopsticks in his hands before dipping them into the broth.

Maci turns to me, adjusting her own chopsticks. The boys engage in another conversation, but Maci still lowers her voice. "I feel bad. He does try to find a girlfriend. He's agreed to nearly every date Lexy and I have set him up on."

I have a hard time believing the man couldn't get a date on his own. Has he looked in the mirror? I glance past Maci, getting a clean peripheral view of Marcus even with Dean in between. His scruff is clean cut, his hair tied back neatly, both drawing attention to his sharp jaw. "He just has terrible luck? I mean, he got a phone number tonight from a stranger without trying."

"He does fit dates into his schedule somehow, but I think he's picky because he never goes on a second date. Plus, the work thing is spot on. Trying to spend a solid amount of time with him is like trying to parallel park in downtown Portland. It's either impossible or takes multiple tries."

"Didn't he just go on a camping trip?"

"Yeah. But that's been a standing tradition for him, Dean and their friend Aden since they were in high school. If he tried to bail, they'd kick his ass." She laughs, spooning a bite of ramen into her mouth.

"It seems like he wants to find someone, though?" I feel bad talking about him when he's only a few seats away, but my curiosity is getting the best of me. I've only had a good impression of the man so far. I can't imagine it would be hard for him to find a girlfriend, despite his work ethic.

She finishes chewing. "I'm convinced he does. We still have seven months until our wedding, but since it's intimate and international, we've been trying to nail down the accommodations. The other day I asked him if he was going to bring a date. He said he doesn't have anyone he'd want to invade our circle, so he'd rather bring no one. But I can tell that sometimes he feels lonely when he's the third wheel–that he wishes that wasn't the case. Are you going to bring someone?"

"Am I going to bring someone to Australia, where arguably the hottest men on the planet live?" I chuckle, swirling the sake in my glass. "Kidding. The last thing I need is to fall in love with someone who doesn't live near me. If we're the only ones riding solo, Marcus and I can keep each other company, I'm sure."

"Yeah, it'll be nice that he's met you now. Weddings are the best with the right people." She spins her engagement ring with her thumb. "Have you ever considered getting married? For real this time."

"I don't think so. My experience with Beau was really traumatizing. The prenup process alone was a nightmare. The way Beau's parents sat across the conference table from me, eyes flitting back and forth between me, the lawyer and the contract, making sure I knew my place in his life, was enough to make me want to steer clear of marriage. I get there are expectations in every relationship, but it feels like too many rules and extra paperwork to complicate things for no reason. That's not what love should be about."

"It would be different with the right person. Unless you stumble into another millionaire, which doesn't seem likely based on how much you avoid them."

"Yeah. I don't know. Regardless, I'm not sure marriage is in my future. You know me, I like freedom."

"But you also want to find someone." She doesn't ask. We've had the conversation before about how I would love to find *my person*, the way she found Dean.

"I don't think commitment and freedom are mutually exclusive. To me, you can be committed to someone, but choose to release yourself from all the heavy expectations placed on that by society. Things that complicate it unnecessarily."

"I get that. We're all awesome at making love more complicated than it needs to be."

"I'm glad you figured yours out," I tell her genuinely, leaning my head on her shoulder.

She tilts her head until it's resting on mine. "I'm glad I had you to help me with it."

An hour later, we're back at home, and the awareness that Marcus is on the couch in the room next to me is at the forefront of my mind. I wonder if he regrets letting me stay here. What if he likes the waitress from tonight? What if he wanted to bring her back here and

I'm preventing that? Maybe *that* is why he seemed put off about her tonight.

I shake the guilt from my head and delay thinking about where I'll go after staying here and what that will look like for my life. Reaching for my Kindle on the nightstand, it slips from my grasp, falling to the floor behind the bed. Shit.

Climbing down from the mattress, I reach my hand in the narrow gap between the bed and the wall blindly. My hand latches onto something that is definitely *not* my Kindle. Curious, I tug on the loop. It takes my brain a moment to register, and I drop the strap immediately. Not because I'm disgusted or freaked out. I think because I'm curious. Because I want to know more, but I'm sure as shit not going to ask. Not Marcus anyway. I pull my phone from the nightstand, gripping it tight to avoid that falling too, and open the girl group chat that Maci started with me and her friends.

Me: *So, I accidentally dropped my Kindle behind Marcus' bed...*

Maci: *OH! Dean got me one of those things you clip to the frame and use a clicker. You need one.*

Lexy: *Please tell me you called him in to help you get it and got *distracted**

Me: *You can't tell him I told you.*

Avery: *Oh my gosh, you have to tell us now.*

Lexy: *Troy knows I tell you bitches everything about our sex life. Guys should expect it. But we won't tell.*

Maci: *Everything is about sex with you, Lex. You don't even have to tell us.*

Lexy: *Tell me you and Dean didn't try that thing I told you about the other day and that it wasn't amazing.*

Avery: *covered in baby spit living vicariously through whatever Brooke is about to tell us*

Avery: *Then let's circle back to the thing you told Maci.*

Me: *I found ties tucked under the mattress.*

Maci: *...like hair ties?*

Me: *Nope.*

Lexy: *Oh, damn. I knew Marcus would be hot in bed, but I wasn't prepared for kinky.*

Avery: *Please tell me you're interested in trying them.*

Maci: *Have you ever?*

Me: *I've literally known the man for like two weeks–most of which he was gone.*

Lexy: *I slept with Troy the fourth time I ever saw him. Stronger argument, please.*

Maci: *Okay, wait. Why did I not consider this scenario? You two would kind of be perfect for each other. OMG please date him.*

Me: *You guys are insane.*

Avery: *She didn't say she wasn't interested.*

Maci: *I'm going to ask Dean if Marcus has said anything to him.*

Lexy: *I'll ask Troy too.*

Me: *No way. I work for him now!*

Lexy: *You're the one who brought up the restraints. At least part of you must be curious.*

Me: *I'm not getting tied up by my boss.*

Lexy: *You better tell us about it when you do.*

Chapter Ten
Brooke

The sharp sound of my phone ringing cuts through the silence of my meditation, jolting me upright from where I was lying on the workout mat in Marcus' home gym. With a newly racing heart, I check the caller ID, only to reach an all new high-speed, nearly beating out of my chest when I see the name.

Beau.

What the . . .

I haven't *talked* to him since I ran away from our engagement. That doesn't mean he hasn't tried. He called multiple times a day for the first few weeks, but I ignored every one. I know it was immature of me not to deal with it then. Maybe I at least owe him the courtesy of a conversation now. Someone must have told him I'm back on the same continent because ever since I returned to the states, he's been texting and calling at least once a day. I should just get it over with.

I still hesitate with my finger over the *Accept*, but give in and pull the phone to my ear.

"Beau."

"Hey, babe."

"Don't call me that," I spit with a tone somewhere between disgust and annoyance. "What do you want?"

"Is that how you're going to talk to me after three years? After everything we've been through together?"

"After everything you've put me through, you mean?"

"Don't play the victim. The story of us you've created in your head isn't in alignment with the truth, and you know it."

"What do you want?"

"For you to come home. It's time."

"Says who?"

"Your mother. And Me. The Cancer Week fundraisers are coming up. Your favorite events at the club." I'm shocked he remembers something about me, despite his poor delivery and word choice.

"I'm not ready to come home yet, Beau," I admit.

"It's time. It's the least you could fucking do, Brooke. Either way, I already bought your flight home."

"You did what?!"

"Brooke, you're coming home. In two weeks. That should give you plenty of time to wrap things up with your little friends."

"And what if I say no?"

"Either you show up, or I'll make sure your mom doesn't have a job to show up to."

I suck in a breath. "You wouldn't," I call his bluff. I haven't talked to him in *years*. I can't understand why he even cares. Maybe he just needs the last word?

"Try me."

Maybe I was too immature then to deal with this the right way, but I've grown now. And he's exactly who he's always been. If he's still that same shady guy, I should take this threat seriously. Even though my mom doesn't support the things I want for my life, she's still my mom.

I don't want her to lose her livelihood because of me. "Fine. I'll be there. Send me the confirmation. Are we done here?"

"Not even close. I'll be seeing you."

I mumble some sort of acknowledgment before hanging up and immediately calling Cam. He's my only friend who has met Mom and Beau. There's something great about people you don't have to explain details to because they just know.

He answers on the second ring. "Hey, babe." The pet name from my best friend hits different compared to when Beau says it. "What's up?"

"Hey." I sigh in defeat, feeling like I'm twenty again, trapped and alone in a bed I don't want to be in with someone I never want to see again.

"Oh no. Hold on." I hear a scuffle, like he's leaving the room he's in, and then the background noise goes silent. "What happened?"

"Beau. He's such a piece of shit."

"Bitch, I've been telling you that since we were sixteen and he wouldn't help us make a pyramid for the *Bring It On* dance."

A genuine laugh leaves me. "He missed a solid opportunity to see up my skirt."

"Always an Aaron, never a Cliff." I imagine him shaking his head as he clicks his tongue.

The next laugh gets caught in a sigh, and there's silence between us for a moment. "He threatened to get my mom fired if I don't come home. Do you think he has that power?"

"What the fuck?" I echo his momentary silence before he continues. "I don't know. The board loves your mom for all the sucking up she does, and the club would honestly fall apart without her. I'd like to think no one would let that fuck boy make a call like that. Especially when his mommy wears the pants in that family, and she's your mom's best friend. But..."

"But what?" I insist.

"They just put in a new fountain on the front lawn of the club. It's so big, it's an orange couch short from being *Friends*."

"What does that have to do with Beau?"

"He paid for it–along with a ridiculously large plaque with his name and credentials carved into the gold. Yes, real gold."

"Do you think he has any idea how tacky he is?"

"Tackier than the whale tail making a fashion come-back."

"Cam," I chuckle. "You're getting off track."

"Sorry, sorry. Look, I don't know how much power he has over something like this. I can ask around, but I wouldn't take his threat lightly. He's done worse for less."

I groan, hating this. "He bought me a flight, you know?"

"Oh, fuck. Yeah, I'd say he's as serious as an owl trying to get to the center of a Tootsie Pop."

"I know you're trying to lighten the mood here, but your sparkling personality is feeling a little extra right now," I tease.

"Blame my date. That man knows how to banter. He's got me at the top of my game."

"God, I'm sorry! This could have waited until tomorrow. Go, go. Give me the details after you sneak out of his place in the morning."

"I'm thinking I might stay for breakfast. Apparently he knows how to stuff French toast."

"CAM!"

He chuckles. "Seriously, though. You might as well come home if you already have a flight."

"Anything from Beau has strings."

"Undoubtedly. But you already promised your mom. Might as well kill a couple of birds with a free stone and not give him any reason to cause problems."

"He's still going to cause problems, but fine. You better clear your schedule for me. I'll need my sidekick."

"I'm all yours. Let me know when and where."

"Thanks, Cam. You're the best."

"I know. Love you, babe."

I return the sentiment and hang up, still feeling slightly concerned about the future of my mom's job and significantly worse now that I have a set return date to hell.

Chapter Eleven
Marcus

Lifting my suitcase over the threshold of my front door, I quietly set it on the tile and walk down the entryway of my house to get to the kitchen without waking anyone. I haven't been this exhausted in a while, but the past week being gone was *a lot*. And to top it all off, my to-do list today doesn't include a nap.

Turning the corner, three pairs of eyes shoot to me. Maci stands at the sink filling a water bottle. Dean and Brooke are sitting on the breakfast stools with coffee mugs in their hands. It's 7 a.m. on a Sunday. What are they all doing awake? From my spot at the side of the kitchen, I scan Brooke's outfit. Tight black leggings, a basic burnt orange sports bra that reveals more of her cleavage than I've seen to date. I blink, hardly awake. Fuck. I run my hands down my face. Her blonde waves are pulled back into two loose French braids that I would kill to tug on from behind.

"Are you just now getting home?" Dean questions, standing from his seat and walking around the counter to put his mug in the sink. His hand falls to Maci's lower back as he reaches around in front of her.

"Yeah. My flight got delayed." I was supposed to get home late last night from my work trip to Salt Lake City, but apparently the plane had other plans.

"You don't have to come with us if you're too tired," Maci says with a yawn. I fight my own. Go with them? Oh fuck. I forgot we had plans to go hiking, and Maci didn't mean her sentiment.

I try anyway. "Raincheck?" I hate bailing on my friends, but I still have a massive amount of work to get done today.

"But it's Brooke's first hike," Maci pouts. "We have to make her fall in love so she comes back after she visits her mom. And we're doing your favorite one." Her eyes turn into damn puppies, and Dean chuckles.

"Okay, okay." Fucking hell. She's not my girlfriend, and I still can't seem to tell her no. Also, Brooke is leaving? Already? I thought she didn't want to go yet, and she just let me hire her. "Give me ten?" I haven't slept all night, but I did promise. She wants Brooke to feel like she has friends here since apparently she doesn't have much of a support system. Spending time with her is definitely not the reason I'm bumping everything on my list. I mean, she works for me now. So, I'll be spending time with her regardless.

"Yeah, we'll meet you outside." Maci latches onto Brooke's hand, pulling her from the stool and dragging her toward the door. I can't fight the grin that slips out. Oh. Wait.

"Did you happen to–" I catch Maci before she's out the door.

She reaches for the backpack on the ground that I skipped over seeing in the entryway. "Pack you a lunch? Yes, I did."

I take a firm grip on Dean's shoulder as he passes. "What's yours is mine, right?" I smirk.

"Always, man. Except for my future wife. So go find your own." His grin is goofy as he runs his fingers through his hair, then pushes past me to follow his girl.

The front door closes behind them, and I make my way down the hall. Knowing Brooke isn't in my room, I pull open the drawer to my dresser and replace my business suit I haven't taken off from last night's dinner meeting with black joggers and a faded forest green Oregon Ducks T-shirt. I yank the elastic from my hair, retying it, then grabbing my Nalgene bottle from the kitchen.

Locking the house behind me, I walk toward my car, only to detour when I hear Dean's truck already running on the other side of it on our gravel driveway.

Sliding into the back seat next to Brooke, I buckle my belt, stealing another glance at her while I do. We've texted back and forth a few times this week with a couple of questions about Emma and Charlotte's company, but I get the impression she's mostly been communicating with them directly. I would have rather been here working with them in person, but this trip was crucial. I was meeting with a manufacturing company. I had set it up after my first meeting with them. I'm confident the deal will go through, but I wanted to finalize everything with the production in person. It's my first time dealing with the logistics of physical products like this. Mastering the learning curve and negotiating a deal was a beast, but it'll be worth it.

I'm about to share my project with Maci and Dean–knowing how supportive they'll be about it–but common sense kicks in. If Maci wants Brooke to have friends, talking about business probably isn't the best way to help that. It's too early, and I haven't slept nearly enough for that anyway. Not to mention it's not exactly a chirping birds and sunshine type of investment.

Maci plugs her phone into Dean's truck using the auxiliary cord, thumbing through her playlist until she lands on the one I know she will. Constantly being in someone's personal space is a surefire way to get to know them, and that's proven true since Maci moved in. I've known Dean since we were five. He's one of the select few I've let in. Troy and I have become close too, now that we own a business together. My friendship with Maci happened by force and accident. And while I love that we coexist in the same house so well, I can't help but wish I could spend the same time getting to know someone meant for me.

An instrumental version of Taylor Swift's "State of Grace" seeps through the speakers, and Maci sets her phone on the dash as the sunlight peeks through the trees on either side. She's made a playlist of piano covers of all her favorite songs because I rarely listen to music with words. It's distracting while I work.

The three of us have created quite a few compromises to make for a peaceful living arrangement–none of which I mind. But finding someone who already shares priorities and preferences? That would be great. Leaning my head back against the seat, I close my eyes, letting the melody soothe me. It's an hour and a half drive, and I could use the peace and a nap.

"I like this version," Brooke whispers, like she's talking to herself. "It's almost like you can feel it more, like the words are trapped inside, trying to get out." I get the impression she wasn't talking to me, so I keep my eyes closed. Though, part of the smile I try to prevent slips out.

The small jolt of the truck coming to a stop and Brooke's fingers grazing my forearm wake me over an hour later. "We're here." Her voice is soft, and I wouldn't mind being woken up this way every day.

I rub my eyes, allowing myself only a quick glance at her before I scan our surroundings through the window. We're at one of my favorite places to hike. It's also a go-to place for my buddies and me to backpack camp.

Jumping down from the truck, I loop my Nalgene bottle through my finger. The full trail is a seven mile loop, so hopefully I don't need more than that.

"Here." Dean smirks as a packet of bug spray wipes hits me straight in the chest. I barely catch it before it slides to the dirt.

I take a step, smacking him upside the head with it at his joke.

"Ignore those two," Maci says with a laugh. "Their bromance is something else. They've got more inside jokes than we'll ever have."

Brooke laughs, zipping her hoodie over her sports bra. "Do I even want to hear this story?"

"Oh yes, you definitely do." Maci nods emphatically.

I groan at the stupidity of younger me but don't fight it, my mind wandering to a curiosity about whether or not Brooke enjoys camping. Would she be a tent girl or insist on an RV? She must have an adventurous side if she lived in Thailand, but there are drastically different ways to live life there.

Maci starts the story without permission. "One time, when they went camping there was an unfortunate marshmallow incident that led to so many mosquito bites that they woke up with welts all over their bodies."

I didn't plan to chime in but can't help it. Chuckling, I say, "You're a terrible story teller. You're missing all the key elements."

"You tell it then," she says over her shoulder, reaching her hand behind her as she walks toward the trailhead marked with a wooden display box filled with a trail map, emergency numbers, and instruction guide for what to do if you encounter a bear.

Dean shuts his door, slinging the lunch backpack over his shoulder and slipping the keys into the pocket of his basketball shorts, replacing them with Maci's hand. All of a sudden this feels like a double date. I glance at Brooke, looking at me with anticipation for the story–not at all giving a sign that she wishes it was a date. I'm her boss now–at least temporarily–and she won't be here long. I definitely don't wish that's what was happening here. It's nice not to be a lone third wheel for once, though. "What happened was this fucker," I motion to Dean, "wouldn't help me put out a fire."

"A three inch fire on your marshmallow," he cuts in.

"I had no choice but to fling it through the air and let the wind help me put it out."

"You couldn't just blow on it?" Brooke asks, scrunching her face at me as we leave the openness of the parking lot to enter a barely wide enough for two people path between the trees.

"THAT'S WHAT I SAID!" Maci exclaims, dropping Dean's hand to turn back toward where Brooke and I walk a few steps behind them.

Shaking my head, I can't help but grin. I am much more intelligent than that, but a twelve pack of beer between the three of us dissolved common sense. "You're not allowed to tell her any more stories about the days we were young and dumb."

"And full of cum," Brooke chimes in.

A laugh bursts out of Maci, and Dean says, "I like this girl."

I stop in my tracks and stare at her.

"What?" She shrugs. "That's how the saying goes."

"Uh-huh," I say, forcing my eyes back to the trail instead of trailing her body at the mention of anything regarding sex.

Dean helps Maci over the giant tree that's fallen across the path as Brooke asks, "What? You're telling me sex was not part of your young and dumbness?"

Biting back a smile, I hop up on the log, instinctively reaching for Brooke. She eyes me for a moment but slides her hand in mine and lets me pull her onto the fallen tree. I hop down gently, not releasing her until she's safely on the ground. "You don't hold back, do you?"

"Not anymore. Not in what I say, anyway."

I want to dig more into her words, but the idea screams trouble. The last thing I need to do is talk about sex with someone who is an employee. The point is to keep me from going there, from preventing me from letting anything overpower the truth: I don't have time for a girlfriend, and Brooke isn't going to be here forever anyway.

Brooke doesn't add anything else, and refusing to continue on the topic, I watch as Maci steps up on her toes to whisper something in Dean's ear. His hand falls to her lower back, sliding around her waist to keep her from falling over as she tells him a secret.

"Those two are disgustingly cute."

I chuckle. "You get used to it."

"You don't have a girlfriend, right?"

I hold back an overgrown bush branch and let Brooke pass me. "Nah. No time really."

"Oh. What about that girl from the restaurant?"

"I met her for coffee."

"That's it?"

"My work schedule doesn't allow for many detours."

"Right. I am surprised you're here. Why'd you even humor her with coffee then?"

Because I'm lonely as fuck, and I *want* to find something more important to me than work. "I promised Troy I'd make more of an effort to meet someone."

"Like you promised Maci you'd come hiking today."

"I'm a man of my word."

"But why agree to do things you don't want to do?"

"Who said I didn't want them?"

She opens her mouth to speak but clamps it shut like she decided against her next question.

Getting to know her feels dangerous, but curiosity gets the best of me. "Do you have a boyfriend?"

She laughs. "I haven't dated anyone in three years, let alone had an orgasm that wasn't self-induced." She glances back quickly, doing a terrible job of masking her cringe before she faces forward again. She continues on her way like she's decided to commit to saying something to a near stranger that girls usually reserve for their closest friends. Thank fuck for that because it means she can't see the deep breath I inhale at her words. I thought my three *month* dry spell was bad. Wait, what did she say? "So, you haven't had sex?" I tiptoe a line that shouldn't even be within sight, but she started it.

She shrugs, sparing me a quick glance over her shoulder. "Not in a while. Turned myself off, I guess. My first few months in Thailand were . . ." She stops so abruptly that I crash into her–not hard, but enough that I stumble a bit, and instinctively grab her to steady myself. She grins at the contact, like she's not bothered, but her shoulders slump under my touch. "Well, to be honest, I was a total tourist slut." She's only a few inches from my face, the tone of her voice severely contradicting the sadness in her eyes. Shrugging again, she pulls away from my touch to continue on the trail.

"Everyone goes through a phase."

"Did you?" she asks, holding her hands out for balance as she walks a log on the side of the path like a tightrope.

When I don't answer, she glances over her shoulder to make sure I'm still here but doesn't push. "What happened after the first few months?" Fucking hell. I mentally high-five my face. What is it about this girl that makes me want to know more? Getting to know people is rarely on my to-do list. I chalk it up to killing time on the hike even though I usually prefer the silence.

She stops in her tracks, but this time I don't crash into her. Hopping off the log she was walking, she takes a few steps to where the trail opens up.

My favorite part.

The path loops around a deep valley with a pool of water at the bottom. Following along it will bring us to the backside of the waterfall pouring over the overhang of the massive moss-covered boulder on our left. I walk past her, assuming she'll follow, but there's no crunch of leaves or other signs of movement from her.

Turning around, I watch her take in her surroundings. Her eyes are locked on the waterfall, but then she slowly scans. She follows the path with her gaze, where the tree-lined trail turns into the rock wall holding up the waterfall. Past where I can barely see Maci and Dean making out like they are sixteen years old behind the rushing water. She spins ever so slightly, the toes of her Nikes grinding against the dirt as she continues to sweep the view, sunlight reflecting against the water, a group of hikers making their way around the next bend.

Her gaze locks on where the tail end of the waterfall meets its resting point, and stills. I hear the roar of the waterfall crashing into the pool below, but it feels like all I see is her. Her hands are in the pockets of her purple zip-up. Her blonde baby hairs are now wavy wisps framing her face, a little sweaty from the hike, or maybe mist from the waterfall.

A bird chirps nearby, and it breaks her out of her trance. She shakes her head, bringing herself back to reality. "Oh sorry," she says like she didn't realize I was still standing next to her.

It's not a problem, but I don't say anything.

"It was just a glimmer." Her words are soft like she's worried they'll be taken away if they're said too loud.

"What's a glimmer?" I step closer in case it's a secret. Even if it's not, for some reason, I want in.

She gives me a half smile. "A small, seemingly insignificant moment that sparks joy, peace or gratitude. Something that cues your nervous system to feel safe or calm. Basically, the opposite of a trigger. It's nothing really."

"Doesn't sound like nothing."

"I know it's just a waterfall." She sighs. "But, I don't know. Nature has so much power, but it doesn't want to use its power to control you. It wants you to have it, to soak it up, to enjoy it. It trusts you not to take from it. Most people who hold power over you want more than to just surround you with the beauty of life. So, focusing on things–nature mostly–that bring me peace helps me feel safe, I guess. Calm." She chuckles, moving down the path again. "It's way cheaper than therapy."

"You miss Thailand." The observation isn't a question. I can tell her sentiment was only partially about that, but I don't touch the part about people abusing power.

"Yeah." She tugs her arms through the sleeves of her hoodie, pulling it off and tying it around her waist, her midsection on full display. Goddamn, she's hot.

Focus, man. "Why didn't you stay?"

"It just felt like it was time to move on." She's not giving me enough, but I drop it, knowing less is better.

We continue the hike without talking. Just the roar of the water. The chirp of the birds. The rustle of the wind through the trees. She slows her pace a few times to take it all in, and I stay with her, completely forgetting Dean and Maci are here until we reach where they are waiting for us at a little side trail on a log by the river.

Maci is pulling sandwiches out of the backpack, lining them up on top of their ziplock baggies along the log she's straddling. She glances up at the two of us. "You both want chips on yours?"

"Yup," I answer and can't help my grin as Brooke says, "Duh. It's the only way." Maci pulls off one top piece of bread at a time, layering each sandwich with Doritos as I sit on the other end of the log. Brooke joins Dean nearby, immediately stripping off her socks and shoes. She moans dramatically when she slips her feet into the crystal clear river water, and I need a fucking distraction from her.

I pull my phone from my pocket, wanting to check on a few work things anyway. By some miracle, I have a bar of service and open one of the thirteen emails I've received since we left the house. Maci holds out my sandwich as I'm punching out a reply to one of them, and I take it from her, setting it on my thigh.

"Thank you," I hear Brooke say on the edge of my awareness.

"So, are you at least excited to see your dad when you go home?" Maci asks her friend. I'm curious about her answer but don't engage. I need to finish this email.

"So excited. It's only been a few months since I've seen him. He came to Thailand at the beginning of the year. But he's the best. Partially makes up for my mom being the way that she is."

"I get that," Dean chimes in. I tune him out as the three of them talk about Dean's dilemma over whether or not to invite his dad to the wedding after what went down regarding his sister, Sophie and her boyfriend, Cooper. I've already run through the pros and cons with him until we were more angry and further from a decision.

I press send and open another email.

"–Marcus?" I register my name at the end of a sentence I completely missed from Brooke. Finishing my email and pressing send, it sinks in that she was talking to me. When I glance up, her face shifts from hesitating on mine awaiting a response, back to Maci who has started to reply for me.

Fuck. She probably thinks I'm such an asshole. I need to get this done. I don't want to drop the ball on Charlotte and Emma's deal and need to keep up with everything else too. The email I just opened was an issue with our tax payment on the bar property–obviously a priority.

Closing out of the app, I slip my phone into my pocket and pick up my sandwich.

"Marcus won the lotto with his parents. I love them. On summer breaks from school, they used to do mission trips to South Africa. They have such good stories."

Brooke looks to me as if for confirmation, and thank fuck I'm paying attention now and figured out what she was asking about. "They're great." I smile at the thought of my parents. I know I'm lucky to have two incredible ones. I feel bad for my friends who don't. My gaze shifts to Dean for a moment, noticing the conversation about his dad took a toll. Not sure if I'm helping or hurting, I add, "My dad and Jack coached our soccer team when we were kids."

"Oh my gosh. I wish I knew you then!" Maci swoons.

Dean chuckles. "I'm glad you didn't."

I hold back my own laugh with a bite of my sandwich. Goddamn, the chips *really* make it.

"Oh yeah?" Brooke instigates. "Why's that?" She splashes her feet on the top of the shallow water, the sunlight reflecting off the skin where her leggings are pushed up.

"We just fucked around all day," Dean responds for the both of us. "I'd always forget my uniform. And Marcus would be missing before every game. Dad would find him wandering through the food carts."

"And yet, somehow, you both ended up with killer bodies, like you actually made an effort in sports." Those words from Brooke's mouth definitely get my attention.

With half a mouthful of sandwich, Dean takes a sip of his water and swallows. "Yeah. Well, girls are much better motivation than orange slices and rice crispy treats." He pinches Maci's side and she giggles, falling into him. It's disgustingly cute, and I want to detour away from relationship talk.

"So, Brooke." I shift my attention back to her and where the sun's golden rays reflect on her braids. Fuck, she's beautiful. "Did you play sports?"

"Yeah." She smiles briefly before it falls as she brushes crumbs off her hands. "When I was younger, I did gymnastics. Dad was my biggest cheerleader. But once I got good, it became too time consuming and expensive for my parents to keep up with."

"That sucks." I have no clue what the fuck else to say because it does. Money makes the world go round. My dad only coached my team with Jack so we didn't have to pay for my spot. I refuse for it to be like that for my little sister. I want my parents to be able to experience her life however they want.

"It's okay." She forces a smile, lifting her feet from the water and kicking them in the air a bit to shake the water off before putting her socks back on. "My best friend and I made up games to play in the woods behind my mom's work. I would never have become a pro at 'capture the five-star dining napkin' if I had been stuck in the gym for five hours a day." She laughs at the memory, and I feel the shift inside my chest. I want to know every detail about the life that created this girl in front of me.

Without giving me the chance to start that right now, Brooke stands. Maci and Dean follow suit, zipping up the backpack and getting ready to continue on our way. This time, they don't skip ahead of us, taking over the conversation with wedding talk, and finding out more about Brooke becomes just barely out of reach.

Chapter Twelve
Brooke

Butterflies tear through my stomach. Or maybe it's junk food. I probably shouldn't have stress binged an entire bag of salt and vinegar chips while I finished going over my presentation in my head. Now my mouth is all torn up on top of the nervousness practically vibrating through me. It makes no sense that I'm feeling this way. I was always the girl in school who barely prepared for speeches and tests. Even with Beau and wanting to live up to his expectations, I was consistently going through the motions to the point that there was no room for nerves. But thinking about Marcus possibly rejecting my idea . . . what if he doesn't like it? What if it's not good enough for him to ask me to stay again? *Why do I care so much about him wanting me to stay?*

Taking a deep breath, I knock softly on Marcus' home office door, praying I don't blurt out something else completely inappropriate like when I brought up my sex life–or lack thereof–on our hike.

It didn't make sense to meet at the bar to go over my proposal since his office there is smaller and shared with Troy. But it feels weird that I just walked out of my . . . well, his . . . bedroom to the room next door for a business meeting. My outfit is professional but cute. I'm wearing nice blue jeans with a loose-fitting lavender blouse French tucked. I have brown wedges to match this outfit, but didn't put them on since I'm inside. Now I'm wondering if I should have? Is it weird I'm barefoot? That's not very professional. This is weird. Why am I overthinking this so much? I'm not even sure why I felt the need to dress up. It's not like this is an interview for a job. It's just me sharing an idea–something completely out of my job description. It would be insane to think I'll become valuable enough that he would hire me full time and long term, especially when I can't stay in Oregon permanently. Can I?

My knuckles rap on the wood more confidently this time and Marcus' deep voice sends a shot of adrenaline straight through me. "Come in."

Am I sweating? God, it's so hot in here. Taking a deep breath, I twist the knob and push the door open. I only got a peek of this room during the tour Maci gave me the day I arrived and haven't been in since. To the left sits a massive oak desk in front of a long window. There's a huge computer monitor on one side. Everything is neat and organized. A three tier metal rack sits on the wood with papers neatly stacked within it. There's a filing cabinet in the corner and a fiddle leaf fig tree that stands just as tall. To the right is a rich brown leather sofa. Marcus sits on one side, leaned back, an ankle crossed over a knee as he examines the paper he's holding.

He was out all morning, which is also part of the reason we didn't meet at Jameson's. I'm not exactly sure what he was doing, but it must have been important if he's dressed like *that*. The charcoal slacks and button up that's a shade lighter hug his muscles deliciously. His hair is pulled to the back of his head and one of his hands runs across his jaw, over his neatly groomed facial hair. Holy hell. And since when does he wear glasses? Just slightly rounded black frames sit on his face, perfectly highlighting his ocean eyes as they glance toward me.

"Brooke." He sets the paper on the coffee table in front of the couch and motions to the space beside him. I cross the room, and it's not until I sit on the leather that I remember this is currently his bedroom. "What's wrong?" he asks, his eyes fixed on my scrunched face.

"It's not that this couch is uncomfortable . . ."

"Gee, thanks." He chuckles.

"No, really. It's great. But this is what you've been sleeping on? I feel terrible. Please trade me. It's the least I can do." I can't believe that while I'm sleeping peacefully on the comfiest mattress I've ever slept on, he squishes onto these way too firm cushions. Okay, maybe I haven't been sleeping peacefully with everything on my mind, but at least I'm comfortable as I lie there awake.

"It's not a big deal. And I've been gone a lot lately, in case you haven't noticed."

Oh, I've noticed. And not just because it feels weird working a job without a boss breathing down my neck. I've been loving working with Emma and Charlotte. They have no idea what to do when it comes to creating an organization system. I'm not a very organized person, but having the freedom to design it in a way that makes sense to me is fun. I keep having the urge to check in with Marcus, to make sure I'm doing things how he wants, but Maci said Dean told her he's been really busy. I don't want to bother him or make him feel like he can't trust me. So, I shoved the insecurity and need for validation on my projects down, despite my desire to text him. "Well, if you change your mind and want your bed back, just let me know."

He holds my gaze for a long enough moment that I feel my face heat.

"Alright, well." I shake my head, clearing the thought of Marcus and the ties under his mattress. "Ready for my proposal?"

"Let's hear it." He takes off his glasses, setting them on the coffee table before leaning back to get comfortable.

I take a breath. I've spent the last week walking through town, scouring lists of all the local businesses and trying to figure out the best idea for bringing in business. I think I landed on the perfect collaboration plan. "Typically, bars rely on their nighttime hours to make the most money." He nods, but I back up my statement anyway. "I talked to Troy, and he said that you've never considered being open during the mornings because there wouldn't be enough profits. But I think we should start there."

"Convince more people it's '5 o'clock somewhere?'" He smirks.

Grinning, I continue. "Not quite. I mean, yes, there will be alcohol involved, but it'll be more than that. One day a week we'll have a Brunch, Booze and Books meetup. I'm not set on the name–it's just an idea. I've talked to a couple of local businesses we could partner with for a mutually beneficial relationship. There's this new crepe place. They are more upscale than what you'd expect at Jameson's–no offense." Amusement flickers in his eyes before his expressionless mask slips on, and he continues listening intently. "But I don't think that's a problem. Who says we can't create two separate vibes? We obviously have alcohol. And I talked to the owner of the cutest indie bookstore in town. So, what I'm thinking is one day of each summer week, we'd open in the morning for this book club of sorts that would be kind of like a secret society thing? Maybe that's not the right word." I sigh, feeling like my thoughts are coming out more jumbled and less concise than I practiced. He watches me patiently, without interrupting or giving any sign of what he's thinking.

"There would be a membership fee. It doesn't have to be a contract or anything. I was thinking $55 a week? Girls spend way more than that just on brunch with their girlfriends on Sunday. But the value would be so much greater. They'd get that week's book club book, a crepe, and mimosas or wine or whatever. We could even create special cocktails for each event. OH!" An idea sparks to life as I'm rambling, and I hardly take a breath so I don't lose my train of thought. "We could make a cocktail that's themed for whatever the book is. It could be a whole thing. Anyway," I try to get back on track, noting Marcus' cool expression paired with god-like patience as he lets me finish my thoughts. "All three businesses would benefit. We could discuss the division of profits however it makes the most sense. But I think this is something women my age would be super interested in. There are about 30,000 women between the ages of 21 and 35 just in Eugene. Marketing at school would be easy, and we'd have both the crepe place and the bookstore advertising for us as well. Plus, it would greatly benefit us if we were the hosts. Each weekly membership could include one mimosa or whatever drink. But after that we could charge. Once girls get drinking and talking about romance, they either want to drink more or fuck."

My hands fly to my mouth as Marcus' eyes go wide like he can't believe I said that.

I squeeze my eyes shut tight, hoping to erase the past fifteen seconds, but when I open them again, Marcus' gaze is still focused on me. Maybe I'm delusional right now, but it looks like he's . . . I don't know . . . trying to figure out which category I fall into. In an attempt to crush the embarrassment, I run straight through it. "Well, it's true. And if you didn't know, you do now."

He holds up a finger to get my attention. "What determines which of those things a woman wants?"

My skin buzzes with the idea that *maybe* he wants to know about me specifically and not women in general. "Honestly, if the smut is good, it's always sex. But if we can't get it–especially if it's a reminder we're alone–a glass of wine takes the edge off. So, again, this is where the bar comes in. They want something we have. Bam. Books, Booze and Brunch."

He quirks a brow. "I thought it was Brunch, Booze and Books?"

"Oh my gosh. That just gave me the best idea. I was thinking like 'BBB' or something short and sweet. My original idea is catchy but kind of a tongue-twister. What about, 'Here for the B?' You know, like a play on . . ."

"I know."

"Oh, right. Wow. This idea kind of took a turn, huh? Is it too . . . problematic? Or I don't know."

He cocks an eyebrow. "Do we need to have the confidence talk again?"

I review his pep talk from when he asked how much I thought I was worth, still surprised by how he seemed to believe in me despite the lack of time we've spent together. "Nope." I smirk. "Not sure there will be enough time between you telling me how amazing my idea is."

"I like it."

"Really?"

"Yeah. It's not exactly conventional, but outside of the box is exactly what gets attention."

"OH. We could even have Charlotte and Emma come to one of the meetings and educate everyone too. They could test their product. Surely it would make it onto everyone's social media. And we'd get content for our own marketing of course."

"Do your ideas ever stop?"

"Honestly, I haven't felt this creative in a long time. Between you giving me control over helping Emma and Charlotte and indirectly free range with no guidelines for this idea, I think the freedom sparked something great."

"I do too." He pauses. "I know you keep telling me you're not staying and that you don't want a long-term job . . ."

He holds his gaze to me as if he's waiting for me to contradict him, but I think I keep showing up so he'll keep asking me if I want to work for him–if I want to stay.

"Take the lead on this project." He doesn't ask. "Feel free to check in if you need something from me."

"You trust me to figure it out?" Bosses don't give their employees this much control.

He gives me a quizzical look. "Should I not?"

"No. I mean, I got this. Thank you," I concede without any fightback. I bite into my lip, anxious to text the girls and tell them. The realization slams into me, fusing a crack in my heart. I've never had a support system. I've never had any sort of group that I felt comfortable around. And I've only known a couple of these girls for three weeks. Is this what it feels like to have someone believe in you?

Marcus stands, and I follow suit. "I can trust you to take care of the details?"

"Sure thing, boss," I say with a light and airy tone.

"Don't . . . Okay." He tugs on the back of his neck. "Good. Let me know the schedule you get worked out, so I can change the hours on our website. I can also create a payment page for when you get those details sorted too."

What was he going to say? Hmm. "Okay. Thank you for this."

His brows scrunch.

"This opportunity," I clarify even though I'm already thankful for so much more. I may still not know exactly what I want to do for work when I go home, but I do know I feel better than I ever did working for Beau, and that's a huge start.

He nods subtly. Without another word, he bends to grab the paper he was reading over before our meeting and walks to his desk. I take it as a cue to leave and make an exit. I swear I feel his eyes on me as I walk out the door, but I don't turn to check.

The second I'm back in my room, I push the door closed, stripping off my jeans and blouse and exchanging them for my elephant pants and a sports bra. Much better. Diving belly first onto the cloud that is Marcus' mattress, I kick my feet in the air and pull up the group chat.

Me: *GUESS WHAT!!*

Avery: *What?!*

Lexy: *He loved the idea?!*

Me: *It seems like it!*

Lexy: *I knew he would. Troy did too. He thinks it's a great idea!*

Maci: *Aaaahhhh. YES!*

Avery: *Thank god! I can't wait. It'll be like a required girls' morning out. I need adult interaction.*

Me: *I'm excited. He's giving me full control too.*

Lexy: *Giving you control at work to make up for the control he'd take in the bedroom I bet.*

Me: *LEXY!*

Lexy: *What?*

Lexy: *He's not my type, but I can still admit that man is fine. And we have a good idea about his extracurriculars.*

Maci: *He really is the best.*

Avery: *Oh, God. Yes, please. We won't even need a book club. We'll just live a real-life story through Brooke.*

Me: *Uhhh hello? Do I get a say in this?*

Avery: *If you start answering our questions. Do you think he's attractive?*

I roll to my back with a sigh.

Me: *I mean, I have eyes if that's what you're asking.*

Maci: *Oooooh. I knew it. You two were so cute on the hike the other day. He couldn't stop staring.*

Me: *You didn't give us much of a choice when you ditched us.*

Maci: *You're welcome.*

Lexy: *I'm so here for this.*

Me: *There is no this. He's my boss now. And I'm not going to be here forever.*

Avery: *Oh my gosh. Can our first book club book be workplace romance?! There's one I've been wanting to read.*

Lexy: *Obviously I'm in.*

Maci: *I'll text Sophie too. She'll want to come.*

Me: *Finally, we're back on track.*

Lexy: *Don't think we're done talking about the other thing, though.*

Avery: *Let us know what you need help with!*

Me: *Actually...*

I want to impress Marcus for some reason. It's different from the way I wanted to succeed when I worked for Beau. That was out of necessity—so he didn't get mad, so he or my mom didn't treat me like I was useless. I don't know why exactly I want to impress Marcus, but it's not for either of those reasons.

Avery: *Hit us with it.*

Me: *I was hoping to recruit all of you. Avery, I was thinking we could make bookmarks with QR codes that link to the website Marcus will make. Lexy, I had this idea today that we could make a themed cocktail that somehow pairs with the book that week?! Maci, you could help me find my way around campus and town to advertise?*

Maci: *Yes!*

Avery: *Eeek. I'm so excited. Let me work on a design this week, and I'll get back to you!*

Lexy: *I already have an idea for a forbidden romance drink. It'll be red, obviously.*

Maci: *Of course it will be.* There's a laughing emoji at the end and I feel like I'm missing an inside joke. It doesn't bother me, though. The fact that these girls rallied around me without a second thought is more than enough to keep me floating.

Me: *Thank you. I owe ya one.*

Lexy: *We accept payment in the form of detailed sex stories.*

I leave a string of eye-roll emojis and toss my phone on the bed.

Chapter Thirteen
Brooke

"Do you know what this party needs?" I ask Lexy and Maci as I stare into the crackling flames of the bonfire. A breeze sends chills across the back of my arms even though I'm standing close enough to the fire to nearly burn my skin through my jeans and tank top.

"What?" Lexy asks, pulling her can of Mango Cart to her lips.

"S'mores."

"Ooooh. Yes!" Maci downs the rest of whatever is in her Solo cup. "We have everything in the pantry. I'll go get it."

I reach for her cup to throw out. "I got it. I have to pee anyway."

"Okay. There are marshmallow sticks in the garage too!" Maci adds as I start my walk up the low incline of the grassy backyard to Marcus' house.

I throw a thumbs up over my head and wonder where Marcus is. I haven't seen him since he was hanging out with his date earlier. He was standing a close, yet respectable distance from her, mostly focused on whatever she was animatedly going on about, but I swear his gaze snagged on mine for a moment when he scanned the party. Maybe it was just a trick of the firelight.

I look back to the fire, spotting a pretty brunette in a jean mini skirt and oversized T-shirt French tucked in the front. She's chatting with another girl I don't know, but Marcus is nowhere in sight. Maybe he's getting her a drink.

Making my way into the house, I open the pantry, finding marshmallows, graham crackers and chocolate bars organized neatly in a wire basket. I pull it from the top shelf and set it on the counter while I search the garage. I've never been in the garage before, but I know the door is in the entryway. As I reach for the handle, I hear two voices, distinct and close, like they're directly on the other side.

"Yeah, she's hot." Marcus. "But she's boring."

"You're a genius. Actually." Dean. "It's not going to be elementary math finding someone to match your intelligence."

I lean against the doorframe, head pressed near where the door is closed.

"I don't think engaging conversation is too much to ask for." The sticky suction of a garage refrigerator opens, and bottles clink against each other.

Dean chuckles just loud enough for me to hear him, and I imagine he's rolling his eyes. "Maybe you're underestimating them. Seriously, man. You work hard. Don't you think you deserve a break?"

"If I wanted one, yes. But I don't. I have goals, and I like working toward them." Released air and a popping sound echo on the other side of the door, and a beer bottle cap hits what I'm assuming is a trash can.

"Alone," Dean notes.

"Look, I want what you and Maci have. I'd kill for it. Anyone would. But unless I meet someone who I enjoy more than my work, why would I stop?"

"They aren't just going to walk into your place of employment."

"Oh, you mean like Maci did?" They both laugh. I know I shouldn't be eavesdropping, but I can't bring myself to leave. Marcus does seem to work a lot. I've been here almost a month and hardly seen him. He hasn't been present for any movie nights I've had with Dean and Maci. He didn't go to dinner with us last night, and I've only seen him in passing in the past few days since presenting my book club proposal.

"Dude. Come on. You have to put in the time and effort. Like you'd do for a business deal. You know that. Agreeing to go to coffee in between meetings with girls Lexy sets you up with hardly counts. And don't forget that it took Maci and me a year and a half to get to a good place and on the same page."

"I know. I also know the *right* girl isn't the one out there. Genius, remember."

"Uh-huh. Well, the right one isn't in here either."

I barely register the few steps they take until the handle is jiggling in front of me. I stand back enough to not fall into them as the door opens.

"Oh. Hey," I mumble awkwardly to the two surprised men in front of me. "I'm looking for the marshmallow sticks. Can you help me out?"

"No idea where they are." Dean slaps Marcus' shoulder and squeezes it before slipping between the two of us. "I'll see you out there."

Marcus clears his throat. "Hey, Brooke."

"Hi. Sorry, I didn't mean to interrupt."

"You're not."

"I don't want to keep you from your date. I'm sure I can find them."

He eyes me as if he's trying to assess my intentions. "It's not a problem." He pushes the door to the garage open, revealing the empty two-car space. There's a freezer chest and refrigerator on the back wall. On the side opposite of us, there's a floor-to-ceiling shelving unit. It's not overcrowded and mostly houses camping equipment. A propane camping stove. A tent. Two sleeping bags rolled and secured with elastic. A row of cast iron skillets hangs from hooks on the wall like he's concerned with the care of his cookware. God, I'd kill for a boyfriend who loves camping. Beau wouldn't even stay in an RV.

The floor is black speckled epoxy that doesn't appear to have tire tracks on it. There are four camping chairs opened in a moon shape facing the garage door like maybe they hang out here when they want fresh air but it's raining.

Marcus reaches the shelves on the other side of the room, immediately pulling the black-handled metal prongs from a shelf at eye level. My feet are still stuck in the entryway as I wait for him to return. When he's close enough, he hands over the sticks. Then he reaches to flick off the light, leaving us in near darkness–him barely inside the garage, me at the edge of the entryway. Right before the lights went out, something caught my eye.

"Do you need something else?" His voice feels close. He *is* close. Closer than he has been thus far and his nearness makes me nervous.

My heart beats so hard I swear I can feel the blood pumping through my ears. What did he just say? Oh yes. "Do you have a telescope?"

He hesitates. "Yes."

"A *good* one?"

"Yes." He flips the light back on, looking over his shoulder to the telescope standing on its tripod in the corner, revealing the truth in his confirmation. I don't know about brands or anything, but it looks extremely nice.

"On the radio earlier, they said you can see Jupiter well tonight."

"Do you want to take a look?"

"Oh. It's alright. I don't want to take you from the party and your date."

"She brought her friend. She'll be okay for a few more minutes."

"Okay then. I would love to see it."

He reaches to press the garage door opener on the wall next to my head. His nearness makes the room feel like it's closing in on me a bit, but he appears unbothered as the door clunks open. He walks toward the telescope, lifting it from its place in the corner and ducking under the still moving garage door to move it to the driveway. He adjusts the tripod legs until they are secure in the gravel, then scans the sky. It only takes a moment to find Jupiter in the distance as if he knew exactly where it would be. Tilting the telescope in the right direction, he looks through the scope before fine-tuning the power ring. He looks back at me. "Turn off the light," he tells me. It's not until this moment that I realize I still hadn't moved as I watched him set up, his jeans tight on his muscular thighs, his black T-shirt riding up slightly as he bent to position the telescope correctly.

I lean the marshmallow sticks against the garage wall and flip the switch. All light disappears from the garage, illuminated minimally by the night sky. When I reach the telescope, Marcus stands back, indicating for me to look.

I quickly tie my hair into a loose ponytail so the strands don't get in the way and adjust the hem of my tank top before bending to look through the scope. I feel Marcus' eyes on me the entire time but refuse to acknowledge them. It doesn't *mean* anything. I close one eye tightly as I press the other to the thick rubber eyepiece and peer into space. Bright stars fill my field of vision. Sound is sucked from the space around me allowing my focus solely on what I see—like I'm underwater, the party muted and distant.

I take a breath, letting the glimmer soak into my soul. I love the universe. But I can't find Jupiter.

Turning my head, I'm made quickly aware of how close Marcus is to me–not more than a foot away. "I can't find it," I tell him when our gazes catch.

He leans toward the scope, invading my space, but I don't back away. With a small twist of the dial, he looks for a few moments longer, then turns back to me. Considering I've frozen myself in place, his face is inches from mine. I lick my bottom lip, all of a sudden dry. The motion snaps him away from me as he clears his throat. "Try now."

I look through the eyepiece again. This time Jupiter is clear, a few of its stripes barely visible. "Can you zoom in a tiny bit?" I whisper, not wanting to move at all. I know I could probably do it myself, but I don't want to mess with his telescope.

There's a crunch of the gravel next to me, and I can feel his well-built frame behind my body. Marcus' arm brushes against my shoulder as he reaches around me, twisting the power ring a fraction and waiting for my update. I hold my breath, afraid of how I'll feel if I breathe too deeply and come flush to his chest. "A little more." I barely breathe out, focusing on the object of my attention. "Okay. Stop."

His hand freezes, but he doesn't pull it back right away. He hesitates, and then a rush of cool night air replaces where he was next to me. I continue staring, taking in each stripe I can make out, the belts more tan in color compared to the Great Red Spot. "It's incredible," I whisper to myself. I start to pull away to give Marcus a turn, but then press my eye back to the rubber for one more look. After another good once-over of the planet, I step back. "Sorry, you can have a turn now."

"I already got a good view," he says, not taking his eyes off me. He shakes his head like he's ridding it of the thought, and contrary to his statement steps into the space in front of the telescope and looks once more.

After what feels like both two seconds and two minutes of me watching him watch the sky, he stands. "Do you want me to leave it out?"

"No. That's okay. Thank you. This was great. I better get back to the party."

"Alright. I'll see you out there." He nods toward the backyard on the other side of the house.

Without a word, I retreat across the garage, pick up the sticks, and find my way back to Maci and Lexy—refusing to think about what other types of stars Marcus could help me see.

Chapter Fourteen
Marcus

Leaning on the doorless divide between the main part of the bar and the back rooms, I take in the event. The usual moody 70s vibe is nowhere to be found. Instead, it's been replaced by romance. Red metallic fringe hangs in front of all the glass window walls at the entrance to the bar. It's nearly one in the afternoon, but the streamers covering the windows create a deep red glow in the room. The usual red shades over the lights only enhance it.

Red heart balloons hang mid-air. *How the hell did Brooke get them to do that?* A row of cocktails lines the edge of the bar. Lexy created a special drink for the morning. I assumed it would be mimosas, but the deep shade of red tells me it might be a liquor drink.

Five giant black rectangle cushions form a circle on the floor. They're big enough for three women to either sit on or lay across–a few girls immediately made themselves comfortable on their stomachs, feet kicked up in the air, chins propped up by their fists. There are more people than there is room for on the giant pillows, but no one seems to mind. Everyone invades the personal space of their friends and acts like the ones they met today are lifelong buddies. There must be at least 50 women here, if not more.

Brooke sits criss-crossed in black athletic shorts and an oversized white sweatshirt. The black lettering on the front says "here for the" in cursive along the edge of a block letter "B." Avery had them made for the four of them. I can't hear Brooke from where I'm standing, but I can tell she addresses the group with enthusiasm. She looks comfortable and happy–so much so that I silently excuse myself and retreat to my office.

I could leave the building. I'm not needed. I'm sure she will give me a full report when the event is over. I stay anyway.

An hour later, a light rapping against the doorframe startles me from the book I'm reading.

"Hey, there, boss."

Fucking hell. There's that word again. Everyone who works for me at the bar has known me since before I owned it. They call me by my name. Everyone I do business with initially addresses me as Mr. Cole until I convince them Marcus is fine. Brooke is the first person who has actually felt like an employee, but even so, that's not exactly what she *feels* like.

And the way *boss* rolls off her tongue so smoothly, I don't mind the name. I shake my head and bring myself back to the moment before my thoughts stray to another place where I'd like to be in charge of her.

"Hello." Picking up my bookmark from the desk, I slide it in place.

"Here, I brought you these." She holds out a plate with a crepe and a rocks glass filled with red liquid.

I take them from her, examining both. The thin golden pancake is perfectly folded into a triangle with a layer of Nutella inside and sliced strawberries shaped into a heart on the top. It's sprinkled with crushed nuts and a dollop of whipped cream. "Thank you," I say, my gaze flitting to her only momentarily before they are on the drink. As I bring it to my lips, I notice the silver glitter swirling in the liquid and frown, my brows scrunching as I send Brooke a look.

She laughs. "It's edible glitter. I promise. I wouldn't poison you. If I did, who would pay me for this kick-ass event?"

A smirk slips out, but I wipe it off my face. I set the drink on the desk, still not trusting a drink that sparkles. "How is everything going?"

"Perfect," she says, moving a step closer to me in the process. The bare skin on her knee nearly brushes my thigh, but she doesn't seem to notice. "There are 52 people here! If my math is correct, our cut alone is enough to cover the included drink for everyone and enough profit to cover all the decorations–that are reusable by the way–and marketing we did. It's impressive considering I've only been advertising for about a week and a half. I think even more people will come next Wednesday. Everyone is having so much fun."

Her animated rambling brings her closer to me and when our legs touch, her excitement cracks me. I lick my lip, biting it to hold back a grin, but it's no use. She's contagious. "Sounds like *you* are having fun." That fact makes me way happier than it should.

"I really am." Her hand lands on my shoulder, and my eyes flick to it on contact. She pulls away immediately like she thinks it was a mistake and steps back to create distance between us. "Thank you again for this."

"I should be the one thanking you. Sounds like this might be better than I even hoped." I wonder if she's ever considered running her own business. She seems to have the talent for it, and it's hot as hell.

She smiles softly, her eyes flitting to the floor like she's shy all of a sudden. Or maybe she just doesn't know how to take the compliment. In the next instant, she pulls her wrist to her line of sight, staring at the screen of her watch. Her chest visibly heaves with a deep breath and she closes her eyes.

"What is it?"

"Just Satan, herself."

"Satan is a woman?" I quirk a brow.

"My mother." She sighs, pulling her phone from where it's tucked into the band of her shorts, showing a sliver of stomach when she does. My body tenses seemingly everywhere but my heartbeat which is running like a wild horse. For fuck's sake, I need to get laid or something. She reads the full text on her phone. "She wants more details about my homecoming."

"To Connecticut?"

"Yeah."

Oh. For some reason, my stomach drops, and I reach for a stray pen on the desk, flipping it in my fingers–a habit I picked up from Troy. "That's far."

"I haven't been back in three years."

A blonde ponytail swings into the office, attached to Lexy wearing a sweater matching Brooke's along with a pair of cut-off jean shorts. "Ugh. Your mom again?"

Brooke turns to her and nods. "She's driving me nuts about visiting."

"Didn't you tell her you have a ticket already?"

"She's throwing a fit about it being a two-way ticket. I'm actually surprised that Beau sprung for a round-trip."

"Round-trip and no first class. How confusing," Lexy says, and I'm definitely confused.

I'm too curious to bite my tongue. "What is going on?"

Brooke starts to speak, but Lexy cuts her off. "Brooke's waste of space ex thinks he can blackmail her to come back."

To him or to Connecticut, I wonder. "Sounds like someone with an ulterior motive."

"Always." Brooke groans, and I'm even more confused.

"So, you let him buy you a ticket . . . why?" I'm taken aback by my uncharacteristic nosiness. Fucking hell, I need to stay out of it.

"Trust me. It was easier this way. Plus it gets my mom off my back."

I'm not quite following her logic, but it seems to make sense to her.

"Hopefully she'll be satisfied once she sees you. Then let you go without a fuss because you just got here, and I'm not ready to lose you yet," Lexy whines.

That makes two of us.

"Doubtful, but maybe. It's so draining just thinking about going. The entire trip all she's going to do is force me toward Beau. Or try to set me up with some other snobby rich guy from the country club." Seriously, what does she have against rich guys?

"Ugh, I'm sorry, babe. Can't you tell her you have a boyfriend?"

"She'll know I'm lying. She might be awful, but she's still my mom. She knows me that well. I'd need too good of a story."

Lexy searches the ceiling as if it'll give her an idea, the two of them having a conversation like I'm not here at all. She snaps her fingers. "I've got it."

"I'm listening." Brooke chuckles, but it's sad.

"The book we picked for next week."

"What about it?"

"It's fake dating."

"Yeah . . ."

"That's the solution."

"Ha. Yeah, let me just find some guy in the next week and ask him to pretend to be in a relationship with me on the other side of the country. No flaws at all with that idea."

Narrowing her eyes and biting into her lip in concentration, Lexy focuses as if it's enough to create said man out of thin air. Another snap of her fingers. "Marcus."

"What?" I drop into the conversation.

"No. You're the answer."

"Excuse me?" I say at the same time Brooke laughs.

"Yes! This is perfect. You already know he's not a creeper. He's a great people person."

This time I'm the one to laugh.

"Okay, well maybe you don't like it, but you're good at it when you have to be. And when you're around people you're comfortable with. And I mean, Brooke is your employee, soooooo."

"He's known me for two months–if that. It's not like we're best friends. I know nothing about him besides the color of his sheets and how he likes his coffee."

"She *is* my employee," I chime in, attempting to clarify it as a reason why this would make it a worse idea instead of better.

"Two very important things a girlfriend would know." Lexy winks, ignoring my statement altogether. "Marcus, come on. You need a vacation. You're long overdue. Plus, I don't want to feel guilty when Troy and I take an extra long honeymoon. This will make me feel better."

"I already assured both of you about taking time off, Lexy. But I can't do this. I don't have the time," I say, on edge that she put me in this situation I can't be in.

Lexy shoots me a glare before softening for Brooke. "Don't worry, girl. We'll come up with something."

Brooke reveals her signature half-smile, full of equal parts hope and doubt, and some stupid fucking invisible string tugs on me. Fuck. I'm not ready for her to leave. *I am overdue for a vacation.* "Troy has been bugging me about taking a vacation."

Both girls' eyes snap to me. "What?" they say in unison and shock. Fucking hell. I hardly registered saying the thought aloud.

I let my justifications race through my mind before committing. It won't be during the fall colors, but a hike on the East Coast would be great if we could get away from her family. I don't mind Brooke's company. A few days hanging with her wouldn't be bad.

"Connecticut. I need a vacation," I confirm, praying panic isn't laced through my voice.

"Trust me," Brooke says. "This would be anything but a vacation. My mother is not easy to convince or deal with in general."

Lexy waves her hand in front of Brooke's face as if she could physically swat away her argument. "Marcus can handle it. Can't you, Marcus?" I run through the points of contention. I'm her boss. She's one of Maci's best friends. If we're in a situation where I should be touching her, how the hell will I ever go back to *not* touching her? This is a terrible idea.

With both the girls' eyes on me, Brooke can't see the smirk on Lexy's. The little devil knows exactly what she's doing. The question is, is it her own game? Or one based on a previous conversation? This is a disaster waiting to happen. But it has been a while since I've had a good challenge. "What's the worst that can happen?"

Ignoring me, Brooke asks, "What about your work? Your non-bar work?" Panic fills her voice as if she can feel her excuses slipping away. "It would probably make more sense for you to go on vacation when I can be here to do things for you."

I pull my phone from the front pocket of my jeans and open the calendar. Scrolling through the next few weeks, I'm surprised by the flexibility in them. "Charlotte and Emma are in production for the next few weeks, so we can't do much there. I only have one meeting that I can't reschedule. The rest I can check on remotely."

Lexy's eyes widen. If she's shocked by my willingness to rearrange my schedule, that makes two of us.

"Oh. Okay. Well . . . if you're sure you don't mind. You heard the part about having to pretend to be my boyfriend, right?"

"I heard."

"So . . . you'll have to act like we're in a relationship."

"That is what being a boyfriend means."

"You might have to . . . I don't know. Kiss me or something."

"Believe it or not, I do know how to do that."

"Oh, yeah, right. Well, I guess we've been working well together already. Just a different kind of work."

"It won't be work," I assure her.

"Oh. Okay. Sure." She stumbles over her words and her face flushes in a way that makes me wonder what else I could say to draw that reaction from her.

"I'm so brilliant," Lexy sasses. "I'll leave you two to figure out the details." With that, she walks away.

Brooke kicks the doorstop out of the way and closes the door, trapping us in the small space. "Seriously, you don't have to do this. Don't feel pressured or anything. I don't want you to be uncomfortable."

"Brooke. I'm a businessman. I don't make deals I'm not confident about."

"This isn't really a deal, though. There's nothing in it for you. I mean, of course I'll pay for everything. But–"

"Stop trying to talk me out of this. I made up my mind. It's enough that I'm helping you. Like I've said before, a friend of Maci's is a friend of mine. And I could use help getting Troy off my back. I haven't taken more than a couple of days off since we bought the bar over a year ago."

"Alright then. Let's get this over with. I'll get your ticket tonight."

"That's the spirit." I deadpan. Is she really *that* against the idea of us spending time together?

"It's not you . . ." she assures me as if she's a mind reader. "I promise. You're great. Perfect boyfriend material, too, I'm sure. It's just . . . my mom."

"Is she *that* bad?"

"I don't know. Maybe not. Maybe I'm overreacting."

"Do you want to do this?"

"I *have* to do this."

"I don't have to join you."

"No. That's not the part I don't want." She chews on the skin at the edge of her thumbnail. "Okay. Let's do it. Thanks, Marcus."

"That's what I'm here for, babe." I wink.

"No." Her pretty pink lips flatten as she shoots me a death glare.

It's impossible to fight my grin. "Text me the flight details, *Brooke*."

Chapter Fifteen
Marcus

Eyes fixed on the leather luggage tag attached to my suitcase sitting in the hallway, I swirl the ice in my scotch glass from where I sit at the kitchen table. How the fuck did I get myself into this situation? Apparently my need over the past five years to think through every part of my plan before I initiate it went straight out the window when Lexy suggested I be Brooke's fake boyfriend last week.

I keep telling myself I don't know what changed, but I am a certified genius, and denying it is only driving me more insane. It's Brooke. It's everyone, really. It's all of the people closest to me finding the person they want to spend their life with. I'm not jealous. I'm fucking ecstatic for them. I'm not alone. If I make time in my busy schedule for them, my friends or family are always there for me. While I'm happy to work them into my free time, I *want* to find that person I'll drop anything for–the one I'll be willing to schedule everything else around. There's this nagging fucking feeling constantly in the back of my mind that maybe Brooke could be that person.

I can't pinpoint why I feel that way, but the thought is there. I'm constantly questioning if I know enough about her to have feelings for her. I've only known her for a month, but I wonder if she's been working her way into my life since long before we met and without her knowing. I've been listening to stories about the adventurous, loving girl from Thailand through Maci, on repeat, for the better part of a year. Some of them are from their time together and others are reiterations of phone calls at the kitchen table with Maci and Dean.

Maybe she was a hazy image in the distance that didn't come into focus until the day I met her with tears streaming down her beautiful face and realized that all I wanted to do was comfort her. I'm always there for my friends when they need it. I've talked Dean off more than one emotional ledge before he and Maci got their shit together. I've helped Maci work through her own doubts. Lord knows Cooper and Sophie would probably still be playing a relationship version of chicken if I hadn't slapped sense into them. But they all came to me. I somehow became an unspoken voice of reason even though comforting someone has never felt natural to me.

But when I saw Brooke wiping the tears from her eyes, masking her sadness with a joke to introduce herself, I spent the next twenty minutes racking my brain for something–anything–that would make her feel better.

Since then it's been every little thing that intrigues me.

The way her hair curls around her face after she gets back from a run.

How calm she looks when she's sitting criss-cross in my workout room in her elephant pants during a meditation–making me wish I could find peace in an unproductive moment.

Her pink lips pressed to a wine glass as she takes a sip, smiling at something Maci has said.

How quickly she thinks on her toes even when I force her into an unfamiliar situation.

Her confidence even when she's not completely sure about something.

The way nature seems to ground her and how I could have done that hike with her ten times over. That extended amount of time I went without thinking about work . . . it's proof there is something about her I should hold on to.

The way she looks at the stars–like they are what makes life worth living–makes me want to slow down for the first time.

I swear she's looked at me a few times like that–when she thought I wouldn't notice.

A few weeks ago, when that waitress gave me her number, it piqued Brooke's interest. I'm confident about that. I'd like to think it's because she was curious for personal reasons, but girls tend to be curious for no fucking reason at all.

"Dude." Dean's voice startles me and I pull my gaze from my luggage in the hallway to where he's standing next to the table, hands pressed into the back of the kitchen chair. He's staring at me like this isn't the first time he's tried to get my attention.

I sit up straighter in my seat, the ice clinking against the side of my glass as I swirl the amber liquid and stare into it before looking at him. "What's up, man?"

"I don't know." Dean chuckles. "You tell me."

"What do you mean?" I take a sip of my scotch.

"You're acting weird."

I raise a brow.

"Are you ready for your vacation?" He eyes the same suitcase I pack and set out the night before a trip nearly every week.

"Yeah, sure." I shift the glass over the table, leaving a trail of condensation over the wood.

"Did you pack condoms?" My eyes snap back to him. "I mean, clearly you're fucked, so . . ." He smirks. Fucker.

"It's a business arrangement."

His eyes raise in question. "Is she paying you to date her?"

"What? Of course not."

"If there's no transaction, then it's not really business." He smirks.

"Semantics," I mumble.

"Uh-huh."

I narrow my gaze. "Drop it."

He holds his hands up in surrender. "I'm just saying you've never had the urge to spend longer with a girl than the time it takes for coffee to get cold."

Don't I fucking know it. "Yeah." I toss back the rest of my drink. "I'm good." I get up, walking past Dean to put my glass in the sink.

"And you never take time off work," he razzes me behind my back.

I press my palms into the counter and take a deep breath. "It's just a vacation. I'm not getting married."

"Take a few in case. You never know."

I push away from the counter, taking a moment to stare blankly at my friend before whacking him upside the head. I swipe my Nalgene bottle from the marble by the loop and make my way to my office couch to attempt sleep, leaving a chuckling Dean behind.

Chapter Sixteen
Brooke

"Is it hot, or is it just me?" My words come out frustrated as my arm gets stuck in the sleeve of my zip-up sweater. I yank hard to no avail. Marcus gently balances his laptop bag on his suitcase where it sits on the concrete in the Uber curb-side pickup area of Bradley International.

"Here, let me help," he says calmly, locking his hands onto my flailing arms. His touch makes me feel like I'm suffocating more, but I let him pull the sleeves off before taking the jacket from him and tying it around my waist. "Are you alright?"

"Yeah, why?" I lean forward, glancing up the street to see if our Uber is here.

"Because it's 55° out and you're sweating."

I redirect my glance to his outfit. He's wearing a black pea coat over his go-to gray jeans and black T-shirt. His deep brown hair is pulled back neatly as if he just did it, rather than slept on a plane for five hours. Not that he slept. I don't know what he did besides pay for the three glasses of wine I drank to put me to sleep. "I'm . . . ugh. Just not looking forward to this is all."

"How many more minutes until the Uber gets here?"

My brows scrunch. Uhh. Okay. I guess he's going to ignore me. I glance back at my phone. "Still twelve more minutes."

"Okay." He scans the area, eyes locking on a walking path that runs between the parking garage and the road separating it from the airport terminal. Marcus slings his laptop bag over his shoulder, then aligns both our suitcases so he can grab the handles with one hand. With his free hand, he reaches for me. "Come on."

I stare at him blankly. "Where?"

He gives me a pointed look that says, "I'm not luring you to your death. Trust me," so I take his hand. It's an innocent hand holding. Our fingers aren't linked or anything. He simply has a firm enough grip to tug me gently toward the path ahead, but the warmth of his hand in mine soothes my entire body like a cup of tea.

We only take a dozen steps before he lets go, gently setting his bag on the cement path. "Take off your shoes," he tells me, kicking each of his off by the heel with the opposite toe. When he reaches to pull his socks off, he freezes, glancing back to where I'm staring at him in confusion. "It's called 'grounding.' Your bare feet touching the earth is thought to help realign your electrical energy."

He tugs his socks off, tucking them into his shoes, then steps onto the patchy grass lining the path. "I started doing it whenever I would change time zones. Someone told me it helps with jet lag by resetting your inner clockwork."

"And it works?" I kick off my shoes and tug on my socks without waiting for him to respond and step onto the dirt patch next to him.

"Might be a placebo effect, but I feel like it does."

"I think I saw something about this on the show *Down to Earth.*"

Recognition sparks in his eyes. "Yeah."

"You've seen it?"

He chuckles. "Dean's sister, Sophie, made me watch it with her when she lived with me." Wait. He's lived with a girl before? But surely not in a romantic sense? Maci would have mentioned if he dated Dean's sister. "It's good info, though. After watching that show, I did more research on it. It's not meant to be a microwave type of fix for anything, but over time and with consistency, it's supposed to benefit you physically and mentally."

"Doesn't seem like there's a reason not to try it then." I wiggle my toes, feeling a few small pebbles between them.

"Exactly."

"Thank you." I look up from the ground to meet his gaze, realizing he's extremely close to me. If I took a step forward and reached out I could easily slip my hands under his coat and lean into him. If someone told me they saw a grown ass, fully dressed man barefoot outside of an airport, I'd think they were talking about a homeless person. But watching Marcus not giving a shit where we are just to try and help me–or even if it's just to center his own body–it's a turn on that I'd never have put on my list in a million lifetimes.

Movement on my phone screen breaks through the temptation to touch him, though. Our car is arriving soon. I flash him a half-smile and my phone screen, and without another word, we put our shoes back on and walk toward the rideshare pickup.

Just in time, a silver Civic pulls up to the curb, the driver confirming it's me before popping the trunk. Marcus effortlessly slides both our bags in the back, then ducks into the backseat next to me. "Hey." His words are barely audible over the annoying rap song the driver has on half-blast. He reaches out like he's going to touch my leg to comfort me. Instead, he shoves both hands in either pocket of his jacket, twisting so he's facing me. "It's going to be fine. Do you want to go over the plan again?"

I nod. I love the idea of grounding, and handsdown, I'm adding it to my daily regimen, but like Marcus said, it's not an instant fix, and not even the power of the earth can immediately flip all my negative energy to positive.

"We kept it simple, remember. Everything is exactly the same as it happened. Except for the dating part. We met a month and a half ago when you came to visit Maci. You've been helping me at the bar, with Emma and Charlotte, and spending so much time together just transitioned into more."

"But we've hardly spent that much time together."

"Enough to know we like each other."

I ignore the flutter tearing up my stomach. He's just talking about the plan. He doesn't actually feel that way. "Okay, but *when* did you realize you liked me? My mom is going to ask you that."

"The day we went hiking," he says easily. "You were so focused on your glimmer that you didn't even notice me watching you. That's when I realized you were mine."

My mouth falls open just barely before I shake my head. This is not real. "Oh yeah. That's good. She'll eat that up. Or at least pretend to."

His eyes shift over mine. "What about you?"

"What about me, what?"

"When did you fall for me?"

"When you handed me a cup of real Thai tea." My answer comes as easily as his, but it doesn't mean anything.

"That was the first day we met." He chuckles.

I shrug. "What can I say? I make impulsive decisions when it comes to my heart."

"Alright then. See we got this. What about your dad? Anything you want me to know?"

A small smile fights through. "Nah. He hasn't spent enough time around me and a guy to know if something is real or not. Plus, I've already told him about you."

Marcus arches a brow.

My dad and I have weekly phone dates, so of course he knows about my boss, and it just made sense to tell him he's my boyfriend when we made that deal. It's not like I was rambling about a crush or anything. "We probably need rules," I blurt, changing directions.

"Rules?"

"Yeah, you know . . . like where the line is. So we're believable as a couple, but you don't feel uncomfortable."

"I'm not concerned. I can't imagine a situation where we'd have to have sex in front of people. Unless this country club is more of the illegal sort of club." He raises a brow.

"Right. I mean, no. It's not. And definitely no sex. You are my boss after all."

"Didn't you just read a book where the girl had sex with her boss?" He smirks.

"Well, yeah. But that was a book."

"Aren't we pretending to date just like in a book?"

"Oh. Hmm. I see your point. Still, no sex."

"Alright." He chuckles. "No sex."

My stomach drops, disappointment shooting through me. Why was I kind of hoping he'd object to that rule? "Okay, next rule . . . No talking to other girls while you're here. My mom can spot sneaky from a mile away."

"I'm not talking to other girls."

"Yeah, remind me why that is again."

"This is my first time having more than two days off in over a year," he states, like that is enough of an answer.

"Right. Lexy said she tries to set you up a lot."

"She does."

"Do you go?"

"Most of the time, I'll take them to coffee."

"And . . ." My eyes drift to the car window behind him. Cotton candy pink wisps through the sky as we drive, the sun an orange glowing ball sinking into the horizon. It's out of this world, and I let its beauty ground me, easing my anxiety from wishing that I could be one of the girls Marcus took to coffee and not because it was part of his newly appointed job as my fake boyfriend.

I focus back on him in time for his words to register. "And nothing."

Nothing what? Nothing in common? No sparks? This man can be infuriating. "Tell me about your family."

"What do you want to know?"

"How did your parents meet?"

"They both worked at an elementary school."

"That's so cool. Did you go to the same school?"

"Yup." It's annoying how he doesn't elaborate. I hate having to dig for information.

"Must have been nice to have them around a lot."

"Your parents weren't?"

"Dad was the best parent he could be while also trying to appease my mom's need for more financial security. At least until they got divorced. Mom has worked at the country club forever. She goes above and beyond for all the guests which is time-consuming."

"Sounds like she's a hard worker."

"That's her argument. But at what cost? She never went above and beyond for me. Didn't come to a single Girl Scout event, or ever volunteered in my class. The only time she chose me over work was prom night. And it was only because I finally picked a 'right guy.'"

"What qualifies as 'right?'"

"Rich."

"That's her only criteria?"

"Basically. She thinks if I marry someone rich, she'll be set for life because they will take care of her too. That's why she always sucks up to the club members. I only ended up with Beau at first because my mom was halfway up Martha's ass."

"Beau is the lawyer." He confirms rather than asks.

I nod.

"Why didn't it work out?"

Hesitating, I contemplate how much to tell him as I pick at my fingernail.

"It's fine. You don't have to tell me. I'd just like to be prepared for whatever happens this week."

Oh yeah. Of course. This is just a business deal to him. He doesn't *actually* want to know. I take a breath and release the bare minimum information. "Long story short? He's an asshole. Imagine your stereotypical lawyer, and you've got Beau. Cares more about his job than any other part of his life. Treated me as if I was his employee all the time, rather than just at work."

"So you dumped him?"

"Something like that."

Marcus stops prying and after a few minutes of silence between us, I wedge my Air pods in my ears and open my meditation app. I leave it playing for the next twenty minutes, with my eyes closed, head leaned back against the seat, until Marcus taps me gently, letting me know we're here.

Chapter Seventeen
Marcus

Tugging mine and Brooke's suitcases from the trunk, I wheel them both forward with one hand, lifting them over the curb outside the hotel where her dad works. Brooke pushes through the front door with far more enthusiasm than I expected, considering how trepid she's been.

She scans the hotel lobby before landing on an everyday man dressed in tan slacks, a light blue button-up and a striped navy tie. "Dad!" she yells like we are the only ones in here and leaps at him, flinging her arms around his neck.

"There's my girl." He squeezes her tight before releasing her just as I catch up. "You must be Marcus. I've heard so much about you."

"Have you now?" I smirk, adjusting my laptop bag on my shoulder with one hand and reaching out the other to shake his. "Only good things I hope."

"The man who doesn't try to clip my baby birds' wings," he says. "I can't wait to hear more about this job."

"It's nice to meet you, Mr. Fields. Thank you for having us."

"Please call me Joseph. And thank you for coming. I know this trip isn't exactly on any bucket lists." He turns away and leads us to the tan marble lobby counter.

"We're happy to be here," I reply. Brooke seems to be out of words, the spark of joy she had for her dad instantly diminishing at the reminder that we are here to spend time with her mom too.

"Alright, well I've got the keys to your room right here."

Room. Singular.

Why did it not occur to me that we'd be sharing a room–sharing a space?

It must not have occurred to Brooke either based on the way her eyes widen. "You know, Dad," she starts. "We can stay in separate rooms. I know you're old-fashioned."

"Nonsense, Brooke." He waves his hand before holding out the white paper packet containing the keycards. "You're an adult. I want you to feel as comfortable as possible during your stay so you come back to see me. If that means having your boyfriend with you to make you feel safe after a day with that wretched woman, then so be it."

Brooke winces at the mention of her mother, and I feel the urge to redirect the moment. "Thank you, Joseph," I say, taking the keys from him and reminding myself of my role. With my free hand, I graze Brooke's lower back, only enough to encourage her toward the elevators. She tenses at my touch but not enough that anyone else would have noticed. Her body relaxes under my hand with her first steps, and she glances over her shoulder.

"See you for dinner, Dad?"

"Sure thing, sweetie. Go get settled in. Meet me in the lobby at 8?"

"Okay."

With that, even though my hand is still connected to the thin fabric of her tank top, she guides me toward the elevator. She taps on the "4" and once I'm inside with the bags, she stares at the stainless steel doors as they close us in.

"I'm sorry," she whispers.

"About?" I shift my gaze to catch hers but she's picking at her light pink fingernail. Weird. I don't think I've seen her nails painted since I've met her. Maybe I didn't notice.

"I didn't think about the bed situation."

I chuckle. "I think we can manage."

"About that."

"What?"

"Well, I didn't even pack pajamas. I don't know why I didn't think about it. I'm not a very good planner."

"You planned an entire successful book event."

"That was important to me."

"I take it pajamas aren't?"

"Not so much."

Fucking hell. Does that mean she's been sleeping naked in my bed every night–not even a scrap of fabric dividing us on the other side of the wall? "Lucky for you, I am a planner. I'm sure I have an extra shirt you can borrow."

"Thanks, Marcus. For all of this."

"You're welcome." I hold her gaze longer than my dick wishes I would, thankfully broken by the elevator jolting to a stop. The doors open with a whoosh to a hallway covered with tan chevron carpet. Our room happens to be the one directly in front of us. I pull the key from its pocket, tapping it against the black box next to the door before pushing through it.

I pull the suitcases into the space in time to watch Brooke toss herself dramatically onto the white comforter, her feet hanging off the edge as she stares at the ceiling. A fresh smile lights her face as her eyelids flutter closed.

"That good, huh?"

"Just a glimmer. Nothing like a freshly made hotel bed, you know?"

"Not really. I've spent a lot of time in hotels in the past few years. My bed is what I look forward to."

"Sorry." Her smile fades. "I've been holding it hostage from you."

"That's not what I meant."

"Well, maybe after this trip, we will be pros at sharing a bed and you can move off the couch." Her words flow with innocence when I wish they were anything but. I debate making a joke, but not knowing how she'd react keeps me from it. "I guess it depends if you snore."

"No snoring here. Hope you don't mind my mid-night kicking, though," I tease, feeling weird about being somewhat relaxed in this situation.

"Not at all," she plays. "A perfect way to test my self-defense skills. If I can't protect myself in my sleep, what even was the point in all those Muay Thai classes?"

Taking off my jacket and draping it over the back of a chair, I sit on the edge of the bed and twist back to look at the beautiful girl sprawled out behind me. "Impressive. Seems Thailand was good for you."

"Yeah." She sighs, sitting and kicking off her Nikes to sit criss-cross on the mattress. "*Thai Brooke* is the best Brooke."

"*Thai Brooke* can't exist anywhere else?"

"Not in a place where my mother also exists."

Goddamn, maybe this woman actually is Satan. There's no avoiding finding out first-hand now.

"Your dad is cool," I tell Brooke as we make it back to the room after a two-hour dinner in the hotel restaurant.

"He's the best." She digs through her suitcase for a toiletry bag before walking to the bathroom. "I would have lost my mind growing up if it wasn't for him."

"When did your parents get divorced?" I ask through the door she's left barely cracked.

"Not until right before I left for Thailand, unfortunately." She turns on the faucet, and I lean against the wall outside the bathroom. "It should have been way sooner than that, but it's hard to leave sometimes, ya know? There can still be comfort in things that are wrong."

"It's safe and not as scary as putting yourself out there." I surprise myself with the admission.

Brooke opens the door enough to stick her head out, purple toothbrush pulled to her lips. "Yeah, that." She gives me a sad smile before stepping back in front of the sink, the cracked door still between us. "I'm proud of my dad for leaving. Better late than never. And it's what gave me the confidence to leave Beau."

"Are you worried about seeing him this week?" I instantly regret the curiosity when she doesn't reply, standing outside the door awkwardly.

I'm about to take it back and admit to it being none of my business when her toothpaste spit hits the ceramic sink. A moment later, a soft, "Not as much as I am about seeing my mom, but yeah," comes from the other side of the door. "He wasn't all bad." Her words are so quiet that I barely hear them–like maybe she's trying to convince herself more than me.

Still leaning against the wall outside the bathroom, I resist the urge to both walk away from this conversation and from joining her in the bathroom. "Oh yeah?"

She sighs. "When we were in college, he was different. Fun. Into me. Like I meant something to him."

I can't wrap my head around why anyone would be in a relationship with someone who didn't mean everything to them. Her silence brings me back to the present. "You don't think you did?"

It's a moment before she answers, like she was lost in thought. "I think that once he became a lawyer, his need to succeed and be the best took priority over loving me. When you ignore someone long enough, anything good just fades away, you know?"

I have an idea–it's why I refuse to waste anyone's time if I'm not interested enough to make them a priority.

"Have you ever been in a serious relationship?" she asks.

Now I'm really ready to exit this conversation. "I dated some in college. It didn't stick." The second the words leave my mouth, I regret them. She probably thinks it didn't work out because work is my priority too. I guess you could argue that, but it was always *them*, not me. They weren't the right fit.

"Well, at least then you can avoid situations like this."

I have no idea how to respond, and she takes the hint, pushing the door closed and cutting off our conversation.

Fucking hell. This girl is making me nervous about tomorrow. As I dig through my bag for athletic shorts for me and a T-shirt for Brooke, it hits me that I have to sleep in bed with her first. I debate seeing if there's bourbon in the mini-fridge even though there's likely not. I know I can handle whatever comes my way tomorrow if it means helping Brooke. It should be easy enough. I know how to mold myself to any situation as needed. But it's been a long ass time since I've been in bed with a girl I'm sexually attracted to and can't touch. If ever. And she's made it very clear that touching will not be something that happens.

I'm tugging my shorts over my hips as Brooke exits the bathroom. She glances my way but quickly shifts gears toward the mini-fridge. She pulls out two shooters before turning around. "There's no bourbon, but whiskey?" Didn't she just brush her teeth? She must be really stressed. Or maybe not as much of a control freak as I am.

"Sure. Thanks. I left you a T-shirt on the bed." I nod toward the black fabric as if it doesn't stand out on its own against the white sheets and leave to take my turn in the bathroom, skipping brushing my teeth for now.

When I return, Brooke is sitting cross-legged in the middle of the king-sized bed in nothing but my shirt. Her blonde hair spills over her shoulders, and the shirt is just long enough to make me wonder what type of underwear is barely out of reach.

She glances up, her hazel eyes glossed over. There's no drink in her hand, but even if she took it as a shot, it wouldn't have hit her that fast. "Oh, hey," she whispers like she already forgot I was here too.

I'm tempted to reach for the whiskey on ice she's made for me and set on the nightstand, but I'm frozen in place. She's so goddamn sexy, but she's also really fucking sad, and I'm really fucking uncomfortable. Just turn on the TV and drink your whiskey and don't get deeper into her problems than you already are. "What's wrong?"

"Nothing." She brushes me off with a wave of her hand and pulls back the covers, flashing me a view of a strip of purple lace perfectly hugging her ass before she crawls under the sheets and reaches for the TV remote. Fuck me.

I join her on the bed but sit on top of the covers, back against the headboard, and reach for my whiskey. The cold amber liquid hits my tongue and before I can stop myself, I down the entire glass as if it were a shot. "It's not nothing," I say, setting the empty glass–aside from melting ice–on the nightstand.

"It's just . . . What if no one believes we're together and my mom . . . I don't know. Forces me alone with Beau or something?"

"They'll believe it. I'll make sure of it. And I won't let you be alone with that douche for even a second."

"What if you have to pee or something?"

I lick my lips, biting back a grin. "Then I guess we'll hit that level of friendship that happens when girls get drunk and go to the bathroom together really quickly."

"Except you're not a girl."

I shrug. "And we won't be drunk."

"Speak for yourself."

Despite being one, I typically am not a fan of rich people either. But they *always* have excellent taste in bourbon. "It'll be okay."

She doesn't say anything.

"Do you trust me?" I keep my gaze locked on her even though her eyes are focused on where she scratches at her perfectly pink and glossy fingernail again as if she could chip the professional polish.

She nods. "I think so." Guilt racks through me, thinking maybe I should mention my net worth. It's never something I tell people–outside of my parents and Dean, it's never been a conversation. But knowing how Brooke feels about the category she'll inevitably place me in, I'm concerned holding back this piece of information will be a nail in a tire.

"Convincing." I chuckle in an attempt to ease the tension.

"I wish Maci were here," she mumbles.

I try not to take it personally. "I don't think she'd be able to sell the boyfriend thing."

A sad chuckle escapes her lips. "No, I know."

"But she'd know how to make you feel better?"

She nods again.

"What would she do?"

She glances at me, then looks at the comforter, smoothing her hands over it. "When she was in Thailand and distraught trying to figure out who she should be with, there was this night where she was all talked out. She didn't know what to say or think or do anymore. We were sitting on my couch listening to the birds chirping outside in the night with a soft breeze coming in through an open window. I pulled her head to my lap and just let her cry and lie there. I could feel the moment her resolve set in. I know it's not what *worked*, but it helped."

My head falls against the headboard with the weight of my options. I'm sure as hell not Maci, and Brooke has made it very clear I'm her boss and where the line is drawn in our situation. Although, it's contradictory to the way she opens up to me. Fuck if I know what that means. "Maybe you just need a good night's sleep."

"Yeah, maybe." She sighs, rolling away from me, giving up on the idea of TV and replacing the remote on the nightstand before she settles in.

Uncomfortable with the tension, I pull my computer from my laptop case next to my bed, deciding to get some work done as Brooke drifts off to sleep without another word.

Chapter Eighteen
Brooke

My arm lands hard as I turn in my sleep, waking me. Clearly that was *not* the mattress. I squint my eyes open. They're distracted by the hotel clock first. *4:08.* I know that's only one back home, but still. Noticing my hand on Marcus' thigh, I pull it back into my own bubble before taking him in. His fingers are frozen mid-typing, and his eyes are locked on my movement. God, he's hot when he's wearing his black frame glasses. "What are you doing?" I ask groggily, glancing at the screen. Even with the brightness turned down, it glares at me. Even if my eyes could adjust quickly, I'd still have zero idea what he was doing. My guess is coding? Because in my head, I picture coding to look like a bunch of hieroglyphics, and this looks just as unreadable. This man is brilliant. But also, maybe a workaholic.

"Working. Did I wake you?"

I shake my head, curling my hands beneath my face on my pillow and gazing up at the way the dim computer light makes his handsome face glow and hoping it's not clear that I was having a dream about him. It wasn't inappropriate or anything–at least it hadn't gotten there *yet.* Surely it's only because I'm sleeping in bed just inches from him. "No. Just restless." I tug the comforter down, leaving me covered only by the sheet and Marcus' shirt. God, it smells so good. I take a sneaky deep breath of the fabric, reveling in the way the sandalwood calms me the way you'd expect lavender to.

Marcus glances at the clock, and I use the second to my advantage to scan him. My gaze catches on the script along his bicep, barely below the hem of his T-shirt sleeve. *Sisu.* "What does that mean?"

He follows my gaze. "It's Finnish," he says, closing his laptop, the light in the room disappearing as it clicks. Setting it on the bedside table, he adjusts, scooting down on the bed until his face is close to mine. I can feel him despite my eyes not adjusting to the darkness yet. "It's a core element of one's psyche. There's no direct translation, but in essence, it means, 'the drive and courage to see a goal through to the end, one step at a time.'"

"So . . . fortitude?" Sometimes I think Marcus is way too smart for me. I only know this word because of my love for *One Tree Hill*.

"Similar. Fortitude refers to the actual strength of the mind in the face of adversity. Sisu is essentially the spirit of someone who embodies tenacity, and it's activated when we feel we couldn't possibly handle any more."

"Maybe you could elaborate on that a little bit so I understand better." Part of me thinks I should feel stupid for asking, but I'm so curious, and Marcus has never spoken to me like I'm dumb.

He nods, a faint smile gracing his lips. "Sisu is a visceral energy that resides deep inside you and fuels your grit, creating your ability to surpass your preconceived limitations. It's usually harnessed in the face of adversity by accessing this stored-up energy or spirit to get you through any endeavor in life, even if you have no idea how you'll make it to the end."

I think that's the most words he's ever strung together in my presence. It's like my interest unlocked his talkative side. When I was younger, I had this impression that being part of a world with other business owners could be collaborative–the whole idea that you're a combination of the people you spend the most time with, so you want to surround yourself with people always asking questions, learning and growing. But since working alongside Beau, I've seen first hand that more often than not, everything is competitive, and no one is willing to learn at the cost of looking unintelligent. Something tells me that Marcus thinks willingness to learn is a sign of intelligence instead. "Oh, okay. That makes sense. Why did you get it?"

Silence.

I let it hang there. Maybe I was totally off base. I'm prepared to let go of the conversation and fall asleep if he's not comfortable telling me, but still, I breathe slowly and wait.

"My senior year of high school, I created an app. I knew it worked and that it was brilliant, but I was too young to know what to do with it. All I knew was that I wanted to help my parents pay for my tuition and thought maybe I could sell it. I placed my trust in the wrong person."

A small gasp leaves me. "What happened?"

"They stole it."

"That's terrible. I'm so sorry."

"Don't be. It's the best thing that ever happened to me. I'm more diligent now. Prepared. Organized. Cautious."

"You didn't fight back? Didn't you work hard on the app? I can't imagine it's easy."

"It took me two years to code. But I didn't get a copyright or have proof that it was mine first. I had no leg to stand on."

"I would have been so upset. Debilitatingly so."

He chuckles. "There might be a laptop in a dumpster somewhere serving as collateral damage."

"So, what did you do?"

"I came up with another idea and made a new app."

"You say it like it was easy."

"Anything but. I didn't see another choice, though. One day at a time. One decision. Week after week until I figured it out and got it done. That's why I got this. It's a permanent reminder that I can tap into sisu whenever I need to so my life and dreams can continue on the path I've chosen."

"Wow. I love that," I whisper in the dark, wishing I could see him better. "You probably think me acting like my mom is some insurmountable mountain is ridiculous then. Not a real problem."

"Adversity is subjective. We're all entitled to our triggers and challenges based on our experiences. It's more about how we overcome them that defines us."

I keep my hands to myself despite their urge to reach for him as if I could extract my own sisu from his. I should feel pathetic hoping he's my lifeboat, but I don't. I feel hope that I can turn this situation around.

He holds my gaze in the dark, the glow of the hotel clock the only thing casting light across his face. The way he doesn't close his eyes and lets them scan my face draws me closer to him. As if I'm possessed, I reach to touch his arm. The way he's laying with his hands under his face like a pillow, the tattooed part of his skin isn't even visible, but I brush my fingers along the outer edge of his bicep anyway. He doesn't flinch. His skin just feels warm under my touch.

"It already exists inside you too, you know," he tells me.

"You think so?" I whisper.

"Positive." He speaks with certainty like he's known me my whole life.

Against my rational thoughts, I let my fingers wander. They slowly scan his arm–down his bicep, along the crook of his elbow, brushing over his forearm to where his face rests on his hands. He doesn't follow my touch–rather keeps his gaze on me, his emotions untelling. My pinky nearly links with his, my hand ending its journey near his mouth. Holy shit, I want him to kiss me. I want his fingers in my hair. I pull my hand away like my thoughts lit his skin on fire.

"Goodnight, Marcus," I whisper, turning over, away from him.

He's close enough behind me that I feel his breath on my hair when he returns the sentiment.

A glow from behind me is the only light in the room when I crack my eyes open. In my line of sight, the curtains over the window are pinched together by the pant clasp of a coat hanger to prevent daylight from seeping through. That's a neat hack. My vision is blurry with a film of sleep. I wipe it away and turn slowly, taking in the way Marcus' laptop screen lights his face. *Again? Already?* Does this man ever sleep? Or do anything besides work? His hair is pulled back neat where his head leans against the headboard, his black shirt fairly tight against his chest.

He glances over at my movement.

"Morning," I manage with a raspy voice.

"Morning," he says, his deep *first words of the day* tone doing something to my insides. It's so foreign, us being together in bed. Yet, it's casual, like we've done it a hundred times. Why is he working so much, though?

"I thought you were on vacation?"

He glances at me again before focusing back on his screen. "You were sleeping. Might as well be productive."

"You don't know how to rest, do you?"

"I like work."

"Uh-huh." I sit, tugging the edge of his shirt down before sliding out of bed to get ready.

"What's the plan for today?" he asks. When I glance up from where I'm ruffling through my suitcase on the floor, his fingers are still hovering over the keyboard like he intends to keep writing.

"My mom is working a wedding. She's in charge of catering, so after she yells at a bunch of people, she'll have time to meet us for lunch. I thought maybe after that I could show you around the club? I kind of hate it there, but it is where I grew up. You probably don't care about that, though. Today is mostly a free day."

"I'd love to see it." He hesitates, but then closes his laptop.

"Okay. It really is beautiful. And I can show you all the places I used to hide from Mom." I chuckle, excited to show him the disabled laundry elevator shaft and wondering if I'll still fit in it.

"Can't wait. How fancy is this place? Does it matter what I wear?"

"It's faaaaancy. I should probably wear a dress, but no thanks. I'll wear this." I pull out a sheer loose-fitting white tank that I plan to french tuck into my jeans from my bag. "Your usual is perfect."

With my clothes in one hand and my curling iron in the other, I retreat to the bathroom.

Thirty minutes later, I rejoin Marcus in the room. He's in the same position he was to sleep in, but fully clothed now. Black jeans are tight around his bulky thighs and his feet are crossed at the ankle. He's swapped out a typical gray T-shirt for a button-up rolled to his elbows.

He looks up from his computer resting on his lap again, his eyes narrowing as they take me in. "You look . . . different."

I'd take offense, but I know I do. I curled my hair and put on more makeup than just light sunscreen foundation and mascara. I did the whole blush and smokey eye thing. The shades of rose I chose do make the green in my eyes pop, but it doesn't feel like *me*. "Yeah, well. Not wearing a dress will give my mom enough to complain about. The makeup and hair are the compromises I'm willing to make."

"And the nails."

He noticed my nails? It's something I also hate making time for, but I knew Mom would drag me to the salon as soon as I got here if they weren't done already. She always says no man will ever believe in my ability to help him if I don't take my working hands seriously. Whatever the hell that means. "Yeah, those too."

"For the record, I like the waves better."

Whether it's to make me feel better or the truth, I grin. "Thanks. It's this sea salt spray that gives the same effect as the ocean in Thailand." I went through seven until I found the perfect one. I can't help but smile at the discovery. A piece of *Thai Brooke* that's easy to hold onto.

"A glimmer?" he asks, closing his laptop and sliding it off him to stand from the bed.

"Definitely. You ready?"

"I updated my will in case I don't survive lunch with the devil. So, I'm ready as I'll ever be."

Laughing, I look over my shoulder on the way out the door. "Don't worry, she prefers slow torture over a quick death. You've got plenty more days left in you."

Chapter Nineteen
Marcus

"Wow." My eyes scan slowly from left to right when we walk to the top of the outside staircase.

"It sure is something, huh?"

The white marble stairs split to either side with three separate pools cascading down the middle. It opens to a white cement runway of sorts leading to a long pergola draped in ivy curtains and orange flower bouquets. The rest of the area is covered by perfectly manicured bright green grass and the edge of the property is lined by tall forest green trees.

I'm not in denial about the amount of money I have, and I could very easily belong to a club like this, or have a house as extravagant. Despite not wanting people to know I'm well-off, I don't have any desire for it. Regardless, there's no denying this property is extraordinary.

I follow Brooke down the right side of the staircase, her hand trailing along the marbled railing. I'd be concerned about whether or not it's sanitary, but the entire structure looks clean enough to eat from.

"There you are!" A woman directing a man with an absurdly large flower centerpiece yells toward us.

Not missing the way Brooke is paralyzed by the moment, I gently encourage her forward with a hand on her lower back. "It'll be okay," I whisper behind her.

"Don't leave me," she begs.

I have never seen someone so anxious about a parent. It feels a little over the top until I watch the lady with a perfectly styled short bob and a classic rich older woman's navy dress appraise the girl in front of me. She unashamedly drags her eyes over Brooke, the look of disgust deepening with each second.

We come to a halt in front of her, and I swear Brooke reaches back for my hand before thinking better of it and dropping it to her side. "Hi, Mom."

"Darling. What are you wearing?"

I thought she hadn't seen her mom in three years. Not even a hug? It's nowhere near the greeting she shared with her dad.

"It's not like I'm attending this wedding, Mother. We're just here for lunch," Brooke tries, but it's no use.

"You still have a status to uphold."

"I don't even belong to this club." I was curious how we'd get in since I was under the impression it was members only, but the second the older woman at the front desk spotted Brooke, she wrapped her in a hug like a grandmother holding her favorite grandchild.

"So, you have no respect for the image I must maintain? I worked hard to gain the reputation I have here."

I clear my throat and reach out my hand. "Hello, Mrs. Fields. I'm Marcus Cole."

She ignores my gesture, scanning me with almost as much disdain as she did with her daughter. "Who are you?"

Brooke groans. "Mom. This is my boyfriend." She says the word more easily than I expected. "I told you about him."

"Oh, right. Your boss."

"And boyfriend," she reiterates.

"Well that's one way to get to the top," she mutters under her breath.

"Brooke is the best assistant I've ever had," I'm compelled to add, feeling guilty as hell for thinking she may have been exaggerating about how bad her mom is.

"See, Brooke, I told you that you needed that degree."

"You sure did, Mom. Thanks. Ready for lunch?"

We follow her mom to the on-site restaurant, stopping multiple times for her to demand a wedding task from a worker. When we get to our rectangle white linen-lined table near a window overlooking the courtyard, I pull the chair out for Brooke's mom. She hardly acknowledges me, but Brooke whispers a thank you with a look of "I'm sorry my mom is a bitch" in her eyes when I help her settle in her chair.

Brooke unfolds the napkin from its triangle shape on the table and places it on her lap. Her fingers don't leave the fabric, though. Instead, she pinches one end of the fabric between her fingers and runs the fingers of her other hand over the seam repeatedly. I reach over, covering her knee with my hand firmly and running my thumb back and forth over her jeans.

She sends me a quick appreciative glance and to my surprise, slips her fidgeting hand under mine, linking our fingers.

Her mom eyes us like we're doing something wrong. "So, tell me, Marcus. How did you manage to afford free time at work when your assistant isn't home to cover for you."

I clear my throat. "That's the beauty of owning your own business. You can do whatever you want. And lucky for me, I was able to bring some work with me."

"Mhmm. I see." She straightens her fork in its place on the table. "I read an article the other day stating that twenty percent of small businesses fail in the first year."

"And what are the odds of someone making it if they've been pulling a profit since they were nineteen?"

She stares, bored. "Entrepreneurship is not a reliable career. It could fail at any time with even a small shift of the market."

"Some people work hard to make a living, Mom. And figure it out if something goes wrong. Most people aren't given trust funds and contacts at prestigious law firms even though they're shitty lawyers."

I lick my lip to cover my smile. I shouldn't be amused in the first place. She thinks she's defending me, but what's going to happen when she realizes I likely have more money than Beau does? There's a chance my net worth is higher than his entire family. Still, I worked for every penny of it.

"I'm just looking out for you, darling," she says, almost robotically, as she scans the menu.

"No, you're looking out for *you*," Brooke mutters under her breath, and I squeeze her hand, torn between believing she should respect her mom regardless while also wishing Brooke never had to spend another second with her.

Her mom glances up, locking her stare on Brooke. Her gaze shifts to me before landing back on her daughter. "Marriage is not something to take lightly, you know."

"Who said anything about marriage?" Brooke snaps. "I'm twenty-four."

"Exactly, and if you don't find someone now, you won't even be young enough to be someone's second wife." She glances back at her menu like she didn't just fire a loaded gun.

This lady is way past losing her marbles. I mindlessly rub my thumb over Brooke's in an attempt to lessen the impact of the bomb I'm about to drop. "I don't want to get married." Both their attentions snap to me. I shrug, squeezing Brooke's hand. "I want to wake up next to the woman I love because I want to, not because I'm supposed to."

Her mom's mouth drops.

A small smile slips from Brooke. "I've never thought of it that way."

I wonder if she knows I mean the sentiment or if she thinks it was meant to piss off her mom. It doesn't matter either way, but I tack on an added thought. "A man I met in Greece said it to me once. It stuck."

"I like it," Brooke says, and now *I'm wondering* if she means that or if she's trying to piss off her mom.

"Oh for heaven's sake," her mom mutters, reminding me we aren't alone in a bubble. "You two are delusional."

"Mrs. Fields," I address her, pulling her attention from the current conversation, knowing it's not a battle we could ever win with her. "Tell me about you. It's a beautiful place you've maintained here."

The compliment distracts her for now, and we spend the next hour over lunch hearing about all her life "accomplishments." None of which, I note only to myself, have to do with raising the beautiful girl beside me.

Chapter Twenty
Brooke

"You trust me, right?" My smile is mischievous as I hold my hand against the sliding cover for the laundry chute and look over my shoulder at Marcus.

He quirks a brow. The old wood panel sticks only a little when I slide it to the right and reveal a wood platform held up by a pulley system. "Uhhhh."

"Come on," I say, stepping on the ledge two feet from the ground and reaching my hand for his as if he actually needs my help.

"There is no sign this has worked in a decade."

The rope does have a cobweb. "Where is your sense of adventure? I promise it'll hold. This thing can carry a two-thousand-pound commercial laundry bag."

He hesitates but then takes my hand even though he jumps up and doesn't give me any body weight. I reluctantly let him drop my hand so he can get settled. I love the feel of his hands on me, like at lunch earlier. Slipping his hand over my knee was such an innocent gesture–especially considering he was just playing his role of fake boyfriend. The thing is, no man has ever done that with me, even when the relationship was real. Especially not Beau–at least not once he became a lawyer. I can't even remember a time he held my hand in public. He'd always claim that since I worked for him, it was unprofessional to bring what we did behind closed doors into public. But by the end of our relationship, even at home, he'd never reach for me unless he wanted sex. After a couple of years of living that way, it would have been such a strange reaction. Yet, when Marcus did it, it felt so familiar and comfortable. I shake the memories from my head.

"Turn on your phone flashlight." He does as I ask while I reach behind him to close the door to the chute, my hand barely grazing his bicep. Pausing, I take him in as he watches me. He's sitting on his ass, his legs bent and a hand linked around his wrist as his arms rest across his knees. His arms bulge where they are being perfectly constrained by the sleeves of his black button-up and a strand of his dark hair has fallen from its tie as he dipped his head to not hit it on the ceiling. I still fit reasonably well, but it's comical how crowded his frame is.

He holds my stare and when my eyes flick to his lips for only a split second, the only indication that he notices is a slight furrow of his brows. I fall back on my butt, sitting criss-cross before reaching for the thick rope on the side of the cart and giving it a strong pull.

Marcus chuckles, bringing my attention back to him. "Of course it's manual."

I shrug, wrapping my hands around the rough nylon for another pull, nostalgia hitting me hard at the feel of the rope against my palms. Grinning, I talk over my shoulder. "This was my favorite place as a kid. One of the maids would load me into the chute with the bag of dirty sheets. Then she would walk down to the room and work the pulley from there. It was the closest thing

I ever got to a theme park ride as a kid. Plus, it was the perfect hiding spot."

With another two pulls, we're at the bottom, and I slide the door to the chute open, this one sticking a little more than the first and sending a poof of dust into the air. We both cough a little as Marcus steps first into the empty cement room and offers me his hand. Once I'm out, he holds up his phone, scanning the room with the light. It's smaller than I remember. It would probably only fit one commercial washer and dryer.

I take a step to see if the light by the door works when Marcus' phone buzzes. It echos off the walls, startling me enough to freeze in place. Through the shadows, I see him glance at the screen and follow his gaze. It's Emma.

"Were you expecting a call from her?"

"No. I should take it."

I nod and he taps the green circle and brings the phone to his ear, the flashlight on the back of his phone still the only light in the room. "Hey, Emma."

What sounds like a cry comes through, but I can't hear what she's saying.

"Whoa, slow down. What happened?" he asks, and then Emma says something else I can't understand. "Yeah, she's right here. Hold on."

Marcus moves the phone between us and hits the speakerphone button.

"Emma? What's wrong?"

Her voice cracks on a sob. "I don't think I can do this." Her words come out rushed like if they come out fast enough she could deny she even said them. "I'm scared to talk to Charlotte. She's so hyped, so positive, so confident all the time. But what if we fail? What if we don't help anyone? What if . . . I don't know. They're just going to make a new drug that our strips won't detect, and then we won't even have a business anymore, and then we won't have any money, and I'll have to sell my car and my house, and I'll starve, and then I definitely won't be able to save anyone, and it'll all be for nothing. Who am I to even think I could make a difference? It's too insane. It's too big." She takes a deep breath and then chokes on a cry. I glance at Marcus and instantly know by his wide eyes he has no idea how to comfort her. It's the look he gave me last night too.

"What you're doing for the world, it matters so much, Emma. Did you know in Thailand Rohypnol isn't even illegal? You can't buy it over the counter, but it's still prescribed and it's not that hard to get a prescription for it as a 'sleep aid.' There's such a lack of awareness, I promise you every single person you inform makes a difference. Especially because with every person who learns more, it's not only one person who is safe from its dangers, but also starts a new butterfly effect."

"Yeah . . . you're right."

"When was the last time you took a day off?"

"Umm . . ."

"Are you at home?"

"Yeah."

"Do you remember the box I gave you last week? The one I told you to only open in case of emergency?"

"Yeah," she says again.

"Go get it." The soft shuffle of feet against the hard-wood floors takes up the next twenty seconds, and I keep my eyes focused on the phone screen, worried Marcus will think I overstepped.

"Alright."

I swallow. "Okay, open it." There's a rip of packing tape from cardboard on the other side of the phone. I direct her toward one of the two things she'll find inside. "There's a yellow shoebox covered with daisies with your name on the top."

With the sound of the cardboard scraping on the box as she pulls it out, I imagine it sitting next to a blue one that I covered with waves and starfish and Charlotte's name.

"What is this?"

"It's your *Thai Emma* box. It's supposed to be things that make you happy, feel confident in being you–because you deserve both of those things."

The other end of the line is silent besides the soft shuffle through the items.

A new ribbon headband covered with evenly spaced silk daisies.

A box of chamomile tea.

A mug that says *The rain helps you grow* in cursive surrounded by wildflowers.

And a copy of *The Little Book of Big Dreams*. A book full of short stories of people who followed their spark in life despite every obstacle and doubt.

"You made this for me?"

"I thought you might need it one day."

"Thank you," she whispers. "I'll let you go."

"Are you sure? We're not busy." I know the deal with Emma and Charlotte is important to Marcus. I know they are important to him too, just like they've already become to me.

"I'm sure. I probably freaked Marcus out."

"I don't think so. I have a feeling he's a big softy, and we just have to prod it out of him. If it takes tears, it takes tears."

Emma laughs, and the glow of the phone reveals the smirk Marcus is trying to hide. "Still. You helped enough. Thank you."

"Anytime, Em. Feel free to call me whenever. And I do mean whenever. Especially if you have a gut feeling my mom is peeling the last of my sanity off like a scab."

"I'll let Marcus handle that part." I can hear the smile in her voice. "Talk to you soon."

We both say goodbye and the call ends, disconnected from Emma's end.

Marcus' large hand grips around the sides of his phone as he drops it to his side, leaving the flashlight on and illuminating the wall space behind him and casting a shadow across his face.

"Thank you," he tells me.

"For what?"

"For comforting Emma."

"It's nothing. You could have easily done it just as well."

"I doubt it."

"With all those mindset books on your shelves at home, I'd bet you're full of pep talks."

"Quieting inner voices is not my strong suit."

"I imagine you'd succeed at anything you set your mind to," I whisper, not knowing how I mean my words–although I know they are true in any sense.

The light from his phone screen blacks out, the decrease in a sense heightening the others. His slow, steady breath pushes the air around us. His nearness makes my skin tingle, a wave of heat rushing through me.

Silence.

A controlled breath from Marcus.

A held breath from me.

"I hope that's true," he murmurs and all of a sudden he feels closer. I can see him–the light from his phone flashlight still dully echoing around the room. But I can't *see* him–not well enough to know what he's thinking anyway. I think his eyes dart to my mouth. I think his tongue barely peeks out to wet his lips. Does he want to kiss me too? I think he grips his phone tighter because a shadow crosses the edge of the light like his finger slipped in front of it.

We're in near darkness, but he doesn't seem to notice. The lack of light makes me feel like I should be cold, but I'm not. A fire flickers through my veins, and while it seems to be burning inside me, it's doing nothing to shed light on what's happening outside. Nothing moves but his chest rising and falling, still in steady breaths. He's hardly affected by this, by me.

In confirmation of my thought, he clears his throat. "Since we don't have anything else to do today, do you mind if I go back to the hotel and get some work done?"

I breathe out a sigh of resignation. I don't know what I was hoping for when I brought him down here. I don't know what I expected from him on this trip outside of his "boyfriend" duties. "Yeah, of course." Marcus makes a move to climb back into the dumbwaiter. "I want to make plans with Cam anyway."

His body shifts along with his phone light as he twists from where he has one foot on the platform back to me. "Who is Cam?"

Did he mean for that to come out with a hint of jealousy? Doubtful. I'm reading into things. "My best friend." I grin at the thought of seeing him. He came to visit me twice in Thailand, but it's been over a year since I've seen him. "Come on." I hop onto the platform, not waiting for him to hold his hand out for mine. "You can meet him."

Twenty minutes later, we're back in the lobby of our hotel. I don't see Dad anywhere but spot my oldest friend immediately. Cam styled himself after the Backstreet Boys when we were thirteen, and he never strayed too far from the look. Somehow, it still works for him, even at twenty-four. The man always has a date lined up.

"Babe! Where have you been my entire life?!" he screeches.

"Waiting for you." I fling my arms around his neck, and he squeezes me tight around the waist.

He pulls back, taking a moment to take in Marcus. He scrubs one hand over his mouth, eyes widening. "Shit, girl. Who is this sweet and spicy apple turnover?" I let out a laugh but don't manage another word before he continues. "He gives you that vibe, right? Like dark and a little mysterious but in a warm and cozy way like drinking hot apple cider on a porch and looking into a dark shadowy forest. I'd go into his forest."

"CAM!" I slap him, hard. He shrugs.

"Can't say I've ever been described quite so poetically," Marcus muses, stepping forward and stretching out his hand with a smirk. "Marcus."

"My boyfriend," I add.

Cam squints his eyes, shifting his gaze back and forth between the two of us. "No. He's not. A tactic to ward off the Mosqueda?"

A momentary panic flashes over Marcus' face, but I laugh it off. "That obvious?"

"I would try a little harder." He looks at Marcus. "She won't bite unless you ask. You could at least stay close enough to touch her. Not sure how you resist this beauty anyway."

I bump my shoulder into Cam's as I roll my eyes. "Stop," I mutter as Marcus says, "I'm not sure either."

Both mine and Cam's eyes shoot to Marcus, a glint of satisfaction on his face for getting our attention. It's all for show. "Alright, well I'll let you two catch up. It was nice to meet you, Cam."

"The pleasure is all mine. I'll take good care of your girl." He winks before wrapping an arm around my shoulder, pulling me to the hotel bar as Marcus diverts to the elevator without looking back.

"Okay, spill," Cam demands as we reach the black marble bartop, simultaneously leaning over it and waiting for the bartender.

"Spill what? You already called it. It's an act for my mom. I needed to get her off my back so she doesn't try to force me back with Beau every chance she gets."

"Oh, she is still going to do that."

"Ugh." I sigh, sliding my elbow across the counter with my chin in my palm. "I know. That's why Marcus is here, though. Hopefully he'll be a good buffer."

"Hmmm." He studies my face looking for who knows what. "You like him."

"No." The bartender greets us and I order two shots of vodka before turning back to Cam. "Not like that, anyway."

He waves his hand an inch from my face, and I flinch back on instinct. "Oh good. Just checking to make sure you didn't go blind."

"Shut up."

"Seriously, why don't you like him?"

"I don't think we'd fit. I don't know how long I'll be in Oregon. He's so organized and professional and all about work. Total opposite of me."

"Opposites attract."

"No. Complementary opposites attract."

"Sounds like you *could* complement each other. He could help you focus long enough to find a passion. You could help him relax a little. I mean, the man is working on a Thursday night instead of hanging out with me." He picks up one of the shots set in front of us, clinking it to mine, then tapping in on the bartop before throwing it back. "And you . . ." We both cough a little at the burn of a first shot, but he raises his hand toward the bartender for another round. "Maybe he meant what he said. That it's hard to resist you. So he's hiding from temptation."

"Doubtful. It's all an act."

Cam picks up the new shot. "Things always get exciting in Act Two."

I roll my eyes and toss back the liquor. Slamming the glass down on the bar top, I turn to my friend. "Question."

"Answer," he states, nodding to the bartender for another.

"Have you ever, you know, been tied up?"

He turns to fully face me, a grin splitting across his face as his hands land on my shoulder. "Please swear on our love for tracksuits in high school that this is not a hypothetical question."

"I mean . . . I'm asking *you* if you've ever been tied up. Seems like a yes or no to me." I laugh, avoiding his implication.

"Nuh-uh. Stop that shit. Of course I have been. Have *you*?"

I shake my head, reaching for the shot placed in front of me and downing it before his follow-up question.

"But you want to try?" He takes his shot too, shaking his head at the bartender when they make eye contact again. He focuses back on me.

"I guess I've never really thought about it before. Beau might have liked to control me, but he was as vanilla as they come in the bedroom–in and out, get the job done."

My best friend makes a face. "I hate him."

"You and me both."

"So, anyway." He waves his hand like he could flick away the memory of Beau. "You want Marcus to tie you up?"

I slap his shoulder. "HEY! That is *not* what I was saying."

"Wasn't it, though?" He smirks.

"I just . . . I have a feeling maybe he's into that kind of thing, but he's my boss. So I shouldn't even be thinking about it at all."

"Or you could keep thinking about it until it manifests. That sounds like a way better plan to me."

I roll my eyes. "I'm being serious, Cam."

"Yeah, I am too. Do you think you could handle it? Being restrained and having no control."

"That's the part that freaks me out. The thrill sounds fun. The having no control part . . . well you know how much that scares me."

"That I do. There's only one way to find out, I guess."

"Yeah, yeah. Enough about me. Tell me about your date last week."

Chapter Twenty-One
Marcus

My internal alarm clock wakes me up, but since we're on the East Coast, I know it's later than normal. Missing my routine yesterday morning, I opted for a late night workout and remote work instead of drinking with Brooke and her friend. He's too intense for my liking, and I imagine alcohol would only make his pushiness about my pretend relationship even more profound. By the time I turned out the lights a little after two, Brooke still wasn't back, and I lay awake, telling myself I wasn't worried until she stumbled into the room an hour later.

She was trying so hard to be quiet that it was nearly comical, but things got serious real quick when she stripped her clothes off. I couldn't tell for sure in the dark, but with the way she was fumbling around in that *trying to be quiet but in fact making a ruckus* way that only happens when you're drunk, I think she attempted to look for my T-shirt to wear before she eventually gave up and crawled under the covers in only her bra and underwear. A rush of jealousy twitched through me, regretting missing out on having fun with her. An urge to be part of her night, to contribute to her happiness nearly convinced me to let her know I was awake. I opted for sleep instead, but it was a long, restless night anyway.

I check the neon blue glow of the hotel clock on the other side of Brooke. *7:58 a.m.* The light illuminates the sleeping girl next to me, the sheets pooled at her waist–a blatant reminder that she wore only her bra and underwear to bed. Fucking hell. The curves of her breasts are mouthwatering, my hands begging to trace her soft skin before exploring her body under the sheets. There's no use in trying to go back to sleep now. I slide out from the covers, slipping into the bathroom for a much needed cold shower. Brooke showed no sign of wanting our arrangement to be any different when Cam mentioned it, so I have to assume that's where her thoughts remain.

My thoughts, however, wander back to yesterday and our phone call with Emma. I would have completely froze if I were in charge of the situation. If you have a boardroom full of entitled executives or an app that's crashed and no one else can fix it, I'm your guy. But not even an entire shelf of mindset books has prepared me for emotional breakdowns without feeling extremely out of my depth. But Brooke . . . she's a natural. She's so effortlessly kind and thoughtful in a way that makes me want to be the same.

By the time I finish showering, I realize Brooke probably won't be awake for a few more hours. Knowing today will be long, I set myself up for success. Using my phone light, I shuffle through the dresser, finding my gym clothes and pulling them on, checking over my shoulder to make sure Brooke is still sleeping. I slip through the door, the only sound the soft and controlled click as I close it behind me and pray I can kick start my endorphins enough to get me through a day of

Brooke's mom and whoever else we have the pleasure of spending time with.

Nearly two hours later, I quietly press open the door to our room, a pep talk from Grant Cardone–about how it's not selfish to want more money, more life, more everything–low and powerful in my left earbud.

The lights aren't on, but sunlight coming through the opened curtains floods the room, giving me a good view of Brooke. She's sitting cross-legged in the middle of the bed in jeans and a tank top, her Hydroflask resting in between her thighs. She's bent over, sucking from the straw while staring at her phone. The door clicking behind me brings her to the present, and she glances up. "Hey," she says, hangover evident in her voice.

"Good morning."

"You didn't happen to bring a suit did you? Or like something that could pass for black tie."

I slip the AirPod from my ear and into the pocket of my athletic shorts. "It needs to be steamed, but I did." I nod toward the closet where I've organized a few of my things.

Her eyes flick toward her suitcase on the floor, her things strewn on the carpet around it. I'm surprised by the lack of irritation it causes me. As long as my things are organized, I'm good. And when it comes to the work she's been doing for me, everything has always been in order. "I didn't plan that well."

I chuckle. "You told me like eight times how fancy this country club was and how much time we'd have to spend there to see your mom."

With a dramatic groan, she flops back on the mattress. "I knoooooooow." She rolls to her side, pulling her water bottle straw back to her lips. "I need to go shopping today. The event tomorrow night is a Casino Night fundraiser. I can't get away with jeans for this. My mom would kill me."

"Can I shower first?"

"Of course. You don't even have to come. I'm sure shopping isn't on your list of fun vacation activities."

"I don't mind. Give me ten."

Chapter Twenty-Two
Brooke

"Am I going to have to drag you in here?" Marcus asks as I stare up at the glowing store letters. We've been to three department stores, and I didn't find anything. I knew I wouldn't. There were a few dresses I loved, but they wouldn't be Mom-approved. They aren't expensive enough, which is why we are now standing outside a store full of glitz and glamor–the kind of store that has individual dressing room attendants and personal shoppers.

"How do you feel about kicking and screaming?" I say with a completely neutral expression.

"Kicking, not so good. Screaming on the other hand . . . If it's in the right scenario." His tongue darts out ever so slightly to wet his lip as he smirks.

I roll my eyes. "Let's get this over with." He's been patient so far, but I can tell it's running thin. I make a bee-line for the dressing rooms and find the nearest attendant. By the time Marcus catches up to me, I've given the lady my size and told her about the event. I'm over making this more difficult than it needs to be.

When she returns with a coat rack on wheels lined with dresses, she gives Marcus a once-over. It's not because he's hot. It's the same appraisal she gave me after noting my plain blue jeans and tank top in such a high-class establishment. Marcus isn't dressed any-more appropriately–although his signature look does it for me. His pea coat is unbuttoned, revealing his dark gray jeans and black V-neck. His dark hair is tied back in a neat messy bun–how he manages to make that oxymoron work is beyond me. The things I would do to that man if I could pull him into the changing room with me and get away with it.

"Miss Fields?"

"Yes?" I notice Marcus' eyes on me in the split second I meet his gaze before turning back to the attendant.

"I'm ready for you. Right this way." She holds out her hand, motioning in the direction of a door where she's already written my name on a miniature whiteboard bordered with pearls.

Looking over my shoulder, I watch Marcus pull his phone from his pocket, checking the screen. "I need to take this."

"Oh, okay." It's not that I need his opinion, but every-thing on this rack is disgustingly extravagant and com-pletely unnecessary. It would be easier if someone could choose for me.

Marcus hardly waits for my response before he wan-ders off, phone pressed to his ear.

The attendant closes me into my room, assuring me she'll be close by in case I need anything. Sighing, I run my hand over the assortment of fabrics hung in front of me, the reflection of sparkles filling the mirror on my right. At first glance, I don't *love* any of them. I imme-diately move the silky, floor-length red one to the end of the rack. I rarely look good in red. Navy blue with a scoop neck and spaghetti straps. My mom will likely be in this color. She's always in this color. Pass. That leaves a black one and a purple one. Purple is my favorite color, but I push aside the plum sequins, wanting to try it on last. I flip the price tag over on the black one. A dollar short of three hundred. The purple one is likely a similar price, and it makes any draw toward them disappear.

I don't have a choice, so I shimmy out of my jeans, tug my tank top over my head, and unhook my bra. I'd definitely have to get some of those sticky pad things. How annoying.

Pulling the black dress from the hanger, I slip it over my hips, sliding my arms into the sleeves. It falls barely below my ass, although long enough to pass as classy because the sleeves are full-length. The fabric hugs my body everywhere and is glittered with silver sequins so small they look like stars in a night sky. Instead of a zipper, there's a keyhole open back, held together by a hook at the top of my shoulder blades that I barely manage on my own.

I spin to face the mirror.

I hold the beach waves off my neck and take in my reflection.

Damn.

The sparkles glisten in the fluorescent lights of the dressing room, and I imagine how pretty they will look in the light of the crystal chandeliers in the club.

I think I *need* this dress. I've never thought that about any article of clothing. I threw away every single piece from my old life without hesitation when I moved to Thailand–outside of my one hoodie. But this dress. I shake away the thought of the price as I take one last look in the mirror before taking it off and carefully adjusting it back on the hanger. My first paycheck from Marcus got deposited this morning. I'll be fine. Plus, I saved a lot more than I planned to while I was in Thailand.

I reach for the other dress simply because it's purple and I'm already undressed. This one is a little more risque. Even though the attendant has probably dressed more people for events at the country club than I could even imagine, I'm not sure it's quite appropriate. It's basically a slip covered completely in sequins.

Slipping it over my silk cheeky panties, I pull the scratchy fabric over my boobs. I can already tell I look killer in this dress, but the crisscross straps in the back are a tad tangled. I peek my head outside my changing room, but I don't see the lady who helped me. Stepping out fully, I make my way to the entrance of the dressing area.

Spinning in a slow circle, hands still lightly pressed against each boob until I know my straps are where they should be, I search for help. I don't see the attendant. Marcus isn't anywhere either. But there is *someone.*

He's standing next to a dress rack, his hand on the top of a hanger as if he was mindlessly looking through a row of dresses. I freeze in place, my hands no longer just holding my boobs in place, but also keeping my heart and lungs inside my body and my entire autonomic nervous system from malfunctioning.

"Beau," I whisper under my breath right as he says my name at normal volume. "Hey," I manage.

He pulls his hand from the dresses and closes the distance between us in three steps. He's wearing khakis, a quarter-zip navy sweater and his hair perfectly styled into place. His signature Armani cologne is as strong as ever. Gag. What did I ever see in him? "It's about time I ran into you." His words might be directed at my face, but his eyes are anywhere but as they drag up and down my body. What the hell is he doing here?

I pull my arms tighter around myself as if it would strengthen some invisible force field around me. But the truth is, nothing is capable. There's something about Beau that makes me weak–not in the "Please take me back and I'll marry you" way. I just tend to revert to the version of myself who isn't strong enough to make my own decisions. The one who answers solely with "Yes" and "I'm on it" in that "I owe you so I'll do anything for you" way even though he's never truly done anything for me. That's what years of my mom's whispers in my ear did. They were like a bug constantly buzzing nearby, no matter how many times I swatted it away. The only solution was to go somewhere they didn't exist. It was wishful thinking to hope that when I came back to the swamp, the bugs wouldn't still be here. Cam's nickname for her–Mosqueda–is all too fitting. "Unfortunately," I mumble.

He flashes his Warner Huntington III smirk like he knows his effect on me. He's a lawyer. It's *his job* to know how to take people down with one look and a few words. "It's good to see you," he says cooly like it hasn't been three years. Like the last time I saw him wasn't the night I texted Cam "SOS" in the middle of the night to have him drive me to the airport with nothing but the clothes I was wearing and my passport. "How are you?"

"What are you doing here?" I'm suddenly intensely self-conscious of my dress. It's practically lingerie.

"I'm here making sure Magnolia chooses something appropriate. You look good. Is that for tomorrow?"

"No. I don't know. Maybe." A flash of a memory invades my mind–my first charity event with Beau as my boyfriend. We used to have fun shopping together. We'd sneak into the changing rooms together when the attendants weren't looking. But the second he started with the firm, it's like piece by piece, they locked away any parts of him I did actually love until that man no longer existed. I was left feeling crazy, like maybe it was my fault I didn't *grow* with him.

"Looks like you need some help with it."

I stare back at the smug look on his face, the one that says he knows I'll let him touch me. The way he has control over me is the reason I haven't let another man have control over me since. Wordlessly, I turn, exposing the tangle of criss-crossing straps to the man I was supposed to marry.

His fingers brush my skin and the contact shoots a wave of chills through me–the kind that makes me nauseous–as he fixes my dress. His touch lingers on my skin. "When were you planning to come see me?" he whispers near my ear.

My thoughts race, worried if I say the wrong thing, he'll still follow through on his threat about my mom's job. "Tomorrow. At the party," I lie, knowing I planned to evade him all night.

"Right." He smooths his hand over my shoulder and down my arm, and I'm so glad I'm not facing him because there's no way I'd be able to hide the disgust on my face.

I take a step toward my dressing room, his hand falling from where it rested on my wrist. Somehow, I escape his force field. I'm pretty sure I blacked out because I have no idea what else I said to end the conversation or how I got inside the dressing room. It was like when you drive home from work beyond tired and can't remember at all how you got from Point A to Point B.

I quickly tug the scratchy dress over my head, but a sequin catches in my hair. I pull at it gently, but without being able to see, it's just getting more tangled. A groan of frustration escapes, and in the next moment, I hear a voice on the other side of the door.

"Brooke? Is everything alright?"

"What do you want, Marcus?" I snap.

"Do you need help in there?"

"No." The word comes out with both venom and a rush of relief as the dress pulls free from my hair. Thank god. I don't even bother putting it back on the hanger and toss it over the rack. I jump into my jeans, hook my bra, and tug my tank over my head, not even caring if it's centered over my chest. Grabbing the black dress from the rack, I push the door open.

Marcus startles back like I nearly hit him, eyes wide when they meet mine.

"I needed help five minutes ago when my ex-fiancé was simultaneously eye-fucking me and using his stupid mind control voodoo on me."

"His what? What happened? I was gone for ten minutes."

"You're not supposed to be gone. You're supposed to
be my boyfriend." I know the words are too harsh the
second I say them, but seriously? This is the whole point
of him being here.

He takes a controlled breath. "Brooke, there is no way
I could have known your ex would be at the mall in the
middle of the day on a Friday. Doesn't the man have a
job?"

I know he's right. But still, "You're not supposed to be
working. You're on vacation."

He taps his phone against his palm before pocketing
it, looking at me like he knows I'm right about this.

"I'm sorry. What can I do? You found a dress?"

"If by dress you mean a week's worth of pay piece of
fabric, then yes." I hate the person that Beau makes me.
I'm self-aware enough to recognize his presence rattles
me, but for some reason, I haven't learned how to not
let it affect me.

Marcus reaches for the hanger, tugging it from my
grip.

"What are you doing?"

"Buying your dress."

"No. I don't need your pity present."

"Not a pity present."

"Then what is it?"

He ponders his answer, a stray piece of hair falling
across his forehead that I fight the urge to brush back.
"A work bonus."

"I've been working for you for like a month." I try to take the dress back, but he tightens his grip, his arm not budging an inch.

"Just let me buy your damn dress."

"Marcus. It's a three hundred dollar dress."

"If it's a three hundred dollar dress, then this establishment probably isn't an appropriate place to be fighting over it."

I drop my hold on my hanger only so I can hang on to some of my dignity.

Chapter Twenty-Three
Marcus

Despite my better judgment, as soon as we got back to the hotel, I opted to leave Brooke on her own again. Even though she was doing her yoga and meditation on the balcony, I grabbed my laptop bag and headed down to the conference room. Today is the meeting that I couldn't reschedule. In theory, it would have worked out fine because there was nothing on my and Brooke's schedule until the wine tasting in the lobby of our hotel tonight that her dad is in charge of. But I can't stop kicking myself for not being there to do my "job." It's not just that I was *supposed* to be there. I *want* to be there for her. Fucking hell, that was bad timing, but still, I dropped the ball big time.

My phone buzzes with a text on the table next to me.

Troy: *Your girl sure knows how to plan an event.*

It's a group chat he just now started with Dean and me. What is he talking about?

Dean: *Seriously. She killed it yet again. Maci said she didn't have to do any work. Brooke had it all organized.*

Oh. The book club event yesterday that the other girls hosted for Brooke.

Marcus: *Not my girl. But I'm glad it went well again.*

Troy: *Tell me I am not the only one benefitting from this book club.*

Dean: *Definitely not. I swear it's like Maci is in college again.*

Marcus: *What the hell are you talking about?*

Troy: *Sex, man. Keep up. These books are full of them. It's like free foreplay. Hell, Brooke might as well start advertising to men to buy tickets to this event.*

Troy: *You might need to edit your fake boyfriend job description.*

Marcus: *She made it crystal clear that won't happen.*

Dean: *According to Maci, that's what all the girls in "fake dating" books say.*

Troy: *And they always end up together.*

Marcus: *That's fiction.*

Troy changed the name of the group to Operation: get Marcus laid

An alarm pops up, and I pocket my phone, ignoring the guys. Having gotten in a few solid hours of work and ordering a late lunch from a sandwich shop up the road, I close my laptop. I'm surprised I got anything done with my distracted thoughts always drifting to brainstorming ways to help Brooke relax so that hopefully some of her vacation actually feels like a vacation. Ironic coming from me, I know, but still, I'm hoping my idea paired with a quick trip to Target earlier lands even better after Troy's unsolicited texts. When I head upstairs to change for tonight's event, I push the door open to see Brooke standing next to the television stand. One hand is propped against it for support while the other hand slides on a strappy gold sandal.

Her dress is tight against her slight curves and a purple similar to the shade of a dress I caught a peek of on the rack at the store earlier. I wonder why she didn't end up with that one. Purple seems to be her favorite color. It looks like a T-shirt, but longer, and fuck if it's not my new favorite outfit on her.

Ignoring the way I want to run my hands over her body, under her dress, I clear my throat, drawing her attention. She taps the pause button on her phone lying on the television stand, silencing the instrumental version of a song that sounds familiar–maybe from Taylor Swift's *Evermore* or *Folklore* album? It's the same album to me.

"What's that look on your face for?" Brooke asks.

"Huh? I was thinking how much I know about Maci."

Her face scrunches a bit, and it's fucking cute. "That's a weird thing to be thinking about."

I nod toward her phone and the opened music app. "She plays this a lot."

"I hate to break it to you, but she's kind of spoken for."

I chuckle. "I didn't mean like that." The realization hits me all at once, like a piece of self-help advice you've been told a hundred times but none of them make a difference until the *one time*, at the right moment. What if I do have time for a girlfriend? Time to learn the little things that make up who someone is? It's probably wrong to think of it in terms of business, but I check off daily tasks that get me closer to goals each day. I don't expect to complete them all at once. I know a person is different, but . . . If I have time to add on investments . . .

She looks at me, perplexed, then sighs when I don't answer. "Okay, well I'm going downstairs to meet up with Dad. I'll see you down there?"

"Yeah. I'll be right down."

I follow her with my eyes until the door clicks behind her, then look at the nightstand. Picking up her book, I flip through the pages, stopping when I reach her bookmark. She's almost to the end. I shake the curiosity of how this book is affecting her, pushing away the memory of when she already admitted to me that they make her want sex. Set in my plan to find out, I take ten minutes to change into gray slacks and a black button-up, clean up my beard and refresh with a bit of sandalwood aftershave.

And once again, ten minutes is all it takes for me to miss the mark.

Again.

Stepping off the elevator directly into the bar area, I spot Brooke immediately from the back. I also see a man who looks vaguely familiar leaning against the marbled bartop. He's standing way too close for my liking, and when it hits me that he's her ex, he's suddenly way too close for comfort. I could pretend it's fake boyfriend duties being taken seriously, but I can already tell that's *not* what this is.

Beau is so focused on Brooke's tits that he doesn't notice me until I'm within reach of them. Not even bothering to eavesdrop on their conversation, I steady myself behind Brooke, taking in a confident breath before grazing my fingers up her arm.

She was already stiff but becomes even more so under my touch. Though, she doesn't retreat from where our skin connects, and I take it as all the consent I need right now. I brush her beach waves over one shoulder before gripping her hip lightly and bending enough to press my lips to her neck. "Hello, love," I whisper.

She spins into me–likely in an attempt to hide her shock from Beau, which is confirmed by her wide eyes, the green and golden specks in them competing for real estate. "Hey," she whispers, her eyes flickering back and forth across my face as if a look alone will help her dissect my unfamiliar actions.

I thread my fingers through her hair, taking a firm grip on the side of her face, hoping she feels my sincerity as I brush my thumb across her jaw. "Sorry I'm late."

"It's okay," she says, and I release her, turning to face Beau.

"Hey, man. Marcus." I extend a hand.

He takes it. "Beau."

"Ahhh. The man with the underwear," I say intentionally at full volume. I can usually keep my snark to myself, but this would have been such a missed opportunity.

Brooke tries to hold back a laugh but ends up with some mix of a snort and a chuckle, and I wish I didn't have to wait another second to kiss her. I contemplate if I could get away with it. She'd probably go along with it for the sake of the plan, but it's not worth it.

"Excuse me?" Beau asks, his rocks glass frozen part way to his mouth. Isn't this a wine event?

"Ignore him." Brooke smiles and play slaps me in the chest. But instead of taking her hand back, she settles it at my waist, pulling herself to me. I wrap my arm around her shoulder, her head fitting perfectly against my chest. Fucking hell that feels good. "Marcus is my boyfriend," she says with a confidence that makes me question why she even needs me to tell this doucheca-noe to fuck off.

"Boyfriend?" Beau repeats.

"You don't mind if I steal my girl for a while, do you?"

He stumbles over his words–something I'd believe is actually rare for him as the well-known lawyer he is. "Yeah. Uhh. Sure. No problem. I'll catch up with you later, Brooke."

"Maybe," she says with a shrug and lets me guide her away from her ex.

"Come on." The idea I came up with earlier today seems even more risky. Adrenaline courses through my veins stronger than the shot of whiskey I took before coming down here. I racked my brain for ways I could help Brooke . . . take the edge off–while also not crossing the line she secured in place when it comes to our physical fake relationship.

"Where to?"

"Do you trust me?"

"Yeah." She doesn't hesitate, and a pang of guilt hits me knowing she still doesn't have any clue what my net worth is.

I lead her down the dark hallway full of doors leading to conference rooms. She lets me take her hand and tug her inside an empty room lit only by the wall of windows to the starlit night.

"What are we doing here?"

"Are you okay?" I question her, pulling her from the door I closed behind us and the peephole window on it. "I'm sorry I wasn't there when you needed me again."

"It's okay."

"No, it's not." I brush my thumb across her cheek but quickly drop my hand. "I hope I didn't cross a line earlier."

The questions in her eyes are visible even with just the glow of the moon.

"Touching you. The way that I did," I clarify.

"Oh. It's fine. You were doing your job, following the plan. Thank you."

"Do you feel any better? Now that Beau knows you have a boyfriend."

"A little. Not sure if he caught the surprise on my face when you kissed me. He may be a dick but he can still read me after a decade of knowing each other, you know?"

"Yeah. We'll just have to keep it up. Make it believable." This new plan forming in my mind is not only to make these people believe we're together but to make Brooke believe that maybe we should give this a shot for real. "Is anyone else here that you know?"

She sighs. "I didn't expect them to be, but they are."

"Who?"

"You saw Beau. But his mom is here too. She's a real piece of work. Especially when she's around my mom, who is also on her way. Why she wants to be at an event thrown by my dad, I have no idea. Just a warning, they might be here in an attempt to get Beau and me together. I can't imagine any other reason they'd 'lower' themselves to a *not* five-star hotel."

"We will just have to show them that's not an option."

She groans. "This is so stressful and so unnecessary. Like, I'm an adult. I should get to choose who I want to be with."

"And you don't want to be with Beau." It comes out as a cross between a statement and a question. Even though she's made it clear, I still feel the need for confirmation.

"I want to be with you."

Her words catch me off guard, stealing my voice. Fucking hell. What way did she mean that? I laugh to jump-start my thoughts. "Probably good considering I'm your boyfriend."

"Yeah." Her eyes search mine.

"On that note . . ." I shove my hand in my pocket, wrapping my fist around what's inside. "I know you have a rule. About the physical aspect of this fake relationship."

"Yeah . . ."

"And that you usually use meditation or yoga or Thai tea to relax, to distract yourself."

"Yeah . . ." she repeats but with even more uncertainty.

"You can't use those tactics at a party."

"Those are really the only ways I block out things that disrupt my inner peace."

"Then you need something strong enough to distract yourself. What's the next best thing?"

She laughs and the sweetness in it sparks something inside me. "I'd say an orgasm, but you can't use those at a party either. At least not this kind of party."

I hold my hand between us, opening my fingers to reveal a purple bullet in my palm.

"Is that a . . ."

"Yes."

"What exactly is happening here?"

"Preferably an orgasm."

Her eyes widen. "Not at a party it's not."

"You said you trust me."

"Yeah, but I can't use a vibrator in the middle of a crowded room."

I quirk a brow. "I can."

"You definitely can't."

I pull my phone from my pocket, tapping on the recently downloaded app. "Sure I can." I smirk, flashing her the screen that clearly shows controls for the vibrator. "I'll be right outside." I nod toward the door. "You get this situated."

"Marcus."

"Yes?"

"No."

I pause at her rejection, curling my fingers around the bullet and searching her face for any tell. "Because you really don't want to?"

Her fallen gaze shoots to mine and locks on. "Because I do."

I bite back a smirk. "I'll be waiting outside," I remind her, reaching for her hand, turning it palm up and handing over the vibrator. "Make sure you put it in far enough."

Her fingers grip my hand, not releasing me or pulling the toy away, and the extended contact makes my dick twitch. Fucking hell. She holds my gaze. "This is a bad idea."

"Is it?" I don't know what else to say because my thoughts have all blurred into inappropriate ones. *I could just touch you myself. We could go back upstairs and have our own party instead.*

After hesitating another moment, she finally pulls away from my touch, taking the vibrator with her. She doesn't make another move. I take the hint, leaving her behind for the dimly lit hallway. Not even a minute later, she slowly steps through the door frame, tucking her sun-bleached waves behind her ear in the most innocent way–like she's overcompensating for what she's about to do. "Ready?"

"With a glass of wine, I will be," she says, leading the way back to the party.

The event is set up like a ten-course meal, but with wine. Instead of being seated, the bar is lined with half-glasses of wine set in a specific order. I hand her a glass of white, holding off myself until the reds.

"Brooke?!" The screech hits my ears before Brooke's wine is to her lips. She turns at the sound, holding her wine back toward me like she trusts I'll hold it for her without asking. I do, in time for a girl who hardly looks old enough to drink to throw her arms around her.

"Magnolia!" She squeezes her friend's neck in the embrace, giving me the impression she's genuinely happy to see her. "I didn't know you'd be here," she says, pulling back and reaching for her wine again with a quiet "thank you" and the smallest moment of eye contact.

Magnolia leans in close enough to whisper, "Not for much longer. My boyfriend is picking me up in a few minutes outside."

Brooke laughs like she's in on a secret. "Not family approved?"

"You know my brother." The girl rolls her eyes, then gives me a once-over. "Not in the way you used to, I'm happy to see."

"This is Marcus."

"Doesn't look like the kind of boyfriend your family would approve of either." She smirks, reaching for Brooke's wine and taking a big sip before handing it back to her. Wait. Is that why Brooke agreed to bring me? Because I'm the opposite of the type of man her mom would want her to go for? Minus the whole rich thing, but that card isn't face up.

"Yeah, well, only because they have terrible taste."

Magnolia nods in agreement. "It was so good to see you. I'd love to stay, but . . ."

"No, I get it. Trust me. I'd leave with you if I could. Go have fun. We'll catch up before I leave."

"Promise." Magnolia takes Brooke's wine back effortlessly, finishing it in one gulp. "Thanks!" She's out of sight before either of us can reply.

"She's . . . something."

"Beau's sister," Brooke tells me.

"Biological?" I quirk a brow, and Brooke laughs.

"Surprisingly, yes. Nothing alike. Magnolia is only seventeen, but we were pretty close. She even mailed me a few things she retrieved from Beau's house when I ran away to Thailand."

I'm about to comment when an older woman approaches. Considering Beau is tacked to her side, I'm assuming it's his mother. We're knocking this all out at once apparently. Brooke is standing close enough that I can feel her immediately tense beside me. Seeing a high-top table within reach, I direct her toward it as a meeting point and a barrier for this reunion.

Brooke follows my lead, setting her empty wine glass on the table. Without the alcohol to relax her, I'll just have to give her something else. "Be good," Brooke whispers like she can read my thoughts. I smirk, unsure if she catches it before addressing the woman in front of us. "Martha, hi."

"Brooke, dear." She runs her eyes over what she can see of Brooke's outfit that isn't blocked by the high table with the same disapproving tone her mother had. "It's so nice you're finally home. You can get back to your life." It makes no sense to me that this woman of status is so set on Brooke being *the one* for her son. Besides the fact that he'd be lucky to have her, the simple fact that she doesn't come from money seems like it would be enough to not encourage it. "And who do we have here?" She looks at me with disdain.

"Marcus Cole, ma'am. It's nice to meet you. I've heard so much." I reach my hand for hers and she takes it begrudgingly.

"Oh, right. Your mother told me about him," she tells Brooke like I'm no longer in the conversation.

Next to me, Brooke's rage is building. I can tell in the way she's squeezing her fist next to the bare skin on her leg as it barely brushes my slacks. She takes a controlled breath before anything she says. The girl needs to relax, and I'm here to take care of that.

I pull my phone from my pocket carefully, angling it under the table just enough I can see the screen. I tested the strength earlier, so I know level one shouldn't feel stronger than a tickle. It startles Brooke nonetheless, and I have to bite back a laugh. She covers the small jolt between her legs with a cough, earning her a confused look from both her ex and his mom. "Are you alright?" Beau reaches for Brooke's arm resting on the table, pretending to care about her. It's all for show.

"Oh yeah, I'm good. Great actually." She pulls away from his touch.

I tap my screen under the table, turning the intensity to the second level. Brooke reaches for her wine glass, pretending to sip from it even though it's clear it's empty. I pocket my phone, running my hand along her lower back and reaching my other for her glass. "Would you like more?"

She pulls her attention to me. "Mhmm." The way she says it and the smirk she tacks on at the end makes it clear she's not just talking about the wine.

"I'll be back." Before she can react, I press the softest kiss to her lips. It's shallow and quick and everything in me begs to stay and make it longer and deeper. I pull back enough to still feel her breath and watch her face for any indication of what she's thinking.

"Okay," she whispers, her gaze stuck to mine until I step away without giving any attention to the other two. Before I'm out of earshot I hear Martha say, "Well that was a little inappropriate given the situation, don't you think?"

I'm tempted to go back and put her in her place, but it's a waste of breath. I'd rather give Brooke something more positive to think about. The bar is close enough that I can see her clearly but far enough away that I can't make out any of the conversation.

I can read body language, though, and Brooke's eyes shifting to me momentarily tell me exactly what she wants. She says something to the two of them, and I hit a button on my phone screen. It should send a strong pulse through the vibrator followed by a few short and slightly less intense ones. I wish it were my fingers under her dress, inside her, but I take what I can get, watching her subtly cross her legs at the ankle under the table. With one arm resting on the table, she folds her other hand over it, her fingers wrapping around her forearm.

I increase the intensity, skipping level three completely and watching her pretty pink nails dig into her skin. I waste a moment glancing at Beau and his mom to see no indication they think something is off. I know Brooke is purposely not looking at me. I'm not sure why, but I'd like to think her biting the corner of her lip and the way her eyes keep darting around the room are a reaction to what I'm doing to her.

Beau says something and Brooke pinches her lips together, from the looks of it barely managing a "Mhmm" sound with her soft nod. I imagine it comes out more like a squeak of pleasure, and I love everything about it except that my role in this is too indirect.

With a full wine glass in hand, and the next adjustment ready on my phone screen, I make my way back to the table. She hesitates before taking the glass from me, pulling her fingers from where they are digging into her skin. "Thank you," she manages, her voice both soft and on edge–like *she* is on the edge.

"Anything for you, love." I wrap my arm around her shoulder, pulling her tight to me before pressing down on where my thumb was hovering over the button in my pocket. The vibrations should switch to steady, long pulses that I'm hoping push her over the edge.

Somehow managing to keep her reactions under control, Brooke's arm bends, her hand linking with my fingers draped over her shoulder. She squeezes barely enough for me to notice, but a jolt of need courses through me. The way she's leaning into me feels like the missing piece of my puzzle. Fuck. "As I was saying, Marcus is brilliant. He can code any app you could ever need." A burst of pride blooms inside me, and I wonder if she genuinely believes I'm that talented.

"He certainly looks the part of a tech guy." His mother's tone makes it clear that's not a compliment.

"There's no consistent money in tech when it could crash at any moment. Completely unreliable," Beau says as he attempts to burn a divide between our hands with his stare.

Technology is quite literally one of the most profitable industries. This guy graduated from Yale? I try to wrap my head around what Brooke could have seen in him, glancing over at her to see if she believes any of his bullshit.

I don't think she even *heard* any of his bullshit.

Her eyes are locked on Beau's as he talks. She's biting hard on the smallest sliver of her lip. If I didn't know what was happening behind the scenes–behind her panties–I would have thought she was entranced by him. It looks like she's entranced by him and his words. It seems he thinks so too as he leans ever so slightly toward her, still rambling on about a technology article he read in the newspaper the other day.

She won't look at me, and while I'm hoping it's simply because the movement would break her control, I can't handle her attention on him this way, not when I'm playing with her like this. I tap my screen under the table once more, maxing out the intensity. An involuntary twitch shoots through Brooke. To anyone else, it would probably seem like a chill, which is exactly how she plays it off. "It's a little cold in here. Could we go get my jacket?" Her fingers tighten against where they hold mine, damp with sweat.

"I'm sure Matthew can be a gentleman and get it for you," Beau's mom suggests. Does she seriously believe her match-making is subtle or effective?

"It's Marcus," Brooke snaps, struggling to keep her composure, but I'd be willing to bet it has nothing to do with her ex-future mother-in-law. Anyone paying attention could see that the way her cheeks are flushed, there's no way she's cold unless she has a fever. "I'm not feeling well anyway, I think it's best if we call it a night."

I give a slight nod to our company, faking pleasantries only to get out of here sooner. Beau tries to say something to Brooke, but she ignores him completely, guiding me away. I imagine she's heading toward the elevator, but instead of pushing the buttons, she veers right, heading down the hallway toward the conference rooms.

I barely have time to slide in the room behind her, the heavy door closing behind us. She twists into the wall, her forehead pressing against it with a heavy breath. Her breathing comes quickly in short pants. If she's this fucking turned on, I have no idea how she was holding it together in a room full of people the way she made me believe she was. With her forearm pressed into the wall above her head, she looks at me sideways. "Turn it off," she practically cries.

"Why?" I know damn well she hasn't come yet, and I refuse to leave this room until she does.

"I can't handle it. I can't . . ." she trails off before adding so softly I almost miss it, "let go."

I take a step, invading her space, close enough to touch her, to feel the heat radiating from her body. "Let go of what?" I'm praying to fucking god she's not talking about the douchewad on the other side of this wall.

"Just let go. It's making me mad," she huffs out.

Ahh. "Stage fright?"

She glares, and I chuckle. "No. That part . . . got me closer than I expected." Her breaths are still shallow like she's genuinely struggling to get a deep one. "But this was supposed to bring me relief. Now I'm just on edge."

"So fall over it."

"You act like it's that simple."

"Isn't it? Most things in life are a choice. A mindset shift." I roll the sleeves of my button-up over my forearms like my body knows what I'm going to do next before my mind does.

"Stop giving me pep talks from your stupid books and put me out of my misery." She sighs, twisting her body away from me like she'll lean against the wall. I slide in behind her, pulling her back flush to my chest by her hips. She gasps. "Wh-what are you doing?" she stammers.

"Putting you out of your misery," I whisper against her ear. I pull my phone from my pocket, lowering the intensity of the vibrator to two before stashing my device again. The moment the buzzing inside her settles, she relaxes against me like she can breathe again.

With my phone back in the pocket of my slacks, my hand takes a firm grip on her waist. "What are you doing?" she asks again, this time in a whisper.

"Brooke," I murmur against her ear. "Leaving this conference room before you come might kill me. What's it going to take?" Testing the waters, I run my hand over her thigh. Her breathing immediately picks back up, and I hope she's too distracted to notice my heart rate doing the same.

"The rules," she breathes.

"The name of the game is getting you out of stressful situations while we're here. Is it not?" A chill rakes through her with my hot breath on her ear.

She nods, her eyes fluttering closed.

I let my thumb brush over the fabric covering the apex of her thigh. "Tell me you want my help."

She presses into me more with a whisper of a moan, her ass grinding against my cock. Goddamn. I've never wanted anything as much as I want to make this girl come right now.

I press a kiss to her neck. "Let me break the rule," I say against her skin.

"Marcus." The sound of my name on her desperate lips makes me never want to hear it said by anyone else again. "Yes. Please, yes."

Fucking hell, her begging is hot. With her confirmation, I increase the pressure of my fingers as I trail them to her inner thigh, my other hand gripping her hip, holding her in place.

I inch my fingers closer, feeling the warmth of her body. When I get to the hem of her dress, I push it up until I've got a firm grip on her inner thigh. I rub my thumb across the silk separating us, damp to my touch. The realization sends a twitch straight to my dick, bringing him to attention against Brooke's ass. A groan escapes both of us as I hook a finger on the side of her panties and pull it across her sensitive skin.

My middle finger makes contact first, rubbing small circles against her clit. Her head falls to my shoulder. I slide my finger down, toying with her opening. Fucking hell, she's so turned on and sexy. It's taking every ounce of self-control I have to not bend her over the conference table and fuck her until she sees stars. But patience has treated me well in the past, and I intend to keep it that way.

She sucks in a breath when I slip inside her. I stay shallow, my palm pressed against her clit and I make slow circles inside her. I add a second finger, switching to pumping in and out of her slowly and deeper with each thrust. "Rules are overrated," she says in a sedated voice before biting the corner of her lip with her eyes closed, her head locking into place on my chest.

The next one is deep enough I feel the small vibration against my fingertips. Her hips buck, and I fuck her with my hand, pinning her against me as I do. She tightens ever so slightly around my fingers–closer, but not there. She presses her hips into my hand, trying to chase the feeling. My other hand tightens on her hip, grinding her ass against my hardening cock. Fucking hell, she feels good. I'm not even inside her, but I decide at this moment I'll do what it takes to make sure that happens.

It feels like forever, and I savor every moment my brain is focused on the present moment in a way it never is. I shift my fingers inside her. Taking my time. Playing. Reveling in her soft skin and the smell of the fresh saltwater spray in her hair. The small twitches from her paired with the faint vibrating coming from inside her. I have all the time in the world for this, but I'm abruptly reminded she doesn't feel the same when her head tips toward my neck in defeat, a groan leaving her as she stops fucking my hand. "I'm sorry."

"Sorry?" Panic spikes through me thinking she's regretting letting me touch her.

"I can't do it. I can't get there."

A sigh of relief leaves me. Fucking hell, she scared me. "Why not?" My tone isn't accusatory. It's curious.

"I don't know. I'm in my head."

"How so?" I don't remove my fingers, but I slow their pace. In and out. Steady.

From this angle, I can see her eyes flutter closed again as she stays nuzzled to my chest. "It's too much work. It takes too long. Your hand is tired. You're annoyed."

"None of those things are true."

"I don't know how to not believe them. There's no way you're not frustrated."

"Why would I be frustrated?"

"Because you're on a mission rigged to fail." She's whispering but her voice sounds louder in the dark.

I chuckle.

She tenses, and I hold my fingers in place, keeping her pinned to me with my palm in case she tries to move away. "Is this funny?"

"Nah. I'm just not worried about it. It's not me. It's you."

She spins in my arms so quickly that my fingers slip out of her. "Excuse me?"

With the fingers that haven't just been inside her, I tilt her chin so she's looking at me. I want to kiss her so damn bad. "I'm not annoyed because I'm confident I can do this."

"Of course you are." She rolls her eyes, trying to take her head with them and out of my grasp. I hold tight enough to her face that she's trapped. "You're Marcus Cole. Successful businessman. You always get what you want." She doesn't say it, but somehow I've just been lumped into a category with her ex. The way she acts like she has me pegged without knowing I'm rich terrifies me for how she'll feel once she finds out.

"What *I want* is to give you the best fucking orgasm of your life, Brooke Fields. So good you'll be relaxed through the end of the trip, regardless of how long we're here. Got it?"

"This isn't part of your job description."

I debate my words. "Maybe not. But I'm going to do it anyway. We just have to break down your block. It would help if I knew what it was."

"I don't want to talk about it." She tugs at the hem of her dress until it's in place.

Fuck. I felt like we made progress tonight. I had hoped that her letting me get physically close would move us toward a *real* relationship, but that doesn't seem to be the case. Not wanting to push her away more, I ask, "Do you want to go back to the party? Hang out with your dad?"

"No. I'd rather go back to the room."

"Alright, let's go." I let her lead the way, following behind her with enough room to give her space, racking my brain for all the ways I could have made that go differently.

When she's done washing her face and changing, Brooke opens the bathroom door in a way that invites me inside. When I join her, she's standing in front of the mirror in nothing but my T-shirt, with her toothbrush in her mouth. Fucking hell, seeing my clothes hang on her body does too much to me. I never want her to take it off just as much as I'm not so sure I can handle seeing it on her much longer.

She glances at me, holding my toothbrush toward me, all ready to go.

"Thank you." I take it from her, brushing my teeth next to her, the only sound in the small space. It's awkward and miserable. If my way of relaxing her isn't working tonight, I'll have to settle for her way.

We crawl into bed from either side, still without a word. She reaches for her bedside lamp and flicks it off. "You don't have to go to bed. I know it's early."

"I'm a morning person." It's still earlier than I usually go to sleep, but I'm smart enough to know pulling my laptop out right now probably isn't the best idea.

"Alright." She's definitely not *alright*.

"Do you want to talk about it?"

"Talk about what?" Her words feel even further away than the three feet between us on the bed.

"Either how you're doing after seeing Beau twice in one day. Or whatever else you want to get off your chest about me."

She glances up from where she was staring at her fingers running over the seam of the comforter. "What about you?"

"Me touching you. Pushing the line you set for us."

She chews on the corner of her lip. "I hate seeing him. I was wrong. I think it's worse than seeing my mom."

It takes everything in me to refrain from a smirk at the way she immediately decides talking about me is actually the harder path. "Why do you think that is?"

She sighs. "It makes me hate myself a little–that I let myself be controlled by someone for so long."

"But you left. Not everyone is strong enough to do that."

She shakes her head. "You didn't see me earlier. At the store. I shouldn't have even let him near me, let alone fix my stupid dress. It's like being in his vicinity activates a spell where any respect for myself immediately disappears."

"I didn't get that impression when we were downstairs."

Her eyes fall back to the comforter. "Because you were there. I don't know, that gave me courage or something. You and your stupid pep talks about confidence and self-worth. Sometimes I truly can't believe I thought I loved him."

"Did you?"

"I'm not really a fan of the whole 'I love you' thing." The way she sighs makes it seem like she thinks the entire concept of love is made up.

"The 'I love you' thing . . .?"

"Love is such a simple word that *should* hold so much power. But it's overused and abused to the point where it feels like it's lost all meaning. Things you do embody love far better than the word ever could, anyway." She shrugs.

"But ignoring the word doesn't make the feeling cease to exist," I argue.

"No. I guess what I'm saying is that I'm the one who abused the word. I said it back to Beau whenever he said it even though I know he did it out of obligation. I said it in an attempt to convince myself it was true."

"Did you ever believe it?" Shut the fuck up, man. The last thing I need to do is talk about falling in love with a fake and *temporary* girlfriend if she doesn't feel like there's potential here for her.

"You know when you see a word too many times and it feels like it's spelled wrong? Or say it too much and it doesn't sound like a word anymore?"

I nod. "Yeah."

"That's how loving Beau felt. Confusing, unclear, made-up. But someone tells you it's right, so you stick with it. The next time I fall in love . . . The words aren't what makes the feeling clear. I'd like to think I'd know if someone loves me regardless of if they say the words or not."

"You will."

Every time she shares her perspective on some aspect of life, I'm stunned. She makes me think about things in ways I've never considered before. It's engaging in a way I've been craving with every single girl I've taken on a date.

"Yeah." She picks at the hem of my shirt she's wearing, revealing her inner thigh but not noticing.

Not knowing what else to say–and in an attempt to keep from ripping her clothes off–I reach my arm out. The motion raises her gaze. She looks at me like I grew an extra limb, scrunching her face at my unspoken demand. "I'm not Maci, but I am her favorite, so I'm the next best thing."

She chuckles, hesitating.

I motion to her with my fingers in a way I wish I could do inside her again. What the fuck was that thought? She continues to make it clear she doesn't want that from me. I'm just her fake boyfriend and only option for a friend right now, and that makes me her temporary safe space. Fucking hell. It's going to be a long week. Hoping she doesn't magically have access to my thoughts, I give her a pointed look. She holds it for a moment, then scoots down on the bed, twisting her body sideways until her head is on my lap. The blanket pools mostly in front of her as she curls up, her backside covered by nothing but my shirt. She takes a deep breath and readjusts a couple of times before she's comfortable.

When she stills, I drop my hand to her soft blonde waves, noting the faint smell of coconut and ocean. She stiffens for a moment at the touch but doesn't move away. Instead, she reaches up, locking her fingers on my thigh where my shorts have slightly pushed up as I run my hand over her hair repeatedly.

Reaching over her for the remote, I flip the TV on and scan a few channels. Junk. Click. Trash. Click. Stupid. This is why I hardly watch TV. Click. Black and white fills the screen, an iconic face and voice filling the screen as Lucy shoves chocolate into her shirt. Brooke glances up at me, and I set the remote down, this time moving my hand to her back. I scratch in small circles, resisting the urge to feel our skin touch.

Before the episode ends, Brooke's breathing levels out, and not long after, I drift off to sleep too.

Chapter Twenty-Four
Brooke

Dear god, my neck aches. My head is sweaty like when I wake up from a nightmare. I move to stretch but freeze when I open my eyes. Even with just a sliver of light peeking through at the edge of the ugly maroon hotel room curtains, I can take in my surroundings well enough to realize I spent the entire night sleeping on Marcus. On my fake boyfriend who is barely my friend.

Maybe it wouldn't be such a big deal if I didn't have a very tiny, hardly noticeable crush on him. But come on! The man let me sleep in his lap for god's sake—even though he's clearly uncomfortable with the entire idea of comforting me. Comforting me in *that* way, I should say. My thighs clench slightly at the memory of his fingers between them. God, it felt good to be touched that way, by someone so sure of himself, so determined to make *me* feel good. I still couldn't get out of my head, though. On top of my solidified belief that my own orgasms are nearly an impossible achievement for anyone, and my insecurities around that frustration, there are too many questions I'm afraid to ask.

I take a deep inhale through my nose to center me. Ugh. He smells so good. The faint sandalwood is fused into the shirt I'm wearing.

I move slowly to avoid waking Marcus, but the moment I'm off him, he stirs, his middle fingers digging into the corner of his eyes and wiping the sleep away. I have no idea how he slept sitting up all night. "Morning." His gravelly morning voice does nothing to help the crush.

"Hi. Sorry, I didn't mean to wake you."

"It's alright. How did you sleep?"

"Honestly, it was the best night's sleep I've had in a while. Thank you."

He offers me a soft smile before shifting off the bed and heading to the bathroom.

I take the freedom as a chance to collect myself. With there being a three-hour time difference, it's way too early to text the group chat, so I give myself a pep talk.

You're only drawn to him because you're in a fragile state, and he's here.

He's doing this as a favor to you.

He's your boss.

This is just a free vacation for him.

The touching stuff is just a challenge for him.

Don't suck the fun by continuing to be in your feels.

Don't make things awkward by giving him any indication that the sight of him shirtless and petting your hair nearly unraveled you.

"Are you alright?" Marcus stands at the end of the bed in nothing but black joggers cinched mid-calf. Holy hell, he's hot. The bright orange and pinks of his koi fish tattoo stand out boldly against the splashes of blue water and his skin. It's kind of weird that it's so colorful considering he doesn't seem to own a single piece of clothing that isn't black or gray–*maybe* a dark blue. His deep brown hair is pulled back and his ocean eyes wait patiently for my response.

"Oh yeah. Totally. Just thinking about the plan for the day," I lie.

"What do we have planned before the fundraiser?"

"I wanted to go to lunch with Cam. You're more than welcome to come. I'm sure he would be happy to have you there."

He raises an eyebrow.

"He said you look like you have a big dick." I mentally slap myself. *What the fuck, Brooke.* I need to stop letting sex-related thoughts slip into conversation, especially when I'm trying *not* to think about having sex with my boss.

"Is that so?" He smirks.

"He said if I'm not going to flirt with you, then someone needs to."

The words shut him down, any playfulness disappearing. Fuck. I meant for that to be flirty. What is wrong with me? "I'll stay back. I'm going to workout. Then I have work to do, anyway. Have fun."

It's fine. This is how it's supposed to be. *A business trip.* Okay, fine. Maybe it's not *work*. But it's just supposed to be two *friends* helping each other out. Walking to the closet, he pulls a black shirt from the hanger and tugs it over his head. As he adjusts the shirt into place, he approaches me, and each step closer makes my heart beat faster. I follow his movement as he reaches for his phone on the nightstand next to me, pocketing it before grabbing his AirPod case and the room key as well. When I think he's going to turn and leave, he leans over the mattress, his fist pressed into the comforter by my leg.

I freeze, phone gripped tightly where my hands rest on my criss-crossed ankles. He holds my stare. "If any-one is going to get confirmation on that assumption, it's not going to be Cam." Then he pushes off the bed, leaving me there running through every single thing those words could mean.

Chapter Twenty-Five
Marcus

Twenty. I press the last rep with my chest shaking. The steel bar hits the rack above me harder than it should, the 225 pounds of plates clinking when I release it. I swing my body up with the very little remaining strength I have, my feet grounding into the floor as I reach for my sweat towel. Fuck. I drag it over my face and drop the wet cloth on the black leather bench between my legs.

I rip the left AirPod from my ear, David Goggins' voice narrating his book immediately stopping. It's not like I was paying attention anyway. Reaching for my Nalgene bottle I stashed under the bench, I unscrew the cap and take a swig. Pumping out the stress didn't make the impact I hoped for. I dig my phone from the pocket of my joggers and send an uncharacteristic text to Dean.

Marcus: *Talk me out of making a move on Brooke.*

We've been friends coming up on twenty years, but we're still guys. Emotional shit is not morning coffee talk for us. I move to set my phone back down, determined to get in another set, but it vibrates in my hand.

Dean: *No can do. I'm on strict orders to encourage that.*

I probably should have just texted Maci. But while that may be a more comfortable conversation, Dean still knows me better.

Marcus: *I like her, man.*
Dean: *No shit. You took a vacation for her.*
Marcus: *Fuck off*
Dean: *What's the problem then?*
Marcus: *She doesn't live in the same state, for starters.*
Dean: *She could.*
Marcus: *I don't want her to have to add me to the mix when she doesn't know what she wants yet. She's stressed about it enough.*
Dean: *What if adding you to the equation makes the decision easier?*
Marcus: *I'm not even sure she's interested.*
Dean: *Is she with you right now?*
Marcus: *No. Why?*
Dean: *Because I'm reading Maci's group chat text over her shoulder.*
Dean: *Pretty confident you should make a move.*

I want to know the details, but I picture Maci slapping him away when she catches him spying for me and decide against it. I shake my head, amused as much as I am determined. I lay back on the bench and reach for the bar.

The bathroom knob turns, drawing my attention from where I'm leaning slightly over the hotel room desk doing a quick Google search on my laptop. I fold it shut so Brooke doesn't catch the magazine feature I have up about helping a woman get past her mental blocks when it comes to orgasming. I'm confident in my ability to make her feel good but smart enough to know helping Brooke feel how she *deserves* is far more important than keeping my pride. I lock away the possibly helpful bits of information from the article and stand, buttoning my charcoal suit jacket over my crisp white shirt and solid black tie that I had room service press.

Hands still on the button, I freeze. Because fucking hell. Brooke looks up from where she's smoothing her hands over the sparkles of her black dress. It's short–short enough to immediately make me recall the memory of having my fingers inside her last night as she was pressed against me. It would probably be inappropriate for a fundraiser event like the one we're attending, but the sleeves are tight and long and the front doesn't cut low. She straightened her usual waves and tied her blonde hair into some sort of messy but controlled side bun, strands of hair framing her face. Her neck is exposed, and I wish I could kiss her.

Her brow furrows. "What's wrong? Do I look okay?" She moves like she's headed back to the bathroom to check herself out, giving me a view of the back of her dress–an intentional cut-out revealing a good portion of her back.

"Brooke." She freezes at the sound of her name, turning to look at me through her eyes, dark with black and gold eye makeup in a way that screams "high-end casino night." "You look incredible."

"Oh." She smiles without a single ounce of insecurity, and I fucking love it.

I take advantage of the moment and press my luck, stepping closer to her. "You're making my job easy."

"What do you mean?"

"I don't have to fake being attracted to my fake girl-friend."

Her cheeks flame, shyness taking over as she scans my suit, my perfectly trimmed beard and neatly pulled back hair. "You don't look so bad yourself."

"We'll look even better together." I wink before turning to the door. "You ready?"

"Yeah, let's go."

Our Uber is waiting for us when we walk out of the hotel lobby, and we slide into the backseat of the SUV in silence. As we're pulling up to the country club, Brooke mutters under her breath, "I don't want to be here."

I don't respond. I have no fucking clue what to say–how to comfort her. I can't fully wrap my head around why she wanted to make this trip at all and why she is concerned with appeasing her mom to the degree that she has. I also have never experienced the type of relationship with a parent that she has, and I'm inclined to believe that if my mom and dad didn't support me, I might want their approval too. I can't wait for them to meet Brooke. They're going to adore her.

Fucking hell, man. This is all fake. A favor for her. The last thing she's thinking about is meeting my parents. I replay my text from Dean earlier, wondering if he has insider information from Brooke's side of it or if his encouragement is simply secondhand from Maci and a wild girl fantasy.

Stepping out of the car, I make quick to the other side, opening the door for Brooke and offering her my hand.

She takes it and doesn't let go once both feet are on the ground, her sigh sounding like an eye roll. We step from the curb to the red carpet leading to the doorway. Then I glance at her, the shimmer of her eye makeup catching in the bright lights from the massive entryway. "Imagine if they donated all the money they spent on this event to the cause. I asked my mom once. She said this event costs over a hundred thousand dollars to host."

"How much money does it raise?"

She shoots me a look that says, "That's not the point," but tells me anyway. "Usually around half a mil."

"That's a great ratio." I regret the fact as soon as I share it, immediately feeling the tension increase. She drops my hand, angling toward me slightly as we continue down the red carpet, ignoring the flashes of photographer lights. "Most major fundraiser goals are a three-to-one return," I stoke the fire for a reason that's beyond my knowledge.

"Whose side are you on?"

"Umm, the children with leukemia?"

She huffs, but her gaze freezes on someone I haven't spotted yet, and she immediately links her arm through mine. "I swear, if he does not get the hint that I'm not available tonight . . ." she mutters under her breath so soft I'm not sure if I was meant to hear.

The object of her bitter attention meets us at the entrance to the club. "Beau."

"Hey there, gorgeous." He leans in and kisses her cheek–while she's attached to my arm. The nerve of this guy. "You definitely picked the right dress." He rakes his eyes up and down her body, reminding me he magically appeared while she was shopping and that I wasn't there.

I pull Brooke closer by wrapping my arm around her shoulder, shifting so I'm slightly between the two of them, clearing my throat. I catch Brooke biting into her lip to hold back a grin from the corner of my eye.

Beau smirks like he thinks my possessiveness is just a temporary roadblock. I'm about to put him in his place when Brooke says, "I'd compliment your suit, but it could pay for a whole fucking day of chemo, and I know you don't give a shit as long as you look like a million bucks."

"At least you said I look like a million bucks." He shrugs, unbothered by her anti-rich person hostility. Unlike myself. How the fuck am *I* going to get past this roadblock? That's the real issue here. Her opinion is so strong, it seems not even a million dollars would sway it. "You're more than welcome to join me at my table or play with my stash of chips. You too." He shifts his glance momentarily toward me. He's acting charitable, but anyone with eyes can see that's not his intention. "I bought three thousand of them." He reaches out to hand a stack of gold poker chips–the name of his law firm on a sticker in the center of each–to Brooke, but she doesn't accept them.

"I don't want your money, Beau."

"That's a shame."

"Is it?" She's so snarky I have to look at her to make sure the same girl I've been getting to know is the one next to me. She's so triggered by something trivial in the grand scheme of things. I mean, if he bought three thousand chips, the man did donate thirty thousand dollars to the cause. It's more than the ten thousand I gave anonymously.

"Are you ready for a drink, love?" I squeeze her shoulder, ignoring Beau completely as I glance toward the bar with a nudge.

"Yes, please. Bye, Beau," she adds with a grin and lets me guide her to the white marble bar with gold trim.

The bartender tilts his head toward us. "Hey, man," I address the man in a tux–equally goofy and sharp, a little like a young Frank Sinatra. "Bourbon neat for me, please." He reaches for a rocks glass. "And," I lock eyes with Brooke, "wine?" She nods. "Cab for my girl."

He pours our drinks quickly, sliding them toward us. I hand him a twenty even though it's an open bar and guide Brooke toward the massive glass French doors across the room that leads outside to the marble staircase winding down to the wedding grounds from the first day we came here.

We navigate through poker and roulette tables, Brooke steering me through the maze when she sees someone she wants to avoid. The room is dark, lit only by golden spotlights above each table. The rest of the room is cast in a purple glow, creating a sexy ambiance. Nothing as sexy as Brooke right now, though, with the silver sparkles of her dress like stars in a clear night sky. Fuck, she's beautiful. I want her all to myself, but that's not why we're here. I stop us on the other side of the room, at the line between the chaos of the gala and the peace outside. "Do you want to play a game?" When I made the donation, they gave instructions on how to claim my chips and apologized for it being too late to have them customized with my business. I didn't want that anyway. I haven't decided how to approach the finance topic with Brooke yet, but I know springing it on her at an event where she already feels trapped is not the place to do it.

She shakes her head. "No. I need to show face with my mom at some point, but," she nods toward the brass handle of the door, "Do you want to go for a walk outside?"

"Yeah. Do you mind if I use the restroom quickly and meet you out there?" I plan to soak up as much time as I can with her, away from the crowd.

"Of course. I'll be right out here on the balcony."

I hand her my drink and push open the gold bar of the glass door, holding it open for her to walk through. I turn toward the hallway behind the main floor. Reaching for the handle of the individual bathroom, a hand cuts me off. *What the–*

I hardly have time to recognize it's Beau before he opens the door and kicks my feet–actually kicks my shoe–so I enter the small room. My instinct is to punch him, but I can't imagine that going over well. So, I oblige the moron.

I step into the bathroom with pristine white tile and an immaculate blue marble counter. Unbuttoning my suit jacket, I slip my hands into my pockets. He stands in front of me looking more like a douchebag than a million dollars if you ask me. "Something on your mind, man?"

Crossing his arms over his chest, his glare tells me he thinks he has the upper hand here. "What's your game?" he demands.

"What game?"

"Don't play dumb. I'm well aware you're not."

I arch a brow. "Is that so?"

"I don't know what is going on with you and Brooke, but I will figure it out."

"Nothing to figure out."

"So, then tell me, Marcus. Why is it that Brooke doesn't seem to be bothered by the fact that your wealth far exceeds anyone in this club tonight?"

The blood drains straight from my face and into my hands, where I grip my hot, swollen fists.

He chuckles. "Oh, so she doesn't know. Interesting. You know, it's a wonder what you can do with money when you know how to use it. I could teach you if you'd like."

How the fuck did he find out.

As if he can read my mind, he says, "I have a great PI." He smirks. "How do you think Brooke would feel if she knew about your donation to this event she's so strongly opposed to?"

"What's *your* game here, Beau?"

"I want her back."

My stomach twists at the thought of her being with him. "Why? No one else is willing to be your doormat?" I feel bad implying Brooke is weaker than I believe she is, but fucking hell this corner is starting to make me claustrophobic.

"I don't know what she's told you, but surely you're missing a lot of details. I've loved Brooke since we were seventeen. Everyone here knows it except for you."

"Yeah, that explains why she fled the country three weeks before your wedding."

"You don't think I let her do that? I know her. She just needed to get her free spirit out of her system before she was ready to settle down. The plan was always for her to come back when she was ready."

There's no fucking way. I see how she looks at him, the way she tenses whenever he's in the vicinity. A small part of me is drawn to believe him. I used to have a bad habit of immediately trusting someone whenever I could see any bit of possibility in their statement. It was a beast to wrangle, but I shove doubt into a cage with mostly ease–just like I intend to do now. I trust Brooke. *But she has no idea about the secret you've kept from her.*

"Here's what's going to happen. You have one day to tell her. If you don't, I will. And when she realizes you're the liar, and that I've *never* lied to her, we'll see if she remembers where she belongs then."

This guy is insufferable. "She's smart enough to see your manipulation."

"We'll see." He unfolds his arms from over his chest to pat my arm. I follow the movement and will my hands to stay in my pockets instead of making contact with his face. "Have a good night."

I stay frozen, watching the heavy bathroom door close slowly behind Beau long after he's gone. When it finally clicks, I turn the lock and pull my phone from the pocket of my slacks. I scroll through my contacts for the man who has been mentoring me since I was twenty.

As the phone rings, my heart thumps in my chest as flashes of what *could* happen appear in my mind–Brooke realizing I kept this truth from her, and not forgiving me. Would she storm off? Kill me with silence? Quit her job or our relationship on the spot?

What if I don't get a chance to tell her how I feel about her, *prove* how I feel about her? The phone clicks on the other end when it's picked up on the second ring. There's a concerned greeting from him, knowing I rarely call. After explaining the situation briefly, he hangs up and immediately sends me the contact info for a private investigator that he swears by. *Two can play this game, Beau.* They say you don't know what you have until it's gone, but I refuse to let that be my case and miss out on the girl I'm crazy about. When all is said and done, hopefully the bright side to this bullshit with Beau will be that it made me man the fuck up and push me toward developing a relationship with Brooke. There's no way the man doesn't have a single skeleton in his closet–not when he's a dirty lawyer with enough money to make any problem go away. If he does, I'll find it, and then I'll be honest with Brooke on my own terms.

I call the contact, leaving a message when he doesn't answer. Not knowing how long it'll be until he returns, I go find Brooke. The longer I'm away, the more chance Beau has to swoop in, and I'd be stupid to trust that he'll give me the twenty-four hours he promised.

Chapter Twenty-Six
Marcus

Gripping the gold bar, I push the door open. As the heavy glass closes behind me, the hoots and hollers of drunken poker night soften. She's standing at the edge of the balcony, her wine glass on the edge she's leaned against, her hands pressed on the white marble. My drink is in its place next to hers. I join her but stay a step back so I can observe. I might not trust a lot of people, but I want to trust her. I don't let a lot of people into my life, but I want her to be all-consuming. I want her ingrained in every aspect of my life. My morning workout routine. Breakfast after we shower–me with coffee and her with tea. Making time for lunch between my meetings and whatever it is she decides she wants to do for work–doing whatever it takes to make sure she has access to her dream once she figures it out. I want to come home to her each night and read with her head in my lap and my fingers in her hair. I want her to be a part of all the things I want to keep in my life and want to make time for all the things that I've never made space for because it wasn't right.

Fuck. Besides the fact that I have about a twelve percent idea of whether or not she has any of those feelings about me, none of it will be a possibility if Beau strikes a match before I have a chance to fire-proof us. I need to tell her. I need time.

She inhales deeply–as if being inside was suffocating her and she's able to take full breaths out here–and gazes out over the courtyard. A soft glow from the stars illuminates it just enough to make out the pergola, now devoid of flowers, and the trees lining the boundary of the property. She tips her head up, eyes wandering over the specs of light like she's searching for the meaning of life–or maybe just a constellation. She glances over her shoulder like she's checking to make sure it's me behind her. "Do you know what I love about the stars?"

"Hmm?" I slip my hands into the pockets of my slacks, forcing my gaze from her and tilting my head toward the sky.

"They're not something you can take a quality picture of with a phone camera. Regular pictures, like selfies with friends, emotion somehow attaches to them in a way where you can feel it once the moment is gone. But the night sky? Most pictures are lackluster. The only way to feel something by it is by being in the moment, by standing under it in silence, in appreciation for its vastness and power. Even the best photographs can't *quite* capture that."

My eyes drift back to her. I love the stars but in the science type of way. I took all five astronomy classes available in college on top of my regular course load for no reason other than interest. Although, I can't say I've ever thought of space that way. But I don't disagree. It makes me wonder if I'm starting to feel that way about *her*. There's so much to her that can't be captured in a picture, so much I want to know that no one else would if they only saw her frozen in this moment behind the glass of a frame.

At my silence, she turns to face me. "Is that stupid?"

I shake my head. "Not at all. The way you see the world is . . . refreshing. I don't make time to see it that way."

She steps away from the railing, bringing us only a foot apart as she eyes me like she's not quite sure what to make of me.

Movement in the corner of my peripheral catches my attention, and I shift my glance away from her just long enough for confirmation on who is pushing through the door to ruin our moment.

"Touch me," I whisper without thinking twice, fear rushing through me that if I don't take this chance, Beau might make sure I never get it.

Her face scrunches. "What?"

"Touch me," I repeat. "Trust me."

She only hesitates for a moment before taking a step that closes the distance between us and sliding her hands under the fabric of my suit jacket, across either side of me, then meets my gaze like she's awaiting the next instruction.

"I'm going to kiss you now."

Her eyes widen, and her chest stops moving like she's holding her breath, but I don't give her a chance to object or respond or think twice. I bring my hands to either side of her neck, my fingers slipping gently into her tied up hair and my thumbs grazing her jaw as I pull her lips to mine.

She tenses for a split second, her fingers digging into my waist, but then she relaxes, tilting her head toward me more, letting me into her embrace and past her lips as I deepen the kiss. She catches a groan I couldn't manage to suppress as her tongue tangles with mine. Goddamn, she tastes good. Like sweet wine mixed with bourbon and something unique to her.

Heat radiates from her as she presses her body against mine, like she's burning up, like we're on fire–a stark contradiction from the cool night air. A sigh escapes her like this is comforting–like I am. I try not to read into it as her arms slip around me, her hands running up my back with enough pressure that I can feel where they touch the edge of every muscle.

My grasp in her hair tightens, and I'm trapped somewhere between never wanting to pull back and getting carried away. I'm lost in her. Present. She makes me not want to be anywhere else or care about anything else except this moment with her. All the work I've been throwing myself into the past few days was mostly to keep me from doing *this*. I might have thought I could pretend it was a distraction and deterrent from her ex, but the moment her soft lips touched mine, it wasn't just more than that–it became something different entirely.

I want Brooke Fields. And not for fake. Because this one kiss will never be enough.

Not wanting to get too deep, not before I know if she wants any of this to be real, I pull back just enough to break the kiss. She's out of breath, her chest rising and falling, her eyes still closed. The gold sparkles in her makeup shimmers slightly in the starlight until her eyes flutter open and she stares up at me, my thumbs still locked on her jaw.

"What was that?" she whispers.

"Beau was about to join us."

"Did he leave?"

I glance behind us to an empty balcony, the only people in sight are the ones surrounding the poker tables on the other side of the glass doors. I nod.

"That's why you kissed me." She says it somewhere between a question and a statement.

I hesitate, looking into her eyes as if the gold or the green in them might reveal what she wants me to say. "If you want that to be the reason."

"Brooke!" The voice of her mother pierces through the night, disturbing the silence, and our moment, as both of us turn to face her. In the process, one of my hands slips from her face, but Brooke doesn't let go of me. She keeps her arms linked around me and leans in closer like I could protect her from this woman. "You need to get inside. What is the point of you being here if you aren't *here*?"

"Mom, relax. I just needed some fresh air."

"This isn't the time for a make-out session with your boyfriend, Brooke. Grow up." Grow up? That's her advice? This lady is about as mature as a fifth grade mean girl bullying everyone on the playground.

Brooke groans, but leans into me more and glances up. "Buy me another drink?"

I grin, wrapping my arm around her shoulder. "It's an open bar."

"In that case, I'll have two." She smiles, and it's brighter than the stars, and my stomach sinks. I'm lying to her right now, and I hate it. The thought of her feeling about me the way she does about Beau makes *me* need two drinks.

We follow her mom inside, and she immediately leads us toward a group of people standing by one of the casino tables. My phone vibrates in my pocket as we're approaching. I slide it out, praying it's who I hope. The PI.

Brooke glances over at me, curious. I know I need to answer, but I don't want to leave her. I choose the long term priority and step away from her. "I need to take this." Hurt flashes across her face–mixed with a little fear, like I ripped her safety blanket from her. "I'm sorry. Five minutes, okay?"

She nods, and I lean in, kissing her without permission and hoping it won't be the last time. When I pull back, her eyes have softened. "I'll be right back," I assure her again.

I answer the call as I'm walking away, right before my voicemail catches it. "Hey," I greet the man. "Give me a second." I scan the room for a hallway, finding one to the side of the bar and walk down it until I find an empty room to slip into. "What did you find?" My voice is hopeful but on edge.

He goes into a few minute breakdown of the *nothing* that he's found based on a surface level search. Apparently Beau is a much better lawyer than we've given him credit for. I spend the next fifteen minutes going over everything I can recall about my blackmailer and things I've noticed since our time in Connecticut and my few chance encounters. We hang up only after he's assured me that as long as there is something to find, we will find it. I call my lawyer and update him. Once I disconnect from the second call, I check the time. Fucking hell. I've been gone for nearly a half an hour. Trying to stay positive, I focus on the gratitude for not only having access to but also being able to afford immediate help this way. I've never simultaneously loved and hated money so much, and I pray it's not what rips me from her. Brooke once told me that her mom says money is the source of all problems. I know she meant the lack of it, and I hate to admit it, but the general idea is not *wrong*.

I pocket my phone and rejoin the event. Scanning the room, my eyes immediately find the most beautiful girl. My pulse pumps in my ears, tuning out the chaos of the party. I consider myself a calm and collected person, but my panic mode is activated as I watch Brooke lean a little too far onto the bar, flirting with the goofy Frank Sinatra motherfucker. She's slipping away from me before I've even gotten to hold her.

As I approach, she's laughing about something he said, swirling her wine mindlessly in her glass. My hand touching her lower back startles her, drawing her attention to me. I shoot the bartender a warning glare, and he backs away.

"Hey." I kiss her cheek, partly for show and partly because I need to be close to her. I need her to know that I want this–want her–before the cards are too stacked against me.

"I think we have a very different meaning of five minutes." She's not being harsh. She's hurt, and I hold onto the feeling that she *wants* me to be with her. I guide her away from the bar and out of earshot of the bartender.

I pull her to me by the small of her back with one hand. I let the other settle at her neck, my thumb holding her jaw in place as I debate what to tell her. Her hands hesitantly fall to my chest. I brush my thumb along her cheek. "I'm sorry. I know I sound like a broken record."

"You really do, Marcus. Look, I know you're . . ." She glances around to make sure no one is near us. "I know you're not really my boyfriend, but I thought I could count on you to be here for me like we agreed upon."

Fuck. I want to lay it all on the line, but this moment doesn't feel *right*. It's not some big romantic gesture confessing my feelings as an excuse for why I keep abandoning her–even if this time is completely different. "You're right."

"What was so important that it had to be dealt with at 11 p.m.?"

I take a breath, running through my options. I'm not ready to tell her. I don't want to here, not like this. I want to be honest about Beau, but if she feels the need to confront him that could backfire. I have to take the chance, though, because I don't want to lie to her more than necessary. "Beau."

"What about Beau?" She scans the room as if she'll find him ready to pounce.

"He cornered me. Said he wants you back. That you left Thailand so you could come back to him."

She laughs incredulously. "You told him to fuck off, right?"

I stare back at her.

"Right? Do not tell me that you believe him."

"No," I say hurriedly. "But there's something else."

Worry fills her eyes as she waits.

I release a controlled breath. "He's trying to dig up dirt on me."

"He what?!" she whisper-yells. "Well he won't find anything so it doesn't matter."

"Yeah," is the only word I can manage to pull from my vocabulary.

She tries to pull away from me. "Where is he? I'm going to put him in his place. That piece of–"

I pull her tight to me, holding her close and hard enough that she can't escape. "No. Let me take care of it." She debates her options. "Can I just take you home?"

She nods. "Okay."

Chapter Twenty-Seven
Brooke

I run my fingers over my lips as the scalding hot water from the shower runs down my body. That kiss. It's still playing on repeat like it has for the past two hours. I thought about how he cradled my face in his hands as my mom ranted about my lack of presence at the party. I relived the way his lips felt pressed against mine as I took a sip from a new glass of wine. I thought about how he tasted of bourbon and smelled of sandalwood as Beau attempted to burn me down with a stare from across the purple lit pseudo-casino while I was talking to my mom's friends. But nothing lights my body on fire the way Marcus does.

It all makes sense now. He's why the room always feels hotter when he's near, and why I break into a sweat when it's cold enough to need a jacket. His presence holds power over my body, and I want him to take control of it more than he already has. There was a dominance in that kiss like he was forcing his way in–not in a breaking and entering way but as if he was trying to rescue me.

That's exactly what he was doing, though. Rescuing me from Beau, from my mom, from these situations and people I don't want. That was evident in the way that he disappeared only to handle my ex for me. I was so mad because I thought that maybe that kiss meant something to him–more than just a responsibility–but then he ran off the first chance he got.

When he found me again, something was different. I swear he was jealous when I was bantering with the bartender about the ridiculous quirks of rich people. Then he clung to me in a way he hadn't before. And was adamant about us leaving. So *maybe* it is more than just doing his job. Or maybe I'm imagining things the way I want them to be. Maybe he wanted to leave simply so he no longer had to deal with the drama.

I lather my face wash in my hands before scrubbing it over my face and rinsing away the remnants of tonight's glitter along with Marcus' kiss. Should I ask him about it? Should I try to kiss him again?

Stepping from the shower into the steam filled bathroom, I reach for the white hotel towel from the hook on the wall and wrap it around my body. Oh shit, I forgot to grab my pajamas–well Marcus' T-shirt. My black sparkly dress lays folded where I left it on the bathroom counter. I could put it back on to go get . . . what is that?

Folded neatly next to my dress is deep purple silk fabric. Twisting my towel securely above my chest, I reach for it, holding it in front of me. The camisole unfolds as I hold it from the spaghetti straps. I lay it on top of my dress, replacing it with the pajama shorts. They're the same shade of plum but the bottom hem is lined with a thin layer of lace.

They're soft and beautiful and . . . I didn't even hear Marcus come in here. He got these for me?

Oh.

Maybe he doesn't want me wearing his clothes any-more. That would make sense. I forgot my pajamas, and he was kind enough to buy me some.

I swipe my hand across the fogged up mirror then run my fingers under my eyes to clear away the last of my residual makeup. Dropping my towel, I reach for the shorts, the silky fabric soft as it glides up my freshly shaved legs. I pull the top over my hair, still dry and in a pretty bun from earlier. I'm shocked it's stayed mostly in place since I took out the pins.

Facing the mirror, I run my hand over it again, clearing away the new layer of fog. It's the perfect size. I'd say it *maybe* errs on the side of too revealing, but I have been sleeping in nothing but Marcus' shirt, and there's no way that falls longer than these.

Panicking, I swipe my phone from the bathroom counter, turning off the music I didn't even register I had playing during my shower.

Brooke: *What a mess.*

Maci: *What's going on?!*

Brooke: *Beau is being a dick, as per usual.*

Lexy: *Troy is great at punching douchebags. Happy to lend you his services.*

I send them a picture of my new pajamas in the mirror that's fogged back over a bit.

Avery: *Is that what you've been wearing to bed with Marcus?!*

Maci: *I hope so! You're a total babe!*

Brooke: *He just bought them for me.*

Lexy: *A gift?! STOP. How fucking cute. Please keep him.*

Brooke: *He also kissed me.*

Avery: *Excuse me?? Why are you telling us about paja-mas and exes?*

Brooke: *It was a fake kiss. In front of Beau.*

Avery: *Was it good?*

Brooke: *I can't stop thinking about it.*

Maci: *IT'S HAPPENING!! Just think of all the double dates we can go on!!!*

Brooke: *I think you're getting a little ahead of yourself. Plus, I probably pissed him off yesterday.*

Maci: *How?*

Brooke: *Well...he kind of, sort of, maybe fingered me.*

Lexy: *How exactly do you kind of, sort of do that?*

Brooke: *Okay, fine. He did.*

Avery: *I feel like we are missing some crucial informa-tion.*

Brooke: *I'll fill you in on the details when we get back. But long story short, I couldn't finish. Has that ever hap-pened to you guys?*

Lexy: *Oh yeah. It was as rare as a leap year for me before I met Troy. Now it's not a problem since he knows me so well.*

Maci: *I feel like it was easier for me when I was in college. Like almost every time. Now, I swear it's harder when I'm in different parts of my cycle. Being a girl sucks sometimes.*

Avery: *I talked to my doctor about it. After Canaan was born, it never happened. But my doctor said that libido and orgasms are strongly linked to stress.*

Maci: *Definitely not something to be ashamed of.*

Brooke: *It's not that. Just frustrated. I think I'm falling for him, and I'm not sure if I should yet.*

Lexy: *Where are you right now?*

Brooke: *Hiding in the bathroom in our room.*

Lexy: *I vote you go out there and kiss him without an audience and find out.*

Avery: *I second that.*

Maci: *Me three!*

Brooke: *What if he doesn't want it and it's awkward?*

Lexy: *Or what if he's out there having the exact same dilemma as you?*

Leaving my phone on the counter, I take a breath and creak open the door before I lose my nerve.

"You decent?" I'm not sure if he's planning to take a shower or if he's already in his athletic shorts and T-shirt in bed. When he doesn't respond, I exit the bathroom to the room, dimly lit by the soft yellow glow of the nightstand lamp, and find him sitting at the desk, leaning back in the chair while reading something on his phone.

He glances up and his finger freezes on the screen. He's still wearing his suit, minus the jacket, and his tie is loosened, the top button of his shirt undone. Holy hell he's sexy.

I fidget with the hem of my new pajama top with one hand, crossing the other arm across my chest and linking it on my tricep. "Thank you."

He tosses his phone on the desk like nothing could be as important as this moment. But surely that's not true. I'm sure he was just doing something mindless. Scrolling. Playing a game. Though, I've never seen him play a game before. Or on social media. "You're welcome." He stands. "Do you like them?"

"I liked your shirt more." The words slip out before I can stop them.

He steps closer. "Is that an insult or a compliment?"

"Both, I guess. And neither. I love this." I glance down at myself. "But I love the way your shirt smells."

"It's sandalwood." His voice is low, controlled, sure.

I look up and take a quick inhale to steady my shaky breath. "It's you."

His arms fold across his chest, his hand coming to his face to brush his thumb across his lip. Both of our arms serve as added barriers between us. Is that intentional? On my part or his? Out of fear? Or uncertainty? I want to cross this line, but I'm still doubtful about if I *should*, if that's what he wants too.

"I can't stop thinking about last night."

Last night? What about tonight? We are not on the same page. My body deflates at the realization, my arms falling from over my chest to twist and link my fingers together in front of me.

His finger locks under my face, his thumb pressing into my chin as he tilts my gaze. "Tonight too," he adds, like he can read my mind, and takes a step closer. His body screams certainty, but his ocean-blue eyes swirl with hesitation.

"What about last night?"

His hand slides along my jaw until his fingers are locked into my hair. "My fingers inside you."

"Oh. That." I run my tongue over my lips, my mouth suddenly dry.

"And how you didn't come for me."

I attempt to look away, heat flushing my cheeks, but he holds me firmly in place. It's not forceful, and I like it despite the guilt racking through me. "I'm sor–"

I'm cut off with a slight shake of his head. "I want to know something." His deep voice rumbles through me, sending a shot of panic through my veins.

"What?" I whisper.

"Do you orgasm on your own?"

"Wh–what?" I don't know what I expected him to ask, but it wasn't that.

"Do you?"

"Sometimes . . ."

"How?"

"What do you mean, how?"

"Will you show me?"

My face flames hotter as I shake my head, averting my gaze.

"Then will you let me figure it out?" My eyes shoot straight back to him.

"What?"

"Last night. I promised you the best orgasm of your life. I'd like to deliver."

"That's really not necessary."

"If you don't want to show me, then will you let me try?"

"You don't have to. I know it's a pain."

"There will be no pain involved. Unless that's how you like it." He winks and a small smile breaks through my nerves. My brain is fuzzy like it's retained the effects of the two glasses of wine I drank nearly three hours ago now. Why is he doing this? Should I ask? Should I just see what happens and deal with the ramifications after?

Marcus' hand falls from my hair, his fingers whispering down my neck, along the purple silk strap–all while keeping his eyes locked on mine. "Can I touch you?"

I nod, and his hand slips further. It brushes along the top edge of my shirt, trailing between my breasts, surely feeling the vibration of my heart nearly beating out of my chest. If he does, he shows no sign of it, continuing on his path, the weight of his fingers pressing the silk against my skin. When he reaches my waist, his fingers breeze across the thin elastic waistband before slipping under my shirt. His palm is heavy and warm, flat against my skin as it works its way up my body.

Marcus' eyes are still locked on mine.

He pulls me closer with his other hand gripped on my hip as he squeezes my breast, rough and controlled. A gasp escapes me, heat rushing through me, knowing what *might* come next as I flashback to last night and his fingers inside me. His lips are close enough that his breath warms me as I breathe him in.

I prepare for him to kiss me even though nothing could have prepared me for the way kissing him unlocked a new part of me earlier–a piece that wants intimacy with someone after not having it for so long.

But he doesn't kiss me.

"Get on the bed," he says against my lips, his tone a hushed demand.

I do as he says, breaking eye contact to crawl to the top of the bed, but I can feel his eyes still on me, tracking my movement. Turning to face him, I pull my knees to my chest, wrapping my arms around them to protect me from the adrenaline coursing through my body.

Marcus stands at the end of the bed, the top button of his dress shirt undone, his tie still loose at his neck. His black belt rests perfectly at his hips where it's looped through his slacks, and I want to yank it off. The mattress dips on the edge as his knee sinks into it. Then more when his shin slides forward and his other knee presses into the fluffy white comforter. The maid must have made the bed while we were gone.

His tongue runs over his lip, and I track the movement, wishing he'd say something while also praying he'll kiss me instead. Kneeling in front of me, my head tips up to keep my gaze on his face as he towers over me. Nothing about this scares me–except that I like it. I like him having the upper hand like this. Maybe because I don't think he'll abuse it? Not in the way the last man I was with did, anyway. Still, I'm not *with* Marcus. The line between real and fake is so blurry, and there's a chance any of the real could all be imagined. Or we could simply have different definitions of real. Real as in actions backed by emotion versus ones laced with lust.

He reaches out, brushing a thumb across my cheek, and chills rush over my skin like a watercolor seeping from the touch of the paintbrush against paper. "What is it?"

"This is weird," I whisper, both vulnerable and safe.

"Why's that?" His hand falls to his thigh, and he shifts ever-so-slightly away from me, his eyes steady on my face.

"You're my boss," I say with a shaky exhale.

"Is that what I am?"

My lips part to answer him, but nothing comes out. Is he my boss? I mean, yes, he is. And when all this started that title was at the top of the list of things he is to me. But now? He's my fake boyfriend. He's my friend. He's . . . the man I'm developing feelings for. That scares the shit out of me.

"What's going through your mind, love?"

"Why are you doing this?"

He hesitates like he's debating the right answer.

"I don't want the right answer. I want the truth."

"Because I want to." His thumb reaches back out to brush across my jaw. "Because you deserve to feel good."

Does that added statement make it better or worse? Does he feel like he needs to do this? I wonder if it's some sort of challenge to him. He's so successful, I doubt he's used to losing.

"Brooke?" His hand covers both of mine, stopping their fidgeting as they rest on my bent knees.

"Yeah?"

"You have to get out of your head."

"I'm not the best at that."

"I beg to differ. I've seen you focus. Undistracted."

"I meditate a lot." I chuckle.

"Guided or music?"

"Music."

He reaches for my phone on my nightstand. "Turn it on."

I hesitate but take it from him, waiting for my face to unlock the screen. "How long should I set the timer for?" I tap on the mediation app on the top left of my home screen picture of the waterfall from the hike we went on a few weeks ago.

"Is there a continuous play setting?"

"Yeah."

"It takes as long as it takes. There's no time limit."

I scroll through the time options on my favorite sound and push play. A soft melody of piano and ocean waves flows from the bottom speaker as Marcus gently pulls it from my hand and rests it back on the nightstand. "Do you trust me?"

I nod.

He loosens his black tie around his neck, tugging it free from the knot. By the time it rests loosely in his hands in front of him, I realize what he's about to do.

I shake my head. No.

He appraises me, his eyes narrowing the slightest bit. I take him in as we both sit there in silence. The sleeves of his white button-up are rolled and tight on his forearms in the sexiest way. The top button is undone, the rest of them begging to be ripped apart. His suit pants are tight over his muscular thighs with the way he's kneeling in front of me on the bed.

The allure is there.

I want it. And him.

But it feels like giving up control in this way is like jumping out of an airplane without checking to make sure my parachute works first.

"Tell me why." He says, but for some reason, I feel like he already knows.

"Control," I admit.

He doesn't say anything, doesn't let his eyes wander–keeps them locked on my face.

"The last time I put it in someone else's hands they abused the power."

He sets the tie on the comforter next to us without breaking our gaze. "There's a difference between someone not letting you be in control so they have power over you and someone being in control so they can take care of you."

I search for manipulation in his eyes, dark and stormy blue. I don't find anything but sincerity.

"Let me take care of you," he commands. It's not aggressive, though. It's a weighted blanket wrapped around my heart.

"Okay." The word comes out as a whisper, but it's enough consent for him. In the next instant, the material is in front of my face. His breath is on my ear as he ties the silk around my head, careful not to pinch my hair. "It's just to keep you from getting distracted, anyway."

"Distracted from what?" I whisper.

"From something in the room. From watching me and whatever worries that brings." He pulls the knot tighter, securing it.

My hands move to the fabric covering my eyes on reflex. I know there's still light in the room, but even though my eyes are open, everything is dark.

"Don't think about me. Focus on feeling. On letting go."

He's kidding, right? My heart thumps so loud in my chest that I swear my entire body is vibrating with my pulse. Whatever he's about to do to me, I'm not sure I can detach it from *him*. Actually, I'm positive I can't.

"Lay back." The words trail off as he pulls away from me, taking a warmth I miss immediately. I do as he says, slowly tipping back until my head rests against the pillow, my knees still bent. The anticipation of not knowing where Marcus is in relation to me and what happens next sends a wave of tingles across my skin and a rush of anxiety through my blood. I'm terrified. I'm excited. I don't feel like myself. Like I'm in someone else's body.

The urge to peek from under the tie almost wins out when his hands land on my ankles. I don't flinch, as if my body anticipated his touch. I'm used to it after this week, I suppose. I flash through all the moments our skin has connected, watching them play out like a movie rolling on the back of this tie. A new set of chills immediately take over as he tugs, pulling my legs straight. Tension stiffens my muscles against my will. He either doesn't notice or ignores it, running his palms up my legs, the pads of his fingers pressing into my skin. Holy turned on. How did we even get here? This is more intimate than anything I've experienced with any man, and literally nothing sexual has happened. Despite my throbbing need for someone else to pleasure me for once, I know I'm still tense. This feeling, it's too foreign, too scary, too . . . He's my boss. He's my *fake* boyfriend. Once we leave here, none of it will be real anymore. Right? Could he really want *this* to go home with us?

His hands ascend, reaching my thighs and continuing on their path until they freeze at the lace hem of my sleep shorts. His thumbs brush under the fabric, feathering along the apex of my thigh before they freeze.

"Fucking hell," he mutters under his breath, and I assume it's because I skipped underwear when I got ready for bed. The reaction temporarily helps my confidence fight through, but the thought that this isn't real–that this is just a mission for him to prove he can make me come—cages it back up, my body locking with it.

His thumb brushes slowly over my center, and I can tell I'm wet with how it doesn't stutter across my skin. How can I be so turned on and so tense at the same time? Then he's not touching me. Without being able to see, it's easier to feel everything—like his weight shifting slightly on the mattress. Panic rushes through me, a heart rate so fast it nearly steals my breath.

And then the bed dips below me on either side of my face, his hands pressing into the bed. The weight of his body hovers over me. I can tell despite there being no connection between us. Then his warm breath is against my ear, sending a new flood of heat between my legs. "You have to relax." His voice is deep and low, his facial hair scratching my cheek ever so slightly.

"I can't," I claim with a shyness in my voice.

He doesn't respond. He also doesn't move. The stillness draws my focus to the crashing waves and the piano playing off to the side. I take a breath. Hold it for four. Release it slowly. It feels like forever, but there's no indication from Marcus that it's taking too long. On the next breath, I whisper, "Okay."

"Do it again," he demands.

I respond by breathing in again, deeper. This time my chest barely touches another body, and I realize how close Marcus is to me. I hold it as long as I can, wanting to be close to him.

Finally, I exhale, and then he's gone. He's moving back down my body, his fingers latching onto the elastic of my sleep shorts and tugging them down my legs. I note every move of his body as the mattress sinks and rises around me, and he crawls down the bed with my shorts. When he pulls them from my ankles I'm convinced he's not on the bed anymore, but his hands quickly find their way back to my calves. He presses them apart, slowly, moving his hands higher . . . higher.

By the time they reach my thighs, he hits the mattress between my legs. His elbows dig into the bed as he presses me wider, his thumbs brushing over my opening as a low groan rumbles through him. I instinctively clench my legs together. Why the fuck am I so nervous? I berate myself, beg myself to get out of my head. What if this makes things awkward? We still have to be here together. What if he gets frustrated I can't finish? What if . . .

His palm flattens against my stomach and stays there. There's no movement from him besides his warm breath against my wetness. I can *tell* I'm turned on. I know I want this. What the hell is my problem? "Breathe, Brooke."

Am I not? His hand isn't rising or falling along with my stomach. Oh. Maybe I was holding my breath. I inhale, relaxing at the weight of his hand on me, but not restricting my movement. I take another deep breath, releasing it slowly. Again and again. His breath is steady between my thighs and his hands unmoving, one on my stomach and the other firmly gripping my thigh.

"Good girl," he says like he's celebrating me taking a fucking breath, the number one thing I should be doing reflexively to stay alive. It seems so silly, and yet, his words lift a weight from me, allowing me to relax into the mattress.

I take another deep breath as his palm smooths from my stomach to my thigh, mirroring his other hand as he presses his fingers into my skin. Then his tongue is on me, flat and warm, running the length of me.

I don't squirm or flinch. It's like my body anticipated it, letting out a sigh of pleasure. He licks me again, this time his tongue dipping barely inside me. Holy shit that feels good.

His grip on my thigh loosens. Immediately worry rushes through me, but his hand slides to my stomach, and I know he's just reminding me to breathe.

I don't count the passing seconds, but I focus on air, on taking deep breaths and imagining it flowing through my body, my muscles, my veins–every part of me. His tongue presses against me again and every nerve ending sparks. Damn. Maybe there is something to this breathing thing.

I take another breath, directing the life force straight to where Marcus' mouth is hot on my skin as he sucks on my clit. My exhale releases as a moan, my voice cracking and unrecognizable. I send my next breath to where his fingers dig into my inner thighs and my sensitivity heightens as he licks the length of me again. And again.

I try to take deep breaths but they come shorter and faster as his tongue consumes me. "Fuck," I mumble under another sharp exhale, losing my breath as he drives his tongue inside me, flicking it, over and over.

My hands move from the bed like they want to reach for his hair, dig in, and keep him right where he's at. But I force them to stay where they are, in tight fists full of tension and holding back from everything I want from Marcus.

His palm slides to my stomach, warm on my skin, bringing an awareness of my lack of breath again. I breathe in deep and the rise and fall of his hand satisfies him enough to move his hand back where I want it.

His tongue drags over me, his mouth back to sucking on my clit at the same moment he drives two fingers inside me.

My back arches on instinct, and Marcus' other hand flies back to my stomach, keeping me in place. I notice I'm holding my breath. Try to relax on the mattress. Direct my breath to the sensation building inside me as his fingers move in and out of me, his sucking steady. The feeling sneaking up isn't too familiar, but I know it. I want it. My fists grip the comforter, my fingers balling around the fabric as the pressure builds.

Then his fingers pull out just barely more than they have been, and I'm knocked back. The sensation fades ever so slightly before building again as he resumes his consistent motion. He pulls his fingers from me, pressing them into my thigh as he replaces them with fucking me with his tongue. Again, my orgasm slips barely out of reach. It's like I'm running toward the edge of a cliff and instead of free falling over I slam into an invisible wall, and I have to start over.

I sigh in defeat. I want this, and I don't understand why I can't have it.

Marcus freezes, a cool air hitting where I'm wet as his tongue abandons its place. And again, his touch leaves me. It's only gone a moment before his weight is over me again–this time enough that his body touches mine. The soft fabric of his shirt brushes my skin where my tank has shifted up a bit.

And then his lips are on mine.

The kiss is soft. And lingering. But he doesn't make a move to deepen it. It's like he's simply trying to ground me. He trails to my ear, his lips softly brushing against my skin until he's close enough to whisper. "I *want* to do this." The confession makes me freeze. Makes me wish I could see. Makes me want to take this blindfold off and confirm he means *sex* and not *me*.

He drops his hips against my core, and I feel him through his slacks, hard against me. "I want this," he repeats, his voice deep and commanding. "I want you. Not just sex. And *not* for pretend."

It's like he can read my mind and my heart. All of a sudden I believe him. Believe this is real. And pray like hell that it's not some sex haze that's clouding meaning. "I want this for real too."

His grin against my ear is brief before his weight shifts away from me. His thumb brushes across my cheek, below where his tie covers my eyes. I should be startled, not seeing his touch coming. Instead, I just feel everything. I feel alive. Focused on nothing but him. His mouth presses into mine mid-breath, and without thinking twice I let my hands do what they want sliding around his neck and pulling him closer. We deepen the kiss simultaneously, his tongue tangling with mine between heated breaths from both of us. His hand trails down my body as he's propped up on his other arm, pressing into me without giving me too much weight. He slips his fingers under my silk shirt, the sensation of him hot compared to the cool of the fabric, only made hotter by him pinching my nipple between his fingers, rough and demanding as he twists and elicits a moan muffled by our kiss.

My fingers thread through his tied back hair, feeling the elastic loosen as I do. He frees my breast from his grasp, sliding his palm against my skin, between us. His fingers toy with my entrance, the pad of one creating small circles and instant wetness.

He breaks our kiss, only to press his lips softly against mine once more. Then he descends again. This time, I relax, as he kisses his way down my throat, across my collarbone, between my breasts, skipping over the fabric of my shirt to my stomach. He kisses me soft, broken by nips at my skin that shoot pleasure closer and closer to my core.

My orgasm builds again even though no part of him is inside me.

Then he is.

Two of his fingers shove inside me.

His tongue laps at me right above where his fingers slide in and out.

The darkness holds all my focus on him. Every place his fingers hit as they drag inside me before pushing back in. The increasing sensitivity of his tongue, hot and steady sucking my clit, then licking near my opening. Suck. Lick. In and out.

Holy shit.

The palm of his other hand flattens against my stomach, holding me down, making me realize I was squirming and reminding me to breathe. I take a deep breath and it hits.

It hits me *everywhere*.

The ball of tension at my core explodes, flinging me off the cliff I've been on the edge of, and I soar. The breath I suck in gives life to every cell in my body, and I'm floating despite Marcus holding me down. The pressure holds me in place, but I'm still everywhere. His fingers work inside me, sending new shots of pleasure that echo through my body with each thrust. His tongue warm against my wet skin, flooding me with a new sensation. Like when you hand surf a wind wave out your car window in chilly air. The rush hits where it makes contact but sends a chill through the rest of your body, and you feel like you're weightless like you're in nothing, yet you feel everything.

His palm smooths over my stomach, and I take another deep breath as my orgasm fades. Marcus' tongue pulls from me, but his fingers show no sign of slowing down. On the next thrust, he bites into my inner thigh, his teeth sinking with the perfect pressure into my soft skin and pushing me off another cliff.

I'm conscious of the way I'm holding my breath, but I *can't* breathe as a second wave of my orgasm floats through me. Nothing has ever felt like *this*. My grip on his hair loosens as my mind returns to the bed, to my body, as his fingers slow. My arms cross over my face, my eyes still covered by his tie, as I inhale deeply, trying to catch my breath.

He releases my thigh from his teeth and replaces it with a kiss. His lips are soft against my skin, contrasting the scratch of his facial hair against my thigh, every place we touch overwhelming me. Too sensitive for him to stay where he's at, I twist my hips slightly to encourage him away. His chuckle is barely audible as he moves away. With my arms still folded over my face, the mattress sinks beside me, as if Marcus is laying down next to me. I shift, one hand tucking under my head and the other curled into my chest, and I turn toward him, his tie still blocking my view.

His fingers brush against my forehead as he tugs on the material, pulling it off my head and dropping it behind me. There's still darkness, my eyes closed even though they didn't need to be with the tie. I hesitate, afraid to open them, of what I'll see when I do–of what I'll *feel*.

Marcus' thumb brushes across my cheek in encouragement. I let my eyes drift open. And there he is, only a few inches from my face, his flushed, his blue eyes dark in the room only lit by the small lamp in the corner behind us. They're locked on my face. "Hi," I whisper, not knowing what else to say.

"Hello." He holds back a grin and instead licks his lip, letting his hand fall to my waist. "Are you okay?"

I nod. "More than." I think. Because this is just the beginning, right? Can I ask him that? Confirm that what he said was real, and not just words in the moment? "Can I ask you something?"

"Yes." His thumb rubs over my bare hip, sending a fresh wave of arousal through me.

"Are you always that . . . I don't know. Gentle?" That is not what I planned on asking him, but okay. I go with it. "It kind of felt like . . ."

He fills my pause with his deep voice. "Like what?"

"Like you wanted to be rougher with me."

"I'm not typically that gentle."

"Oh. Why were you then?"

"Because it's what you needed."

"But if it wasn't?"

"If it isn't what you need the next time, I'll show you."

"Next time?" I hold my breath, searching his eyes for sincerity.

"I meant what I said. I'm done with this fake shit." He moves his hand from my hip, back to my face, brushing his thumb along my cheek. "If you are."

"Even when we get home?"

"Which home?"

"Yours." My heart races. "I mean, I can find my own place to live. I meant Oregon."

He presses his lips to mine to quiet me then pulls back. "No matter where we are, I want this to be real. This *is* real."

I breathe a sigh. "For me too."

He grips the back of my head, pulling me closer and kissing my forehead. "It's late. Are you ready for bed?"

I nod, even though for as tired as I am, I've never felt more awake. "Wait. What about you?"

"What about me?"

"It's your turn." I sit up, happy to repay the favor–excited even.

He reaches for my hand, stopping me. "Another day. There's no rush."

"Are you sure?" My worried eyes search him. More than I'd have to search my mind for a time when Beau made my orgasm a priority, it would be even harder for me to think of an instance where *his* wasn't a necessity.

"I'm sure." He flicks the light switch next to the bed, and the lamp turns off. The sliver of light from behind the curtains gives me just enough to watch him un-buckle his belt and kick his pants off. It registers for the first time that at some point while I was blindfolded he took off his shirt. He shimmies the comforter and top sheet from under us and lies on the mattress, in only his briefs. "Come here." He holds his arm out, encouraging me toward him. I reach for the covers, pulling them over me as I get comfortable with my head perfectly between his shoulder and chest, and curl into him, my arm wrapping around his waist. I love this. He squeezes my shoulder, holding me close like he wants me here. I just hope when we wake in the morning he feels the same.

Cuddled into his warmth, I close my eyes, allowing myself to truly relax for the second time tonight as I replay the day's events. When we left the hotel, all I wanted was for the event and this night to be over. But now, I don't want it to end. Still, the comfort in my closeness to Marcus pulls me toward sleep, a haze consuming me.

"Brooke?" he whispers my name but it sounds far away, and I'm fading quickly, the long day catching up to me. Maybe I'm imagining it. Maybe . . .

Chapter Twenty-Eight
Marcus

Fucking hell, my shoulder hurts. How can it hurt when it's numb? I open my eyes, but the room is still dark aside from the sliver of light infiltrating through the blackout curtains. Straining to look at the source of my pain, the most beautiful girl is tangled in me. Her head is heavy on my chest, her hair fallen from her bun and splayed over the pillow under my head. She's tucked into me, her leg over one of mine and her arm around my waist.

She's covered by the comforter, but she's wrapped around me so closely that I'm reminded she's not wearing underwear, and every moment of last night replays in my mind. Can thinking about sex release endorphins the way having sex can? I'll research that later. Either way, my shoulder numbness is now on the backburner. We didn't even have sex, but goddamn was it good.

I run my thumb across my lip, remembering her lips on mine and my tongue on her. I was hopeful but still surprised she let me blindfold her. It's something I'd thought about doing with her in the fantasies I've been pushing away the past few weeks, so it worked to my benefit that one of the articles I was reading suggested taking away a sense to heighten the others.

I'm elated that everything I tried worked. I mean, I would have kept researching, trying, doing whatever it took to give Brooke an orgasm like that, but holy hell was it satisfying watching her fall over the edge the way she did. It was more than experiencing her build up the tension and let it all go. It was her getting comfortable with me, letting me into her safe space, *trusting me*. I was conscious of it happening, but it wasn't until she curled into me, sex-sedated, and comfortable, that the guilt hit fucking hard.

It's not like my secret is horrific and dark. I could never work another day in my life and be set. It's my secret that feels like a crime when it comes to her. I'm proud of my worth. I worked hard for it. I need her to see the good in that, but it's like she's wearing . . . whatever is the opposite of rose-colored glasses. I need her to take them off long enough to understand, to not want to bolt at my apparent red flag.

I almost told her last night. I don't want her to think I misled her, took advantage for sex, but she was so peaceful falling asleep. I couldn't bring myself to disturb it. Especially not when we have a busy day today. Another event at the country club. It's not that I can't see why Brooke has the opinion she does of rich people. The ones she has experience with are insufferable. I just have to show her the other side. After she fell asleep, I stayed awake for another three hours. Thank god my phone was within reach from where she held me captive, so I was able to do some digging of my own. I went down a few rabbit holes and ultimately followed a trail of court cases for clients all from the same family–ones where Beau was the lawyer. Based on what was available to the public, it doesn't make sense Beau won the case. It should have been a shoo-in for the plaintiff. Might be nothing. I could be missing crucial information. Also might be something. I sent my lawyer and PI an email around four in the morning before finally joining Brooke in an uneasy sleep.

I brush my hand over her arm across my chest, whispering my fingers against her skin until she stirs. Her eyelids flutter open as she takes in her surroundings without moving. "Morning, love," I say, my voice rough from its first use of the day. She lifts her head a bit to meet my gaze, studying my face as if my greeting means what she thinks it does. "Yes, I still mean everything I said last night, don't regret anything we did, and absolutely want to do it again."

She gives me a sleepy smile as she sits. Before I can stop her, she swings a leg over my waist, straddling me. "I was really hoping that would be the case." Her hands fall to the V of my abs, disappearing under my briefs, and mine run up her thighs, her skin soft under my fingers. With the comforter behind her, she's on full display and not shy about it at all–not that it's bright in here, but still. Fucking hell. It's sexy.

I groan, already regretting my decision. "But not right now. If we start, I won't stop. And we have an event to get to."

She pouts. "It's just a little cooking competition. It's not like Gordon Ramsay will be there."

I chuckle. "I thought Bobby Flay was your favorite celebrity chef?"

"He is, but no one puts on a show like Gordon."

"That's true. We still have to go." I squeeze her thighs.

She snaps the band of my briefs lazily. "Who is your favorite chef?"

"Anthony Bourdain," I answer without hesitation. "Was, anyway." She's silent, her eyes drifting to information in her mind. That death fucked me up. It hit so hard, it was one of the catalysts to shifting my mindset around making money, around focusing only on things that fulfilled me and that made a difference.

"I love learning new things about you." She leans in to kiss me, her lips pressing against mine and sealing the sad memory away.

She pulls back, sitting up again, moving slowly against my already hard cock. "Brooke."

"What?" She feigns innocence.

"We're going. You were actually excited about this event."

"Okay, okay. But I'm still returning that favor later."

"I'm not keeping score." I grip her hips, debating staying here in favor of her riding me, but our first time will not be a quickie. "Come on." I nudge her off me, and she tumbles to the mattress dramatically before swinging her head up for momentum and jumping off the bed. I chuckle, shaking my head. This girl.

She's mine.

In twenty minutes, I'm ready to go in my go-to black jeans and gray V-neck when Brooke walks out of the bathroom. She's in jean shorts rolled at the bottom and a loose-fitting maroon T-shirt that says "wander" in bold serif across the front with "forever" scripted below. Her hair is thrown in a messy bun with a folded bandana as a makeshift headband. It's an outfit that her mom will surely comment on, but she's perfect. Somehow more desirable than last night when she was all done up.

"Why are you looking at me like that?" she asks, crossing the room to the nightstand to grab her phone and slide it into her back pocket.

I meet her where she's at and pull her to me by her hip with one hand, the other gripped on her neck as I kiss her. It's soft at first, but then I need more. Her hands cling to my waist as she lets me deepen the kiss. I break it too soon, knowing we can't be late, and she immediately whines at the loss of contact. I can't help but grin.

She leans her head back, still holding tight to me, and I don't want her to let go. I already know she's the girl I've been waiting for, the one I've been hoping will cross my path every time I see my parents together, or Dean and Maci. Troy and Lexy. Cooper and Sophie, even. "I'm going to be thinking about that kiss all day." She sighs like it's a bad thing. "And last night." The brown of her hazel eyes appears to be winning the daily battle today as she stands directly in the stream of light coming from where I've cracked the curtains.

"Good. I intend to keep it that way." I plan to remind her all day of the things we'll do together later, now that I don't have to pretend I don't want more with her.

She slaps playfully at my chest. "Marcus! We have to be around kids all day."

I shrug, pulling away from her. "I happen to know a secret hiding place that only one kid ever knew about." I throw her a wink over my shoulder as I head for the door.

We arrive at the country club in pure chaos. There's no one at the front to even check us in. Brooke navigates us through the lobby, the help scurrying about carrying baskets of vegetables, fruits, and other assorted pantry goods. We make our way outside, a perfect view of the setup from the top of the marble staircase. Memories of kissing Brooke for the first time last night replay in my mind. The same must be happening for her because she turns back, leaning into me as if she'll know I'll wrap my arm around her. "I'm so glad you're here," she tells me, and I consider whether or not I'm capable of keeping a kiss PG in front of all the kids with their parents.

I'm about to respond when her mother's shrill voice pops our bubble. "There you are. I've been looking everywhere for you."

Brooke turns her head but stays close to me. "Right here, mom. Like I said I would be."

"And really? That is what you're wearing?" Predictable.

"Mom, we're hanging out with kids all day and cooking. I want to be comfortable."

"Well, there's nothing we can do about it now."

I bend to whisper in Brooke's ear, not giving a damn if I'm being rude. "I'll take them off you if that would make her happy." Brooke grins up at me.

"I've got your station all set up with Beau." Both our gazes snap back to her mom. Brooke stiffens next to me, my possessiveness building as I process what she said.

I relax only slightly as Brooke does, laughing at her mother. "Yeah, not going to happen. Marcus is my boyfriend. Either we work together, or I won't be helping at all."

"I had to play safe, Brooke. We both know you can't cook, and I couldn't count on him knowing how to."

Brooke glances back at me. "Please tell me you can cook."

"As well as I can eat." I shoot her a wink.

"Better find Beau a new partner, Mom," she says, not succeeding in holding back her smile.

"I'll take one for the team," a voice comes from behind us, and Brooke's grin breaks free. I turn to see her friend, Cam, in khaki shorts and a navy polo with his hair dyed and gelled like he's in a boy band. Brooke told me he comes from money but doesn't act like it. His parents have forced him to attend all the charity events since he was a kid, and he's been Brooke's sidekick ever since. I wonder what locked Cam into the category of rich but not hated for Brooke? Figuring that out could help my case.

"Fine, thank you, Cameron. Please try to rub off your attitude on my daughter."

He smirks. "I'll try my best." With that, she turns, leaving the three of us alone.

Cam appraises us with a pointed look like he's trying to determine what pissed off Mrs. Fields. "Holy shit! You two fucked, didn't you?!" He slaps Brooke's arm. "Bitch, why didn't you tell me?!"

She rolls her eyes, but her face flushes too. "No, we didn't. Come on, you know I'll tell you."

Her friend looks to me for confirmation. "Not yet. Sorry to disappoint." I chuckle.

"I'm stuck with Beau for half the day. You owe me a good story."

Brooke links her hand with mine, locking our fingers together as she grins at her friend, and I fucking love it.

"Seems like there already is a story considering this thing," he wiggles his finger between us, "Is definitely not pretend anymore."

"It never was," I say, Brooke glancing at me in surprise. I shrug. "Let's get to cooking, shall we?"

"We shall," Cam says, linking his arm with Brooke's and pulling her away from me. Her laugh fades as he forces her quickly down the marble staircase. "Tell me everything," he says and she glances over her shoulder at me.

I follow far enough behind them that Brooke can tell him whatever she wants. I've overheard enough conversations between Maci and Lexy to know that nothing is safe when it comes to best friends, so there's no point in trying to stop it. When we get to the field at the bottom of the staircase, it's lined with makeshift mini-kitchens, just like you'd see on an outdoor episode of *Masterchef*. The space under the pergola has been redesigned into a temporary pantry. It's impressive, and I can see the allure of a place like this. Maybe some people are here for show and status, but it's not like they aren't making a life-changing contribution to society.

From what Brooke told me, these events are connected. Last night's gala was to raise money for children with leukemia, and today, some of the kids who are well enough get to participate in a cooking competition. Each group is assigned a kid to help make a dish.

Once I make it to the back of the tables from my slow walk to give them space, Brooke reaches for me. I give her my hand and she leads me to the front of the set-up, a table to the far left facing the pantry. "You can really cook, right?"

"Yes." I chuckle.

"Okay, thank god. I'm excited. Thank you for being here." We stop behind our makeshift kitchen. "Oh, shoot. I forgot to ask if you have any meetings today. I guess I should have considered that before forcing you to be stuck with me without an escape."

"No work. I left my phone in the room."

"On accident? Did I distract you? I'm sorry. Do you need to go back and get it?"

"I'm out of the office." It wasn't an accident. It was intentional. Until I figure out how to talk to her about the amount of money I make, I have to do everything I can to prove that it doesn't consume my life negatively. Her being part of my life has quickly become a priority. I know it's a risk that my lawyer and PI can't get a hold of me for a few hours. But if I have my phone, I'll check it every five minutes, and that's not going to serve anyone. I figure that as long as I'm present with Brooke, I can prevent the snake from slipping in unnoticed while I pray my money is enough that the men I hired can handle it on their own.

"Have you ever been 'out of the office?'" She chews on her lip with her eyes locked on mine.

My gaze is stuck on the strands of hair she's pulled in front of her bandana headband, and I fight the urge to touch her face. It's like I'm pulled to make up for lost time with her, weeks of wishing she was mine. "No," I answer her honestly. Even when I'm camping, I rarely disconnect unless nature's control over service towers forces me.

She opens her mouth to speak when a young Asian girl pops up in front of us. She's wearing a pink flowered sundress. Her hair is pulled into pigtails, but there are chunks missing, giving her a bald spot in the front, like she recently started chemo. Brooke immediately bends to her level. "Hi. Do we get to hang out with you all day?"

The little girl nods.

Brooke reaches for the straps of her dress, lightly running her fingers over the bow holding it together. "I love your dress. It's so beautiful."

"Thank you." The girl tucks her chin to her shoulder shyly. "I like your headband," she whispers. "I wish I had one to cover up my hair."

Even from standing, I can see Brooke's heart breaking in a tear sitting on her lashes. She reaches to her head, loosening the knot at her neck and undoing the bandana. "You can have it if you'd like."

The girl's eyes widen. "Really?"

"Yup." Brooke reaches to tie the white paisley fabric around her head, fastening it with a small bow directly over her bald spot. The girl touches her head and smiles. "What's your name?"

"Amara."

"That's a pretty name. Did you know in Thailand it means 'immortal,' like an angel?"

She nods. "My yai told me that. She lives in Thailand, but I can't go there. Mae says I'm too sick to go right now."

I squat to their level, my forearms resting on my knees. "You know, Brooke used to live in Thailand."

"You did?" Her voice whispers amazement.

Brooke nods, and the girl's gaze comes back to me when I ask her, "Do you want to make food from there today?"

"We can do that?"

"We can make whatever you want," I tell her. Once I started investing, I signed up for weekly cooking classes so I could learn how to make authentic dishes for anyone I'd get into business with. It sealed the deal on more than one occasion.

"I wish we could make Pad Thai, but I'm allergic to peanuts, so I'm not allowed."

"What if we make it without them?"

Amara glances at Brooke. "Can he really do that?"

Brooke smiles, standing and reaching for her hand. "I think we should trust him. What do you think?"

She nods, placing her little hand in Brooke's and reaching up for mine. "Okay, let's go to the pantry!" she exclaims, tugging us both forward.

Chapter Twenty-Nine
Marcus

Sitting across a picnic table from Amara, Brooke's chin is in her palms watching her eat her plate of Pad Thai–made with cashews instead of peanuts. The girl hardly takes the time to breathe as she shovels it into her mouth, her little fist wrapped around the fork handle. We double checked her allergies with her mom before starting our dish, and even though all the kids are supposed to share and try each other's food, Amara doesn't want anything else. She's so excited about her Pad Thai, you'd think it was her favorite food. Maybe it is now.

Brooke leans back, shifting my attention to her. "You're good with kids." My heart rate spikes at the potential directions of this conversation, not ready for a discussion we're too early in a relationship to have, one that might scare her away before I've fully won her over.

"Yeah, I have a sister."

"You do?" Her eyes light with recognition. "The girl in the picture on your bookshelf?"

Pressing my palms into my thighs, I nod. "Yeah. Her given name is Samira. But we call her Mira."

"She's adopted?"

I nod again, letting a smile crack through. I fucking love my little sister. She's one of my favorite people. She's sassy and smart, follows me around with file folders filled with drawings that she pretends are work. "From Haiti. My parents adopted her during my second year of college, when she was a baby. She's five now."

"Wow. That's amazing. Isn't it expensive to adopt?"

My palms press harder into my thighs, straightening my posture. When all was said and done it cost me almost fifty grand. My parents never would have been able to afford it on their own, and I didn't see a point in them going into debt for their dream when I could easily afford it. Plus, it's the least I could do after all the support they've given me. Maybe now is the right time to tell Brooke. "Yeah, actually . . ." Dammit. I cannot use Mira's existence in our life as leverage for Brooke shifting her mindset. Manipulation is the top reason I think most rich people are shit. "Yeah. It did cost a lot."

"See. It's not fair. People who do real good in the world are the ones who deserve money. Not all these people who throw it around for show, taking from donations to host events in the first place."

Today is not the day. Not after last night. Not on our first day of being real, and certainly not while her mind is closed off the way it is right now, surrounded by people she despises. I want to tell her when the time is right, not just because her piece of shit ex is forcing my hand. "But she's worth it. You'll love her."

"I can't wait to meet her."

"When we get home," I decide and hope we don't fall apart by then.

Brooke's gaze catches on something in the distance. "Hey, do you want to get out of here for a while?"

I follow her gaze to where her mom is talking to a few high-society women but glances toward us like she's headed our way next. I stand, reaching for Brooke's hand. "Let's go."

We say a quick goodbye to Amara, and Brooke weaves me through the tables. I peek back and smirk, watching Mrs. Fields try to exit her conversation without success. I follow Brooke toward her abandoned laundry room, sliding the door to the shoot open with more ease than the first time when it stuck. She steps onto the pulley cart, keeping her eyes on the hallway. I climb in after her, ducking my head and scrunching to fit.

Brooke closes the chute door as I reach for the thick rope, working it through my hands to bring us to the floor below. The platform jolts, the only indication we've hit the cement beneath us, considering I can't see a damn thing. I also don't have my phone this time. Her screen comes to life, the photo of the waterfall from our hike barely illuminating the space around us. She flips on the flashlight and hops out of the chute. I follow her lead, ducking out from the cramped space and stretching into the room. It's exactly how it was earlier this week–four cement walls, no windows, a switch by the exit door that presumably turns on the overhead single lightbulb and an outlet and dryer hookup on one wall.

Placing her phone face down inside the chute, the flashlight shines up the pulley shaft. Her next move brings her in front of me. Her fingers slide under the hem of my T-shirt, and she presses against my abs with her palms. I oblige her for now, letting her back me against the wall.

"Hi," she whispers before pressing a kiss to my lips.

I weave my fingers into her bun, messing it up enough for her hair tie to snap free, and pull her closer. Fucking hell, she's good. Her lips, her hair and how it smells of salty ocean air, and . . . I groan, Brooke's hand cupping me over my jeans.

"My turn," she breathes against my mouth as she undoes the button of my pants. The metal of my zipper unthreads in a slow, smooth motion like she plans to torture me. *That's the last thing that will be happening.* Maybe I've only known her for a few weeks, but it feels like I've been waiting for her forever. Her hand slides under my briefs.

Goddamn, it feels good to have her touching me. Our shadows play on the walls next to us, but I keep my eyes on her. Her fist grips my base and she runs it the full length of me, hardening with her stroke. Gripping the hem of my shirt, I tug it over my head in one pull, then drop it to the cool cement floor.

It's not that I *expect* what she'll do next. But she's going to have my cock in her mouth in the next thirty seconds, and the least I could do is provide her some comfort before I stretch her legs over my shoulders in a few minutes.

She barely adjusts my shirt under her knees before she drops them to the ground. Looping her fingers over the edge of my jeans and briefs, she gives a hard tug, my erection springing free in front of her. I kick my shoes off and step out of my jeans. Without wasting more time, her hands smooth around my thighs, and without warning she sucks my tip into her mouth and slides the length of me until I hit the back of her throat.

Fucking.

Hell.

A groan escapes me. I gather her fallen hair in my hand, pulling it over her shoulder to get a better view. My grip tightens in her waves, and I pull her back, her tongue dragging along the underside of my cock as I do. She sucks as I push her head forward, my balls tightening from watching me disappear inside her mouth. She lets me take the lead, obeying my unspoken commands and takes me deep with each thrust.

I pull her back, and she sucks hard on the tip, her tongue twirling around. I hold her in place, not sure if I can handle being deep in her throat again. She looks up at me through her shadowed lashes from the glow of her phone flashlight across the room and that alone forces me to tip-toe the dangerous line between *wanting* to come and *needing* to. I tug her away, encouraging her to stand.

Gripping her lower back, I step her across the room, my hard cock pressed against her. The back of her legs hit the wall behind us, her ass level with the edge of the laundry dumbwaiter platform. I lean to whisper in her ear as my fingers unbutton her shorts. "If I'm going to come, it's going to be inside you, with you pulsing around me."

Chills immediately shiver through her, the bumps covering her skin just as evident as I slide her shorts and thong down her legs. She grips my shoulders as she steps out of them, then I pin her against the hollow frame behind her, holding her upright with my hand tight to her back. My other palm runs flat over her, my fingers teasing her entrance only for a few small circles before driving inside. Her gasp unsteadies her, and her hands fall to the support beams on either side of the laundry chute opening. I finger fuck her hard, thrusting inside her until she's wet enough to take me.

"Fuck, I don't have a condom." It's meant to be a thought and a personal beratement, but the words come out as a growl.

"It's fine." Her breath is heavy, lost in search of ecstasy already. "I track my cycle. I checked a few days ago. We're good. If you trust me."

I consider questioning her, but fuck, it's hot that she's thought about this, that she's prepared for it. And a few days ago? Before I even kissed her? I groan into a kiss, wanting the connection everywhere possible. Without breaking it, I hoist her up on the ledge by her hips, then drag my hands tight over her thighs.

When I get to her knees, I break our kiss and reach for her calves, stretching her legs over my shoulders. She makes the smallest indication that her legs are too tight, and I pause. "You do yoga every day, love. I know you're flexible enough."

"You got it, *boss*." She pairs her words with a challenging smile, and all my patience for being inside her disappears. Thank fuck she relaxes her legs, her ankles hooking on my shoulders with ease. I grip her left ankle, kissing the inside of her calf and leaving a new trail of chills across her skin. Running my hands back up her thighs, I step closer, the tip of my cock teasing her wet entrance. Goddamn, the anticipation alone might pull me under.

"Marcus," she whines.

I wait for her to make eye contact. "I'm not fucking you for fake. If we do this, it's real." I'd stop if she told me otherwise, but I'm thankful as fuck when she nods.

"It's real."

"Then hold on tight, love."

I note the white of her fingers, tight around the wood beams, and drive into her.

She screams out, her cry echoing through the elevator shaft. It's the hottest thing I've ever seen until her head falls back on my next thrust, the light from her phone flashlight a halo around her head. My fingers dig into her hips, holding her in place as I pump in and out of her. She's tight, but so fucking wet, and the perfect friction builds, a precise fit each time I slip deep inside. It's like the air is being sucked from the room, pulling me tighter to her, deeper, connecting us more. I thrust again, too hard to kiss her, but her eyes are focused between us anyway, watching where she consumes me and lets me go just long enough before pulling me back in.

She's pulsing around me, tightening as her orgasm builds. I hate that her shirt still separates us, wanting to twist her nipples and palm her perfect breasts the way I did last night. Fuck that. I hold her tight to me, relishing the stillness of being inside of her. Her brows scrunch together. "Take your shirt off," I demand, my thumbs brushing the apex of her thighs, not wanting to let go.

Releasing her grip on the beams, she tugs her shirt over her head and tosses it on the floor behind me. She reaches behind her to unclasp her bra, leaning away from me just enough that the light behind her creates a soft glow over her body.

I run my finger across the skin below her breast on the right, over the script inked into her. *Amor fati.*

"Love of one's fate," she tells me between heavy breaths, her hands abandoning their mission to get her naked and falling to my waist. Her thumb rubs over the bottom of my koi fish tattoo, her eyes locking on mine. "Everything that happens in our lives, good and bad, is essential."

"Acceptance," I say.

"Gratitude."

I want to learn every inch of this woman. Under-stand the depths of her brain. Everything–the good and bad–that made her the goddess she is in front of me. But right now, I need her.

Smoothing my thumbs below her breasts again, I reach around her back, unhooking her bra and watch-ing the straps fall off her shoulders before tossing it aside.

So much fucking better. I groan, pulling her closer with a grip on her lower back, holding her steady as I resume my thrusts. She's heaven.

I take her nipple in my mouth, biting enough to elicit a moan from her sweet lips. Her hands fall to my hair, her nails scratching against my head as I swirl my tongue over the hardened peak. Fuck it's hot how turned on she is.

There's no friction left as I drive into her hard enough that she finds her grip on the beams again to steady herself. I reach between us, my thumb finding her clit and rubbing fast circles, my hips steady with the way they fuck her. She bites into her lip, her eyelids fluttering closed. She releases a cross between a sigh and a cry, and I know I've got her. A tingling sensation tightens my balls, rising through my cock. Then I explode, and it's like the room is filled with oxygen, relief and life all at once.

My uncontrolled twitch slows my pace enough that Brooke lets go, and I let her legs fall from my shoulders. With her legs now locked around my waist, she grips either side of my neck with her hands and crashes her lips to mine. Our tongues tangle, refusing to leave time for a breath as our kiss deepens, as if it'll draw out our ecstasy. She's contracting hard around me, intensifying my release in a way I've never experienced ever. With anyone.

I slow my hips, our kiss slowing in sync. It's less frantic but just as intense.

I'm so fucking gone for this girl.

I decide right then that she'll never be anything but mine, and I'll do whatever it takes to make sure that's true even when she finds out my secret.

Stopping my movement, I break our kiss. Brooke's forehead presses into mine, our sweat hot against each other, and I fucking love it.

"That was . . ." she starts but drifts off.

"Incredible?"

"Worth every bad moment I've ever lived to get to this one."

I press my mouth to hers, soft as I pull her tight to me, not wanting to disconnect yet. I feel her smile on my lips. "I guess we should get back," she whispers against them.

"Too bad you gave your bandana away. Might have helped hide the sex hair." I run my fingers through the sweaty strands framing her face.

"Or could have helped you tie me up."

I smirk, running my thumb over her lip before gripping her chin and kissing her again. "I definitely have something to help with that."

"The ties under your bed?" She grins.

"You've been snooping through my room?" For as private of a person as I am, I don't care at all. This girl could get away with murder when it comes to me at this point. And knowing she's curious about and interested in being tied up. I'm confident I've met my dream girl.

"I prefer to call it research for what I'm getting myself into."

"Oh, you have no idea, love."

Chapter Thirty
Brooke

Haphazardly throwing our clothes back on, we ride the pulley back to the main floor. I check that the coast is clear before sneaking us into the maid's private bathroom down the hallway. It's an open room with two sinks and a long counter, along with one stall. I go to the bathroom, cleaning myself up while Marcus waits patiently.

I unlock my phone, expecting to see missed calls or texts from my mother.

Yup.

There are two missed texts and a little red four over the green phone button.

I check the texts first.

The top one is from my mom: *Where did you run off to, Brooke?*

The second is from Maci: *Hey, call me as soon as you can, please.*

Weird. I check the calls. I skip over the one from Emma, noting three missed calls from Maci. My heart thumps in my chest, my breaths getting short. What happened? I fling the stall door open to Marcus leaning against the counter, hands shoved in his pockets. He looks devastatingly handsome with his hair re-tied back, and his casual go-to look with his feet crossed at the ankles.

I don't have time for ogling.

"What's wrong?" he immediately asks when he looks up.

"I don't know. Did Maci call you?" I hit call on her contact name and bring it to my face.

"I don't have my phone, remember?"

It rings once in my ear.

"Oh yeah."

"Brooke! There you are." Maci sounds more relieved than panicked on the other end, and I sigh.

"Yeah, sorry. We were busy. What's going on? Is everything okay?"

"Yeah. Dean is trying to get a hold of Marcus. Is he with you?"

"He's right here. Hold on."

I hold my phone out for Marcus. "Dean," I tell him as he takes it from me.

"Hey, man," he says into the receiver.

I can't hear what Dean says on the other end.

"Yeah, sorry. I left my phone back in the room."

Silence.

"No shit?" His eyes widen, and he straightens his stance. "You're not fucking with me?"

Pause.

"Thanks, man. We'll make it work. I'll call them now."

He pulls the phone from his ear, checking the screen to make sure the call is disconnected before handing it back to me.

"What's going on?"

His face splits into a grin. "Emma and Charlotte. A major morning show in New York had a last-minute opening. They invited them to fill it."

My mouth drops, tears instantly filling my waterline. "No way! Oh my gosh. This is so exciting." We've been marketing like crazy. A post even went viral, and we gained nearly sixty thousand followers overnight, but dang that was *fast*. "I knew they would do big things. When is it?"

"Tomorrow."

"You're going, right?"

He looks at me quizzically. "No? We have plans to-morrow."

"Marcus!" I hit his arm. "Did they invite you to come?"

"Dean said they did. That they wanted me to call them."

Sliding my phone into my back pocket, I link my arms around his neck. His hands wrap around my waist. "Then we're going."

"But–"

"No. This is a huge deal. You deserve to be there for this. I know they want you there too. Anything else can wait. We can rent a car and leave tonight. It's only a three-hour drive."

"Are you sure?"

"Positive." I kiss him. "Now, let's go tell my mother we're leaving and make today even better than it al-ready is."

He chuckles. "Thank you, Brooke."

I smile and pull him toward the door.

Forty-five minutes later, we finally tracked down my mom and somewhat contained her meltdown about us leaving earlier than planned. She started to throw a fit, but lucky for us, a few country club members needed to steal her away. We said goodbye, and I promised I'd be back before three years–although I'm not confident I'll keep that promise.

"Okay, can you call us a car from the front desk? I'll text my dad to let him know we're coming back and checking out. Then I'll find us a rental. Dad can probably drop us off at the car place. It's close to his hotel. You can call Emma and Charlotte on the way back."

"Yeah," he says hesitantly, scanning the room before walking the few steps away from where I'm sitting on the lobby couch. He smiles at the front desk lady. She's new since I've been here, but we've already developed a mutual fondness for each other. She picks up the cordless phone from behind the counter and punches in a number for him before handing it over.

Focusing back on my task, I shoot a text to my dad, then pull up the rental car website. As it loads, the space on the couch next to me sinks. I look over to find the culprit. I thought I already got rid of this dead weight. I roll my eyes, more annoyed that I don't have time to fight him.

"What do you want, Beau? Here to cause more trouble?"

"I don't know what you're talking about." He smirks. "Whether you see it or not, Brooke, I'm always looking out for your best interests."

"Sure you are."

"You act like I don't know you at all. I may have been busy working to provide for us for half a decade, but I still paid attention. You forget it's my job to know every little detail."

"I'm not one of your cases," I snap.

"Doesn't mean I can't help you."

"There's nothing you can do for me at this point except leave me alone and move on."

"I beg to differ. You know your boyfriend–"

"Has a car waiting for you." Marcus cuts him off, appearing in front of us and holding his hand out for mine. When I glance up, Marcus is shooting Beau a death glare. I kind of like the possessiveness, but I take his hand and break the tension anyway. My boyfriend immediately relaxes at my touch, pulling me to him and toward the door without a single look back–even when Beau yells after us, "I'll talk to you very soon, Brooke."

Chapter Thirty-One
Marcus

Fucking hell, that was a close call. I tried to get Brooke out of the country club as soon as we informed her mom we were leaving, but word spreads quickly at a place held together by money and gossip. Beau tried to get in a final word, I'm sure a final ditch effort of spilling my secret in person. Thank god Brooke was none the wiser when I pulled her away.

When we got back to the hotel, we packed our bags. I checked my phone–still no update from my lawyer or PI. Brooke made arrangements for a rental car, and we're in a Ford Focus halfway to New York. Beau has tried to call her at least four times since we left the club, each time she declines it with a groan or a frustrated sigh. Thank fuck for that grace from the universe.

I didn't know how to get out of not connecting my phone to the dash cam, so when my PI's call comes through it covers the GPS screen with his name. Fucking hell. The timing.

Brooke is unbothered by the pause of the piano version of Taylor Swift's album *The Dead Poets Society* or something. Glancing over my shoulder, I check my blind spot, then move to the exit lane, getting off at the one directing toward Seaside Park.

Brooke glances at me in question. "I need to take this really quick." Stopping at the light at the end of the exit, I hit accept on the last ring. "Hey, Frank. Give me a moment."

He says nothing, staying on the line while I pull into a parking lot lining a roadside beach. Brooke shifts her attention to the family in front of us, the kids standing on the bulkhead as the parents lather sunscreen on them. I turn the car off, automatically switching Frank to my phone instead of the car speaker. "Hey, sorry about that," I tell him.

"You're good. I've got something."

"Shoot," I say, my confidence immediately spiking. I glance over at Brooke to see if there's any indication that she can hear the other end of the line, but she's not even looking my way. She's got her eyes locked on the car that pulled up beside us. There's a girl in the front seat jamming out to her music like no one is watching, and the biggest smile fills Brooke's face. I love when she sees a glimmer. Her joy from the smallest things makes me so fucking happy. Fuck, I'm pretty sure I love her.

I tune back in quickly, only missing Frank going over a few basic things I already knew about Beau. That's when he hits me with new information. Apparently the cases I found *were* a lead. He managed to get in contact with an estranged friend of one of Beau's clients who spilled all the dirt we needed to nail the coffin of his blackmail against me shut–proof that he'd been paying off witnesses to build his "win" percentage. I ask a few vague questions that he answers clearly, catching on to the fact that I'm trying to be discreet. I ask him to call my lawyer and fill him in, knowing he'll already know what to do, and request the final bill be sent to my email. Thanking him, I hang up, shooting a text to my lawyer as backup. He already has all of Beau's contact information as well as *his* lawyers, and I know he'll take care of this for me. He gets paid to take care of it.

Hanging up with a fresh breath of air filling my lungs, I turn the key in the ignition, and the car roars back to life. I reach over, running my hand up Brooke's thigh, and she glances my way like she was too entranced by tens of glimmers in this park to notice I was ready to get back on the road. She shifts her smile back to me. "Everything okay?" she asks.

"It is now." I give her leg a squeeze.

As I back out of the spot and pull back onto the parkway, I promise myself I'll tell her as soon as the filming is over tomorrow. Even with the threat of Beau telling her gone, she deserves to know, and I don't want to keep anything from her anymore.

Chapter Thirty-Two
Brooke

"I'll text Emma and Charlotte and let them know we're on our way over." I unlock my phone as Marcus pulls the hotel room door closed behind us.

Marcus shoots me an appreciative smile as he guides me into the elevator.

"Have you ever been on TV before?"

He shakes his head. "No. You?"

"One time for the local news station in Phuket." The milky white "1" button glows red when I push it, and the elevator starts its descent from the seventeenth floor. "And a few times in the background when Beau was getting interviewed for some high-profile case."

He hums, leaning against the rail. "Can't say it's something I've ever *wanted* to do."

"Well, it's a good thing you don't have to cross that off your to-don't list today. It's nice you're supporting Emma and Charlotte, though."

He gives me a sideways glance. "It's the type of investor I want to be."

"Well, I know they appreciate it. I definitely would if I were them."

"I'm sure they'll be just as happy to see you."

"Us." I grin, reaching over and linking my arm through his. "Do you think everyone will be excited?"

He chuckles. "You haven't told them already?"

The elevator comes to a stop and the doors whoosh open. He lets me out first and I glance back at him with a smirk. "There might have been a group chat text."

"Might have been, huh?"

"There definitely was. But you know how Lexy gets when she wants answers. It's not my fault."

"You can tell them anything you want, love." He jogs ahead a step to open the door from the quiet pristine lobby to the dirty hustle and bustle of Times Square lit by the orange and pink glow of the sunrise.

"I don't want to tell them *everything*. Some things I want to save just for us." I smile up at him as he takes my hand and leads me through the chaos of the crosswalk.

"Whatever you want," he tells me, but there's an undertone in his voice that I can't quite place in his silence as we finish crossing the street.

"Are you okay?"

"Yeah. We're here." He opens the door to the live studio building.

Something feels off, but I can't quite place it. Maybe nerves. This *is* a pretty big deal.

Even though we won't be on screen, we both dressed to impress. Marcus is in the suit he wore to casino night, looking like he belongs in one of these high rises. I'm wearing black skinny jeans with a white flowy shirt, short brown boots and a navy blazer–the same thing I wore the first day I met Emma and Charlotte. I don't look as fancy as he does, but I still look great. Plus, I curled my hair and did my makeup this morning.

We follow signs to the right room, on the second floor, and down a few hallways. Marcus opens the heavy metal door, letting me walk through first. The lighting is dimmed everywhere except the stage in the distance, but when we scan the room, we both lock on to two pairs of eyes staring back at us. I glance at Marcus, but it's clear by the surprise and grin on his face that he was not expecting to see his best friend or his fiancée. "Hey, man." He reaches to bro-hug Dean. "What are you doing here?" He takes a turn with Maci who hugs me as soon as she releases him, whispering a 'hi.'

"Miss your TV debut? Not a chance."

"I hate to break it to you, but I won't be on screen."

Maci interrupts. "Emma and Charlotte said they aren't letting you get out of it. That they couldn't have done any of this without you."

"Don't worry. I also got you something to improve your outfit." Dean smirks and Marcus' eyebrow quirks. Dean pulls a rolled up tie from the back pocket of his jeans. As he holds it up, the tie unrolls, revealing the most incredible and hideous fabric I've ever seen. It's a picture of who I'm assuming is Dean and Marcus as kids printed in repeat over the tie. They're both wearing soccer jerseys. Marcus is standing with a hand on one hip, a foot on top of a soccer ball. His hair is long and blowing in his eyes a bit. Dean holds a soccer ball under one arm and has his other looped around his friend's neck. They both have goofy grins on their faces. They're probably not any older than six or seven.

"Fucking hell," Marcus mutters, shaking his head, but he's holding back a laugh as he reaches for the tie. "Where did you get this atrocity?"

"It's been sitting in my dresser since high school. I told you I believed in you, man."

It feels like we're in the middle of a secret Maci and I aren't in on, but by the way she's holding back her amusement, it seems she's a little more clued in than I am.

"I'm not there yet." The way Marcus' gaze shifts to mine momentarily after he says it only heightens the unease slowly taking over.

"I don't think you'll be able to say that after this quarter." Dean is confident. What the hell are they talking about? "So, you're wearing that. A deal is a deal."

I shift uncomfortably, feeling like a stranger trapped between two friends chatting on a bus.

Marcus chuckles, running the fabric of the tie through his fingers. "I don't want to take away anything from Emma and Charlotte. I'll wear it to dinner tonight."

"Deal." Dean shoves his hands into the pockets of his jeans.

Maci leans in to side hug Marcus again. "I'm so proud of you."

"Thanks." He squeezes her shoulder with his hand not holding the tie. "Do we still have some time? Can I talk to Brooke for a few minutes?"

Maci glances up at him and pulls away. "Yes!" She smiles. "Brooke, meet me over there by the cookie table when Marcus has to go. We can watch the show together."

"Okay." I force a smile, but I'm nervous all of a sudden. Nervous and very confused. Dean and Maci excuse themselves, and Marcus turns to me.

"I need to talk to you."

"Oh. Umm. Okay." I draw out the last word. He takes my hand, glances around, then leads me to the side of the room, out of earshot of any of the people prepping for the show. "Is everything alright?" I'm starting to worry.

He takes a deep breath. Pauses. Loops the tie over the top of the random clothes rack next to us. I follow the movement, then look back to where he grabs my hands again and runs his thumbs over my knuckles. I've never seen him like this. I haven't known him that long, but still.

"Brooke."

"Yes?" I tip my head slightly.

"I don't think it's a secret anymore that I have real feelings for you."

I shake my head slow and confused. "I've been starting to get that impression . . ."

"I . . ." He takes a breath. Damn. What is so serious right now? "After I tell you, please know that even if you feel like I lied to you, nothing else I have said to you is a lie. Especially when it comes to how I feel about you. And the only reason I haven't told you this yet is because I feel so strongly, and I wanted you to give us a shot before you made up your mind."

"What is it? You're scaring me." Panic squeezes my heart.

His breath is so deep, his chest nearly heaves in front of me. "You know how you hate the people at the club because you think their money makes them entitled snobs?" He says the last two words as if there are air quotes around them."

"Uh-huh . . .""Well, I might have as much money as them." He grimaces. "I'm actually pretty sure I have more."

"What?"

"I have a lot of money," he paraphrases.

"Umm." My thoughts are swirling. This isn't what I expected. I don't know what I expected. My thoughts flashed through a dozen possibilities, but this wasn't one of them. "Like, what kind of rich are we talking about?"

"I guess it depends on who you ask."

"How much money?"

"A lot."

"What's your net worth?" The question feels completely inappropriate coming out of my mouth, and I feel guilty when he cringes. Yet, I can't seem to stop myself. "A couple million?"

He stares back, his thumbs freezing against my knuckles. My hands are clammy now. "A little more than that . . ."

"Tell me, please."

He glances at the tie, then back to me and takes a deep breath. "When I was fifteen, I coded my first app. It wasn't anything fancy. But I figured it out on my own. And it worked. I showed Dean. He slapped me on the back and said, 'You're going to be worth a billion dollars someday. Don't forget about me when that happens.'"

My eyes widen, my hands tensing in his.

"I brushed him off, but he pushed back a bit. He said, 'Fine, when you're rich, I'm making you a tie covered with that picture of us that Sophie always makes fun of. And you have to wear it in public as my *I told you so.*' It became an inside joke. When I sold my first app. After I made my first investment. When I bought the bar. At the time it felt like it would only ever be a joke. But the numbers kept going up . . . and if Emma and Charlotte's company takes off the way most do after airing on national television . . ."

"You're going to be a billionaire." I can't wrap my head around this. How is this even real?

"Yeah." He looks upset.

"Hey, are you Marcus?" We both turn to find a cameraman with a headset approaching us.

"Yes," he answers, dropping my hands.

"We've got to get you ready. Can you come with me?"

He looks to me, as if for permission. "Yeah, of course. Go. Good luck."

He hesitates, then brushes his thumb across my cheek. "Please don't leave," he pleads, kisses my forehead and walks past me.

I stand there for a few minutes, at least, feeling motion sick. Off balanced. Unsettled. What am I supposed to think? Every single thought I've ever had about an entire group of people is being challenged, countered, and attacked right now. I can't untangle this tug-of-war rope on my own. Turning, I scan the room until my eyes land on Maci. She's leaning against a table covered in snacks, and I make my way to her.

"Hey, Brooke!" She smiles as I approach, then takes a bite of a Red Vine. "I can't wait to hear about everything with—" Her eyebrows scrunch. "Are you okay?"

I nod. Then shake my head. I don't have any clue. "Did you know?"

Her eyebrows scrunch. "Know what?"

"About Marcus' money."

"Oh. I mean, not really. It's always been pretty clear to me he doesn't have financial struggles, but I didn't have even a guess at what that really looked like until Dean made us stop by his parents to get that tie before our flight last night."

"A billion dollars." I sigh. "That's more than Beau's entire family has. More than anyone I know at the country club–to my knowledge anyway. There's like . . . less than three thousand known billionaires in the world. In the *world*, Maci."

"That's really impressive then. Don't you think?"

"Yeah, it is . . . but."

"But you've conditioned yourself your entire life to believe that money is bad."

My heart feels like it's actually thrashing against the inside of my chest. "That."

"In the grand scheme of things, money can make up such a small factor." Maci's eyes wander to the corner of the room as she chews on her lip like she's searching for the right words to help me process this. I reach for a Red Vine, biting off the end of it, having no idea how to work through this on my own. I'm reeling, my ears ringing as I try to work through the logic. It should be simple. It doesn't matter that he's rich. He's a good man. A man that I've connected with in the past month. But how can I say that when I didn't even know about one of the biggest parts of him?

"Remember the first time we hung out?" Maci's voice breaks through my spiral. "In Thailand, when you invited me over and convinced me to share every detail of my dilemma choosing between Dean and Mack?"

"Yes." I can't imagine where she's going with this. It's a completely different situation.

"Our excuse is always that we're protecting our heart, right? I mean that's how it was with Mack. He was always the secure bet. He would have loved me until the end of time if I let him–no matter what problems we encountered. That was the risk in choosing Dean. He had never proven to me that I could count on him. For the longest time, I thought Mack was the safe choice because I *could* count on him. And I guess in a way, that is protecting my heart. That's how it would be leaving Marcus behind, I think. Choosing the route that keeps you safe from a world you've had a bad experience with, the way Mack could have kept me safe from heartache. Choosing Dean was scary because it felt contradictory to what I thought I needed.

But sometimes we have to shift the expectations of what we have for our life. When we're younger, we don't know better. We don't see all the options because our view of the world is limited, confined to whatever we've happened to experience. What has Marcus done that's anything like Beau?"

Outside of his net worth, I can't think of a single way he's not the complete opposite of my ex. In replace of a response, I take another bite of Red Vine.

"Hasn't he already proven there are exceptions?"

"Yeah . . . he has."

"There's this concept in psychology called mismatching experiences. The idea is that you free yourself from visceral emotional responses tied to prior experiences. You disconfirm your expectations by repeatedly matching them to its opposite. For example, in your relationship, Beau treated you like you were his assistant, or less than him, even outside of the office. What does Marcus do? In similar situations."

"He gives me control, lets me take the lead." Except in bed, I add to myself.

"And you've been thriving. Loving your work. Right?"

I nod. I noticed that too. My dad even said something about it.

"Your purple hoodie is the only thing from your past. Why's that?"

I chuckle because it feels like she's been preparing herself for this with how fast she's shooting off questions. "Beau replaced everything in my closet one day. He said if I was going to be by his side, I needed to look the part. I tried to fight him, but he went on about the beauty of money and how I should appreciate it for things like that. I'd left that sweatshirt at Cam's house that day."

"Do you think Marcus cares about how you look next to him?"

"I'm pretty sure Marcus bought a bulk pack of black tees and cycles through them. He didn't seem bothered when I went with him to the grocery store in my elephant pants and oversized T-shirt."

"Did Beau even go to the grocery store?"

I shake my head with a chuckle. "Definitely not."

"Didn't you tell me once about how at a photo op Beau stood in front of you like you were just his assistant?"

"Yeah. He didn't want people to see anything that could be considered PDA. He said it was unprofessional since I worked for him."

She hums. "What about Marcus? You work for him. Is he the same?"

I scan through every interaction with Marcus that I can remember like a flip book. Thinking about it in retrospect, in each image, he gets closer to me. "This entire trip . . . he has been touching me. But we were fake dating for most of it. That's probably why."

"I don't know. I've never seen Marcus be touchy with girls past anything cordial. Even Dean said once that he's not into PDA."

"That's hard to believe . . . It feels so comfortable when he's touching me. Natural. Like it would be weird if it was any other way. Like he knows exactly what he's doing."

"Maybe it's just because you make it easy for him."

"I love how it feels when he touches me," I say softly, not necessarily to Maci.

She fights back a smile, twirling her Red Vine. "How did Beau make you feel?"

"Less-than. A means to an end. Like shit, but also like I didn't have a better option than him."

"How does Marcus make you feel?"

I search for the right words, even though I'm not sure they exist. "Sometimes, when I look into the night sky, at the swirls of stars and the planets, I feel so small and insignificant. But other times, I think that if I exist in a place where I get to witness something so extraordinary and powerful, there's meaning in that. That I'm a part of what makes life spin on its axis. Marcus makes me feel like that."

"That sounds like something you shouldn't give up." She smiles, her hand landing gently on my shoulder.

"So, at what point do you abandon this idea in your head for something that makes more sense?"

"He makes everything make more sense." I tear my Red Vine in half, not bothering to eat it. "I just wish he would have told me."

She stares in a way that feels like an eye roll. "Can you blame him with how much you outwardly hate rich people?"

I sigh. "No. You're right."

"I went through the same thing with Dean, resenting him for not telling me he was leaving. But consider it this way. What if you hating rich people so much made him feel like it was something he needed to be ashamed of or concerned about? What if not telling you was simply his way of protecting himself and what you two have?"

He did look upset when he was confirming he's nearly a billionaire. Even though I'm new to his life, it doesn't take more than that to know he worked extremely hard for that. "Shit. I messed this up."

"Trust me, you didn't." She points, and I follow her fingers to the monitor behind me showing Marcus and the girls on a couch on stage. They aren't live yet, but you can tell Marcus isn't present. He's rubbing his hands over his thighs like he's trying to work out worry. "Marcus doesn't get stage fright," Maci adds. There was a sliver of me that thought *maybe* that was it. "He's never nervous. Dean and I went to see him speak at a tech conference for thousands of people, and he seemed as comfortable as sitting at our kitchen table."

"I don't want him to worry," I say it more to myself, but Maci nudges me toward where Dean is standing closer to the stage, watching his friend.

I join her future husband a few feet from the stage, glancing up at him. His hands are shoved in his jean pockets, flannel rolled to his elbows as he meets my gaze, looking guilty. "I'm sorry I let the cat out of the bag. With the way he's been talking about you, I assumed he'd told you."

"It's okay. It's not your fault," I assure him.

"Try not to blame Marcus either. This is a big deal for him."

"I know."

"I hope Maci talked some sense into you. She's the better of us at pep talks." He glances back at Marcus.

I nod, assuming he can see the motion from the corner of his eye without my verbal confirmation.

"There's no one better to have in your corner."

"I don't know how to tell him that's what I want." I stare in the same direction he is, watching Marcus continue to rub his hands over his slacks as he listens to something a cameraman tells him and the girls.

"He doesn't need much. A look should do it. Nothing too intense, though. Slacks are not forgiving pants."

I laugh. "I'm not sure I could have quite that effect from here."

"Oh trust me, if the past week of payback for how many times I brought up Maci when we first met is any indication, he has very little control left."

I don't respond, but I listen and wait for Marcus to glance in our direction. He finally does when the cameraman walks off stage, and his eyes lock on mine. His hands freeze. God, he's handsome. His charcoal suit looks just as good on him as it did the night of the casino fundraiser, his hair perfectly in place. The only thing off is the worry etched into his brows.

I smile and give him a small, nervous wave. My hand drops to my side along with a visible exhale of relief from Marcus. He runs his hands up his face, back down, then leaves one clasped over his mouth like he's trying to hide a smile. He drops his hand, linking his fingers at his bent knees and shakes his head slightly–like he can't believe his luck. Then he turns back to Charlotte and Emma, saying something to them I can't hear.

A shoulder nudges me from the side. "Told ya."

Chapter Thirty-Three
Marcus

The recording light turns off and the lights on the stage dim with a click. I release a breath. Fuck, that was exhilarating. "You two killed it," I tell Emma and Charlotte, willing all my focus on them.

"We really did, didn't we?" Emma smiles brightly as Charlotte embraces her from her seat on the couch.

Charlotte turns her head back toward me without releasing her friend. "Thank you for being here, Marcus."

"Yeah, thank you. We're so thankful for you." Emma's gaze shifts past me. I turn to see three of the people who mean the most approaching the stage. "Brooke!" Emma leaps from the couch, Charlotte tumbling off it after her. "We're so grateful for you too!" The girls tackle her with a group hug that Brooke accepts happily. Her arms are tight around them, but her eyes meet mine as I stand to make my way over. Her smile doesn't fade. She doesn't seem anxious. Seeing her before the show did enough to quell my nerves. I still couldn't help but wonder if it was an act because she wanted to make sure the show went smoothly for the girls. But seeing her now. Fuck. Maybe it's all going to be fine.

Dean reaches for my hand, and I grip it before giving in to a bro-hug. "Proud of you."

"Thanks, man." I release him, distracted, my eyes still locked on Brooke.

"You're good," Dean tells me. "Take a fucking breath. It's all yours."

My gaze flicks to him for a moment. Then back to Brooke. The girls have broken apart, all four of them chatting excitedly reviewing the show. But Brooke's eyes find mine and her focus on the group fades away. She steps out of the little circle they'd forced and the room goes silent. Maybe it doesn't. There are a hundred people here breaking down the set, cleaning up, preparing for a new show tomorrow. I don't hear or see any of them, though. It's just her.

There's only a vague recollection of the rest of them turning to watch as Brooke walks toward me. "Hi," she says with a smile when she's within touching distance of me.

"Hi." I chuckle.

"You did amazing. That was amazing." She closes the distance between us, slipping her hands under where I've unbuttoned my suit jacket and pulls herself to me. "*You* are amazing."

I run my hands along her neck, fingers threading through her curls, thumbs locking on her jaw.

"Even though I'm rich enough to buy you a lifetime supply of the rainbow bagels you're now obsessed with?"

She fights a grin with a nod and confirms with a single word.

"Really?"

"As long as you stay exactly the kind of man you are."

I seal the promise with a kiss. "I'm still sorry I didn't tell you."

"It's okay."

"I wanted to, but every time, I'd stop myself. The way I spend my money . . . it felt like if I told you about those things in the same breath as revealing my wealth, that I'd be taking advantage of things that are important to me–people who are important to me. Using them for gain in this situation."

"Like what?"

I nod toward Charlotte and Emma, not caring that they are all pretending not to watch us even though it's clear that they are. "Investing in this company, for starters."

"I knew there was a deeper reason when you told me they had no proof of sale. What's the reason?"

I don't want to betray Maci's trust. I glance toward her and Brooke follows my gaze, confusion immediately hitting her beautiful face. "Maci?" she asks.

Maci must hear her because she looks up from the pretend conversation she's having with the rest of them a few feet away. Her eyes shift between Brooke and me, piecing together the situation. She glances at Emma and Charlotte, then back to me. Brooke follows Maci's line of sight. It all happens in a split second but feels like forever. Then Maci nods toward me, permitting me to tell her story.

I lock back on Brooke, brushing my thumbs across her cheek. "Avery was roofied once. Sort of attacked Maci after the drug hit her system."

Brooke's mouth falls open. "Oh." She glances back at her friend, and Maci smiles, assuring her everything is okay.

"Yeah. I'll let her tell you the rest." I let my hands run down her neck, over her shoulders, locking on her arms. "Good causes exist on every corner. But I think the ones you'll make the biggest impact supporting are ones that hit home more."

She nods, her eyes wandering to the corner of the room and widening slightly over and over again as if little details are clicking into place. "What else?"

"You know about the bar. Making the dream come true for Troy."

"You paid for the whole thing?" Her eyes gloss over.

"Yes. He's slowly buying me out for his half."

"What else?"

"My sister's adoption fees."

A tear escapes, but she doesn't bother brushing it away. She just wraps her arms tighter around my waist. "I'm so sorry, Marcus."

"You're sorry?" I chuckle.

She nods. "For making you feel like the things that make you incredible needed to be hidden from me."

"It wasn't worth losing you," I say easily. "You sure you're okay with this?"

"The rich people shit-talking might take some time to get under control, but yes."

"Good. Because if you don't walk away now, I won't let you."

"I'm not going anywhere." She smiles. "Except maybe out of New York. This city isn't exactly my vibe."

"We can go anywhere you want. I am rich, you know." I smirk.

"Maybe this won't be so bad after all." Her smile barely has time to escape before she stands on her toes and presses her lips to mine. It's a quick kiss because for as much as I want to get lost in it, I'm acutely aware of the four pairs of eyes watching us. I laugh, breaking the kiss and pulling Brooke into a hug.

"Oh, wait. One more thing," I say into her hair, wanting to get everything out in the open.

She pulls back, curious.

"All last week, Beau was trying to dig up dirt on me."

Her eyes widen, but then she shakes away her shock like she's not surprised. "You told me that."

"Yeah. But not that he was blackmailing me. Wanted to tell you I was rich before I had a chance. So, I hired a PI to bury him."

A grin splashes across her pretty face. "Oh, I have plenty of dirt on him. I could have saved you the trouble and the money."

"I guess I'll have to keep you around then." I smirk, kissing her temple. "Alright." I turn to our friends. "Where are we going for lunch? My treat," I tell our crowd, Brooke turning in my arms enough to look at them too. "We've got a lot to celebrate."

Chapter Thirty-Four
Brooke

I slide my key into the front door of Marcus' house after a long day with Emma and Charlotte. We've been back from our trip for three days now and thinking their product would take off after being on a national morning show was a severe underestimation. Bar owners and managers all across the country have been calling us non-stop, giving us no time to come up for air, and withholding any opportunity for Marcus and I to connect away from the chaos.

As much as I love that my temporary living arrangement includes one of my best friends, I would kill for a night alone with Marcus. We've shared his bed, but not in the way I've been craving considering we haven't slept more than four hours a night and Maci and Dean have been here. That means we also haven't had any time to discuss our future, including plans for me to move to Oregon permanently and what that looks like. Tonight isn't the night for it either, though. Despite my desire for alone time, I am excited to meet his sister.

I twist the key in the lock, turning the knob as I do. A young girl's voice comes from down the hallway. "Uncle Dean!" she screams at the same time Marcus' deep voice booms past the wood divider, "We're in here!"

Closing the door behind me, I slip my flats off and walk down the entryway hall. When I reach the living room couch on the right, the back of Marcus' head comes into view. It's covered with plastic pastel butterfly clips—the kind my mom never bought me because she said bows were more classy. There's a little girl sitting in front of him on the floor, half of her hair in a perfect French braid, and the other almost completed as Marcus twists the dark brown strand a shade lighter than her skin. It's the cutest thing I've seen and *almost* makes my ovaries explode.

Marcus turns, pinching the partially braided hair in his fingers. "Brooke." His rough voice strongly contrasts the image of him with butterfly barrettes clipped into his hair tied loosely in a knot at his neck. He shoots me a tired grin, happy to see me.

Mira turns too, nearly pulling her braid from Marcus' hand. He tries to quickly band the elastic over the end before she squirms away from him and stands but fails. With a chuckle, he tosses the hair tie on the coffee table in defeat.

"Hiiii," she says as she runs toward me, halting right before she crashes.

Before I have a chance to speak, the front door clicks open again. "Hello!" the man's voice bellows, and with a kick of his foot against the wood, the door opens further revealing Dean.

"Uncle Dean!" the girl yells, forgetting completely about me as she hurtles toward him, the strands at the end of her untied braid unraveling slightly. He barely has time to set down the ice cream on the entryway table before sweeping her into his arms and spinning her in a circle.

"How's my favorite girl?"

She giggles. "I'm not your favorite girl. That's Aunt Maci."

"You were my girl first," he says, kissing her on top of her head before gently setting her feet back on the ground.

"Oh yeah. First is way better," she points out confidently, then turns to check out the ice cream.

Dean glances up to me at the end of the hall. Marcus has made his way to me, standing a step back. "Who is ready for a sleepover?" He looks back at Mira.

"Me, me, me!" she screams, trying to pry the top off the ice cream carton with her little hands.

"How was today?" Dean asks, referring to the meeting Marcus had with the warehouse about speeding and multiplying production.

"Good," Marcus says, exhausted.

I watch Dean take us both in. "You two look like you could use a nap." He turns to Mira, bending to her level. "Mira." The girl's focus stays on the pint of ice cream she's managed to get the top off on her own. "Mira," Dean repeats.

"Yes?" She turns toward him as she digs her finger into the top layer of bright blue dessert.

"What do you think about coming with me? We can have a sleepover with Aunt Maci instead." "Can we invite baby Canaan too?" she asks.

"She's with him right now."

"And we can bring the ice cream? And my butterfly clips?" She looks at him with wide eyes.

"Duh. It's not a sleepover without them."

"Yay!" She squeals. "Is Marcus coming too?"

"I was thinking we could let your brother take a nap with Brooke. They're really tired. What do you think?"

The mention of my name reminds her she hasn't actually met me yet, and she reluctantly abandons the ice cream to make her way to me. "Hi, I'm Mira."

I bend to her level. "It's nice to meet you, Mira. I'm Brooke."

She throws her arms around my neck, squeezing me tight. I wrap my arms around her tiny waist, hugging her until she pulls back. "I don't have to take naps anymore." I laugh at the irony of naps being acceptable for the ages that don't appreciate them. "Do you want me to leave you some butterfly clips? Marcus is really good at doing hair after it gets all messed up from sleeping."

The boys both chuckle, but I keep it together. "That's okay. You can bring them to Maci. Thank you, though."

Her eyes widen at my mention of my friend. "Do YOU know my Aunt Maci?!"

"I sure do. I met her in Thailand. Do you know where that is?"

"Is that by Spain? Uncle Dean and Aunt Maci brought me back presents from there."

I laugh. "No. Why don't you ask her to show you pictures when you get there?" Part of me *wants* to hang out with her, get to know her. I know she's important to Marcus, but more of me just wants a quiet house alone with him. By his lack of objection, I'm guessing he wants the same.

"I will! It's nice to meet you, Brooke. I hope you have a fun sleepover." With that, she tugs on Dean's hand. "Let's gooooooooo. Bye, Marcus." She waves at her brother with her free hand.

Marcus leaves the room, coming back only a moment later with a small My Little Pony backpack and hands it off to Dean.

"Avery and Miller are out of town for the night, so Maci and I will just stay there. We'll meet you for breakfast at Brail's in the morning?"

"Sounds good. Thanks, man. I owe you one."

Dean smirks as Mira tugs on his hand again. He lets her pull him toward the door.

"Be good," Marcus calls after his sister. Once the door closes behind them I turn to him.

"I feel bad about bailing. We should hang out with them."

He steps closer, pulling me to him. I press my hands to his chest and meet his gaze. "Nah. Dean's got her. She loves him just as much."

"I don't know," I say, reaching to pull a butterfly clip from his hair. "She seems pretty fond of you."

"I'm pretty fond of *you*."

"Is that so?" I grin, plucking the other four clips from his hair as well and tossing them on the couch behind him. "I happen to be partial to you myself."

"It's been a good week." He tucks a wave of my hair behind my ear. "*A long week.* I haven't seen nearly enough of you."

"Well, I suppose it's a good thing that Dean forced a nap into our schedule the–"

And then his lips are on mine, like a response would take too much precious time away from kissing me. He pushes me backward, my back thudding against the hallway wall.

I break our kiss, but only enough to speak. "Hey, what if I actually needed a nap?" I smile against his lips, but he doesn't show any signs of playfulness.

"I'd say too damn bad."

"Oh, yeah? What would you rather do?"

"Let's just say you'll be tied up for the foreseeable future." He smirks.

"Finally." I grin and kiss him again. A gasp escapes when he grips my thighs and hoists me up. I wrap my arms around his neck and my legs tight around his waist. Burying my face in his shoulder as he carries me down the hall to his room, I bite his neck, and he groans. I sooth it with a kiss, anxious to have his hands all over me–and his mouth.

Chapter Thirty-Five
Brooke

When we make it to his room, he kicks the door shut behind us so hard my heart rattles in my chest. We reach the foot of his bed, and he releases me, my toes touching the carpet first, my bare feet slowly falling to the floor.

My tank top rides up, leaving a gap between it and my leggings, and Marcus' hands immediately find their way to my skin. His palms run over my stomach, up my sides. Hands flat against my skin, he lets his thumbs catch on the edge of my shirt, pulling it up as he smooths his hands up my body until it's over my head. He tugs his shirt over his head before focusing back on me.

"Fucking hell, you're perfect," he says, tracing the top edge of my bra down each breast until he reaches the clasp in the middle. He unhooks it with ease, then drags it off my shoulders and tosses it to the floor behind us. His hands find my breast and hold firm to them as he leans in. "Do you want your meditation?"

I shake my head. "No. I don't need it." He squeezes hard, my nipples stiffening to his touch and a soft moan escaping my lips. "Marcus," I whisper, my hands still linked around his neck.

"What is it, love?" His hands run back down my sides, gripping my hips and pulling me against him, our skin flush.

I want to be completely consumed by this man again, but I already feel in too deep and want to be sure that it's time for me to fall. "This is real, right?"

"Yes."

I search his face. "I want to stay."

"I *need* you to stay," he counters.

"I don't have a place to live. Or a job. I know technically I'm staying here and am temporarily working for–"

"You are living here. That part isn't negotiable. As for work, whatever you want to do after we get Emma and Charlotte taken care of, I'll help you figure it out."

A sigh of relief leaves me, replaced by a contentment I've never felt before. The lights aren't on, but enough glow from the sunset filters through the window behind the bed. He holds my gaze, his eyes loving and patient and needy all at once. "My entire life it feels like I've been running *from* something or running *toward* somewhere–but I never could figure out what it was. I was chasing an elusive peace while trying to escape the parts of myself I didn't love." His grip on me tightens, his thumbs brushing over the skin above my leggings. "The ocean, yoga, my meditations, glimmers–they helped. But they're no match for you. You're what I've been wandering forever trying to find because you–your voice, your calmness and control, your skin on mine–is what settles my restlessness."

His hands run up and down my back slowly. "You are everything good that money can't buy, Brooke Fields. I can't wait to experience every piece of you."

"Starting right now?" I grin.

He smirks, his fingers hooking on the edge of my leggings. With my hands on his shoulders for balance, he pulls the fabric down my legs slowly, kissing my skin, soft and steady. He's always steady and in control in a way that makes me safe to give mine up.

I step out of my leggings, completely naked in front of him, yet feeling far from vulnerable.

He returns to my level, kissing my lips once. "You're sure you're good with this?" he asks as he reaches behind me and pulls a loop free from between his box spring and mattress.

"Positive." I sit on the edge of the bed and scoot myself backward to the center.

He reaches for my leg, pulling me over the comforter toward the lower left corner of the bed until he can place it on top of the padded velcro strip. "You're not going to have any control."

"I know," I tell him with my gaze intently focused on where he secures the loop around my ankle. He runs his hand up my calf, sending a wave of chill through me. "I trust you to have it."

His gaze bores into me with intensity. Like that fact alone turns him on. He flicks his sight to the edge of the bed long enough to grab another restraint. Tugging my leg toward it, he opens me wide for him. The coolness of the air hits my core, my arms instinctively pulling to my chest to try and warm myself.

Marcus chuckles as he secures the velcro tightly around my ankle, then makes his way to the head of the bed. He reaches for my hands, prying them free from where they are clutched to my chest and brings my fingers to his lips. He presses a kiss to my knuckles and straightens my arms above my head. Locking both of them in place with the loop, he pauses to watch me. I tug my arms down on instinct, my body resisting the restraint against my mind's will. I strain my neck to watch Marcus reach for the strap connecting the loops to the bed and tighten them with a smirk.

Once I'm tied up completely, he gives me a once-over, his gaze heating my body and removing any chill that resided before. Climbing onto the bed from the space between my legs, he runs his hands up my thighs. Eyes locked on where his hands touch me, his thumbs brush over my opening, spreading me apart enough for a jolt of arousal to shoot through me.

A moan escapes me, and he glances up. His hands smooth over my body, up my stomach, gripping my breasts with his knees pressing on my inner thighs, pushing me wider. The stretch hurts in the best way. "I love you laid out for me like this." He wasn't talking directly to me–more to himself as he leans forward, taking a nipple between his teeth and sucking until it hardens. The pressure between my legs throbs with each suck and nip at my skin. He moves to the other side, repeating the pleasure. Holy shit.

I could live the rest of my life being the object of his affection.

I whine, wanting more, *needing* more–anxious to find out what he'll do with his power over my body. He glances up, locking his gaze on mine. "Patience is a virtue, love. I'm going to explore every inch of you and what makes you feel good before I let you come."

I bite into my lip, keeping my eyes on him as he shifts his stare.

He kneels on the mattress, straddling one of my legs, as he drags his fingers down my stomach. They whisper along the apex of my thigh before barely brushing over my opening. "Fucking hell, Brooke. You're already so wet for me." I moan as he spreads me with more pressure. My voice gets caught in my throat as he slips two thick fingers deep inside me, sending a jolt of pleasure through my entire core.

His fingers slide into me slowly. It's heaven and torture all at once, feeling where he connects inside of me as he pushes deeper. When they are as deep as they can go, he pulls them out, watching his movement. "Goddamn, Brooke," he mutters under his breath, his hand shaky as he withdraws his fingers, like he can hardly resist slamming them back inside. *I wish that's what he would do.*

I crave feeling him inside me, in whatever way he'll give me. There's something about it that makes me feel undeniably connected not only to him but to myself. The way he touches me—like I'm precious—it makes me love myself more than I've ever felt. He makes me feel grounded, safe, ecstasy—physically and mentally.

He presses his lips to my thigh, glancing up and catching my gaze for only a moment before his focus is back on where his mouth meets my skin—hot as he trails kisses down my leg, slow and controlled. When he reaches my calf, he pulls back and digs his thumbs into the muscle, massaging the entire length of it.

I let out a moan because holy shit that feels good. And it's not even really sexual? Is it? Who the hell knows. The tension in my leg is released as he presses deep with his palms, only to be replaced by a new tension building in my core.

Adjusting himself between my legs, he works his strong hands into the other, repeating the motion, and I respond in the same way–an uncontainable moan leaving my body along with a week's worth of stress. He runs both hands up either thigh, digging into my skin in a way that leaves a trail of goosebumps. With a tight grip on my hips, he breathes a hot breath over my center, and fuck, I can *feel* myself getting wetter. He doesn't give me what I want, though. He licks the skin just barely away from where I need his tongue, and the wetness combines with his next breath and sends a rush of chills through my entire body.

He nips at the apex of my thigh, his hands running up my side. They each grip the side of a breast, his mouth hot and heavy behind them, latching onto a nipple. He sucks it into his mouth at the same time he squeezes. His teeth clamped around my nipple and his fingers digging into my skin sparks every nearby nerve ending to life in an overwhelming way. The one without his teeth sinking lovingly into my hardened peak gets twisted between his fingers. He's straddling me now, hovering enough above me that I can't find relief from him, but close enough I can feel how hard he is through his jeans. He grinds against me, eliciting a whimper as the rough denim rubs against my sensitive skin.

He chuckles, his breath coming out warm against my chest. Kissing up my neck, his fingers trail behind. He sucks on my neck, dropping more of his weight on me as he brushes his hands up my arms tied above my head. Stopping when he gets to the loops, he runs his grip back down by arms, nipping at my earlobe and grinding his hips again. My thighs burn as they tug at the restraints, wanting to wrap around him.

I let out something between a sigh and a breath. "Marcus," I whine quietly, knowing it will probably just drag out the torture. His lips curve to a smile against my neck and kisses his way to my lips. He presses a hard kiss to my mouth, demanding access. I let him deepen the kiss, straining to lean up, to get closer to him. Fuck this is hard not being able to touch him, not run my hands through his hair. His tongue dances with mine as he locks his fingers at the base of my neck, controlling the kiss as much as he does the rest of my body.

Pulling back, he straddles me again, taking his sweet time dragging his fingers and his eyes down my body. It's like he's learning my body, memorizing it. "The things I want to do to you." His voice is deep, his eyes dark as they focus on where I'm aching to have him inside me.

"Do whatever you want," I breathe with my eyes locked on where his thumb brushes over my skin beneath him, sending a throb of arousal through me, my core clenching. He repositions himself to a previous position, straddling one leg. One hand runs flat over my stomach until it locks on my hip. The tip of his finger presses against my opening, teasing me as he pulses against it. He rubs small circles against my wetness, slipping further inside me with each one. My pulse beats in my pussy against his finger, and I let out a soft whine.

Giving in, he plunges a finger deep inside me. A cry breaks free from my throat, my arms pulling on the restraints, begging to reach for the comforter to cling to. Failing to free myself, I grip my own hands, tangling my fingers together and digging my nails into my skin as Marcus pulls his finger out only to drive it back in along with a second.

But they don't continue in a straight and steady thrusting motion. It *feels* like he hooks one of his fingers so that every time the other one bottoms out inside me, that one hits my G-Spot. Over and over. His hooked finger does some sort of "come here" motion in just the right spot–one that nearly knocks the breath out of me with every sweep. Holy shit. Ecstasy vibrates through my body with each thrust in and out–hitting so deep that my vision goes spotty.

I'm entranced. Watching him watch what he's doing. My teeth sink into my lip as his head dips. My stomach contracts in anticipation of his tongue on me.

And then it is.

His tongue hot and flat across my opening, above where his fingers fuck me. He sucks my clit into his mouth. His other hand grips my hip tighter across my stomach, and he devours me. He eats at me at a pace that matches his fingers deep inside me, his tongue licking across my wet, hot skin. Something about the way he licks me from the side. I have no fucking clue why or how it's different other than that, but it is. And holy fuck is it good. I writhe under his touch, squirming under the intensity of how he's eating me out, alternating between sucking my skin between his lips. He keeps me pinned with his arm across my stomach, but my legs strain, aching to wrap around his head.

He speeds up the thrusts of his fingers but slows the seductive lick of his tongue and my core tightens, both holding back and wanting so badly to fall over the edge. I tighten around his fingers, and he must feel it because he slows his movement, pulling his mouth away from my skin completely.

I whimper, wanting to come. When he breathes a hot breath against my wetness, a chill runs over my skin, then seeps into my body as arousal. He pulls his fingers from me, rubbing them over the apex of my thigh. His tongue follows the path, licking my skin. My pussy clenches as if the contraction could pull his lips and his fingers back to it. My orgasm stays on the edge rather than running away like it usually does.

Marcus nips my inner thigh and pleasure shoots straight to my core, heightened more when he slams two fingers back inside me. I'm tied down so tightly that I can't squirm away from the intense pleasure, so I welcome it. He slams them inside me, bottoming out, and I love the way that I can't escape, can't back out of his reach to lessen the intensity. Then his fingers change direction again, to a bicycle movement that lights up every damn nerve inside of me. What the— My head tips back into the pillow, pulling my gaze from watching as my teeth sink into my lip. His fingers continue, alternating hitting my G-Spot and deep inside me as they cycle around as he thrusts inside me.

"Fucking hell," he curses against my skin. And then his mouth is on me again. Hot and needy, he sucks my skin, releasing it with a pop and a groan. Then his tongue licks me from the side again. And again.

His fingers work magic inside me.

Steady and consistent since the first cry escaped me.

"Holy shit, Marcus."

His name stuttering from my mouth between heated breaths throws him off for only a moment before he's back on track. The next twist of his fingers deep inside shatters me into a thousand pieces as I fly over the cliff.

My breath gets caught in my throat, but it feels like I'm full of air, light and fluffy as my entire body convulses as much as it can while being restrained. My pussy throbs against his fingers, waves of my orgasm trapping them. He pulls them away once the waves start to settle but doesn't hesitate before replacing them with his tongue. He snakes it inside me, licking and sucking my sensitive skin and another jolt hits me.

I cry out again, although it's barely audible under my strangled breath. He continues to lick me slowly, his tongue swiping inside like he's savoring my release. The groan that vibrates through me only extends my orgasm.

When I finally relax on the bed, Marcus pulls away from me.

I shake my head as he walks to the end of the bed, ripping apart the velcro from the restraint at the bottom. Relief from the tension in my hips immediately pulls my legs together. "Holy shit." The urge to cross my arms over my eyes and hide from the intensity of my orgasm is strong, but with the restraints preventing me from doing so, I choose to lock my eyes on his instead.

The decision brings me closer to him somehow, like I handed him another fear and he obliviated it.

He brushes a thumb across my cheek. "You good, love?"

"Not until you feel the way I do right now."

He runs his tongue over his bottom lip, hiding a hint of a smirk. "That can be arranged." With a quick kiss on my lips, he grabs either side of my waist and lifts me a few inches up the mattress, creating some slack. His hands grip both hips tightly, and without any more of a warning, he flips me on my stomach. Despite his roughness, I land softly on the mattress, my still wet and throbbing pussy against the comforter, my hands tied above my head. I thought I'd *like* this, but I had no clue how much I'd *love* it.

Chapter Thirty-Six
Marcus

With a perfect view of Brooke's backside, I can't help but slap her ass. The smack is loud and stings my hand, but any worry that I'm too rough fades when the most perfect sound escapes Brooke's lips–muffled by the pillow under her face. Fucking hell.

Gripping her hips, I give them a sharp tug, pulling her ass into the air. I smooth my hand over the red mark on her skin, kissing it for good measure. Tugging my jeans and briefs off quickly, I return to my position behind her. As I reach for my nightstand drawer, Brooke adjusts her head to look at me–as much as she can while she's tied up. Goddamn, do I love seeing her this way. Mine. With complete trust in me to love her body however I want to. I blindly grab a condom from the drawer, half-ass shoving it closed.

It's not until the foil is pinched between my fingers, ready to be ripped, that I realize I grabbed one out of habit. *I don't want to use it, though.* We didn't the first time and recalling how it felt to be bare inside her. Fucking hell. The thought alone is nearly enough to make me come.

I raise my gaze to look at her beautiful face, flushed from her orgasm, and her tangled hair falling over her back. She eyes me curiously, and I hold the condom out in question.

She shakes her head, not wanting a barrier between us either. I groan at the anticipation of being inside her bare. "We're going to talk about this after," I force out, knowing we should talk about it, realizing how unlike me it is that we haven't–that I trust her in such an irresponsible way.

She nods this time, and it's the end of the conversation for now. Thank fuck. I'm already hard as a rock from devouring her minutes ago, the taste of her release still on my tongue, the memory of my hands exploring her skin fresh in my mind. I toss the condom aside and move my hands to the back of her thighs. She's on her knees, her chest pressed into the mattress as her pussy waits on display for me. My hands run up her legs, letting my thumbs rub over her opening. We both groan at the contact, and I push her apart as I line my cock up with her entrance.

The connection sends a tingle of arousal through my dick, guaranteeing that every bit of it is ready for her. My tip slides in easily, coated with a combination of pre-cum and her own arousal. Too anxious to wait, I hold tight to her hips, digging my fingers in a way I hope leaves a mark, and thrust into her. There's a little resistance as my head pushes inside, but I force my way in until I'm fully seated inside her.

She cries out, but I barely hear it over my own groan. She feels too fucking good. Her warmth envelops me. The way she surrounds me, traps me inside her–I know right fucking now it's going to be a feeling I indefinitely chase. I pull out slowly, her wetness touching every atom of my cock, the ache I've had for her since the first time finally satiated.

Her pussy is already clenched around my cock like she's close already, and it creates resistance as I pull out, begging me to go deeper instead. With just my tip still inside her, I thrust my hips, pulling her deep with my grip on her.

"Holy–" she cries out, her voice cracking before she bites into the pillow beneath her. God, she's hot as hell.

I lean forward, my hands traveling up her sides and grabbing her breasts along with the next thrust. I twist her nipples between my fingers-they're hard in comparison to the rest of my handful. I pull out slowly again, loving the sensation of my dick dragging against her sensitive skin, and aching for her as soon as I'm not fully inside. With another penetrating thrust, my restraint shatters. My climax is so close there's not a chance in hell I can stop myself from coming. I plunge inside her again, one of my hands smoothing down her stomach to find her clit, *needing* her to come with me.

I rub erratic circles against her skin, matching the way I'm slamming into her, nearly out of control. Her arousal lets me slide in each time with ease, and her mounting orgasm clenching against me pulls me deeper. "Come for me, love," I breathe against her back before pressing a kiss to her sweat soaked skin.

My words send her over the edge. She cries out as her pussy tightens around my cock, pulling my orgasm from me with each pulsing wave of hers. I pull away from her back, gripping her hips again to slam into her again and again. Until I'm certain we've ridden through to the end of our climaxes. Even then, a delayed spasm shoots through my entire body, my cock pulsing once more inside her.

She shudders, and I run my hands up her back adding full fledged chills sparking across her skin. On a heavy breath, I pull out of her slowly, immediately missing her warmth but knowing she's probably ready to be untied. Crawling over her, I undo the velcro and her hands relax onto the mattress. Her breathing is steady but heated as I collapse on the bed next to her.

She scoots across the mattress, still on her stomach until she's pressed up against me, and my new life plan is to never leave this fucking bed.

"I might not be able to move until tomorrow," she whispers, exhausted. Her arm reaches across my chest, warm and heavy against my abs.

I reach over, my fingers weaving into her slightly damp hair, brushing it away from where her face is pressed into my chest. "Lucky for you, I love you right here."

She sighs. "I think I just love you."

My heart slams against my chest. "In a way that feels like a made-up word and doesn't make sense?"

She tips her head, glancing up at me. "In a way that makes everything more clear than it's ever been."

I brush my thumb over her cheek. "I've been falling in love with you since the day I bought every Thai tea ingredient in bulk to ensure you never ran out."

"Good thing you're rich enough you can afford that, huh?" She smiles, and I know I'll do whatever it takes to make her do it a million more times.

I smirk, my thumb still smoothing across her skin. "Yeah, good thing."

"I guess we should get this conversation out of the way–seeing as we probably should have had it last week."

I tense up, all of a sudden nervous, knowing what I need to confess. "Yeah, probably a good idea. Was that . . . okay? Hormones make it easy to act like irresponsible teenagers." I chuckle, trying to ease the tension in my chest and joking like this is a poor decision I've made with anyone else. I've never *not* used a condom. It's advice my mentor gave me as soon as I sold my first app that I took very seriously. *You can't trust anyone*, he told me on repeat, *especially when this amount of money is involved*. But Brooke is different. I know it. It's why I want to have this conversation with her even though I've never had it with anyone.

Her laugh vibrates against my chest. "Yeah. But I meant what I said the first time. I'm not on birth control because that shit fucks you up. But I'm really regular. And religious about tracking my cycle."

"Even though you haven't had sex in three years?" I worry maybe I remembered that tidbit of information wrong.

She nods against me, and I breathe and sigh of relief. "Yeah. I mean I always use condoms too. But. Ummm. Actually..." The tension is back, but this time I feel it in her too.

"What?" I encourage her with another brush of my thumb against her cheek.

She cuddles into me more, intertwining her leg with mine. Suddenly, I'm reassured because whatever she's about to say, she's nervous, but leaning in instead of away. She takes a breath. "I don't want to get pregnant. Not just now. Ever."

I take a second to process. "You don't want kids?"

She shakes her head slowly, looking at me, her eyes filled with trepidation. "No. I don't." She takes a breath. "Look, I know this can be a dealbreaker, and I totally understand if–"

I cut her off by tipping her face toward mine and pressing a kiss to her lips. I pull back just enough to whisper, "I don't want kids either."

Her eyes widen, and she pulls away from me, sitting up. "Really?"

I chuckle, the tension dissipating. "I was about to tell you the same thing."

"Really?" she repeats.

"Yeah. I love my sister. I'll be the best fucking uncle when Dean has a kid. But every time I set goals and intentions for my life, kids are never part of it."

"Even after you reach all the other goals you've set?" I can't tell if she's testing me or checking my sincerity.

"I'm already so far gone for you, Brooke Fields. I'll give you anything you ever want or need within the realm of possibility. Except this."

She brushes her fingers over my abs and the sensation of her skin fluttering across mine sends a rush through my entire body. "I can't believe it," she mutters.

I freeze, panic rising in me again. "I'm sorry, but it wouldn't be fair for me to keep that from you if it's something you were set on."

Her eyes light up with her smile. "I meant that disbelief in a good way. It's unreal. You're telling me I found the perfect guy and he's not only *cool* with living childfree, but *wants* it?"

I let out my caged grin at her words and pull her back to me. She obliges, cuddling into my chest and wrapping her arm around my waist. "I'm still perfect even though I'm almost a billionaire?" I poke her side, taunting her, but it only makes her squeeze my waist tighter.

"I'll happily be tied up in riches if it means I'm tied to you."

"Physically or . . ."

She laughs. "Definitely that way, too."

"So, you don't think you'll ever change your mind about kids?" Maybe she was testing me a moment ago, but I feel the need to do the same. We haven't been together for long enough to warrant a lot of serious conversations, but this is the one thing that can't be compromised down the road.

"I'm positive. Kids love me. And I don't mind them. As long as I can give them back. I've never had that maternal instinct or a desire for a 'mini me.' Maybe that's selfish—"

"You are *anything* but selfish, Brooke. I think it says a lot about you that you're self-aware enough to make a decision like this based on how you feel and not what society tells you is supposed to happen."

"So we're on the same page?" she clarifies again.

"Same page, love. Same book. Right place. Right time. The one we've been looking for."

Chapter Thirty-Seven
Brooke

"Do you need me to roast your marshmallow for you?" I tease, shoving two white balls of sugar onto the ends of sticks as Marcus rearranges the fire to reveal more embers.

He smirks, taking a seat in his camping chair and scooting it closer to the one I'm sitting in. "Give me that." He reaches for one of the sticks but kisses me before pulling it away.

I hold my marshmallow over the burning coal and look back at my boyfriend. "Thank you for this week-end. I love when it's just the two of us." It's been three months since we got home from Connecticut and New York and our first full weekend off the grid.

"Of course, love. It's just the first one. We'll do this every month. There are some incredible resorts I want to take you to once it's too cold to camp." He sets his stick down, leaning it against the edge of the firepit, and I do the same.

I take his cue, joining him in his chair. Not caring that it's probably not meant to hold both of us, I straddle him. It creaks but holds up, and he runs his hands up my thighs to my lower back to pull me closer. "I can't wait. These past few months have been so crazy. We could both use the break."

"I couldn't agree more."

I feign shock with a gasp. "Marcus Cole, did you just admit to needing time off work?!"

He smirks. "Watch it, love. I'll take it back."

"You will not," I say, looping my arms around his neck. "You love how things are now."

"I do. I should be the one thanking you." His thumbs rub against my skin under my Columbia jacket.

"Nora is great, isn't she?" Nora is the new assistant he hired to help him with a lot of the paperwork for both his investments and the bar. It's taken a huge amount of work off his plate.

"She's not you, but yes. I'm very happy with her work."

The entire first month after Emma and Charlotte's product was featured on national television was insane. We hardly had time to do anything but secure production and shipping, finalize contracts with bars across the country, and figure out a system to track it all. On top of that, I still ran weekly *Here for the B* events and picked up shifts at the bar to help out temporarily since there was also a boost there from when Emma mentioned it on air.

After that, things started to slow enough that we could take the time to hire another bartender to help Lexy and Jess. It took me about a month after that to help Marcus find the right person to help him, so I could step away from that too.

"I'm sure she's happy with you too. You are the best boss."

"Is that so?"

"Mhmm. As long as I'm the only one receiving bonuses."

He runs his tongue over his bottom lip, and I grind my hips into him.

"Are you ready for next week?" He fends off my pass at him.

"Yes. I can't stop looking at the website you made me. It's so beautiful."

"Fitting. For you. And your company."

I grin. I can't believe as of two o'clock this afternoon, I'm officially a business owner. *Brooke's Boxes*. I put together custom boxes for all kinds of people. I started locally–and unofficially–creating ones for bridal parties and baby showers. I formulated a very detailed–possibly annoyingly so–questionnaire nailing down exactly the vibe of their recipient. No two boxes are the same, each filled with unique or personalized goodies designed to make someone feel extra loved. It's been successful enough that I'm confident it can be profitable on a larger scale–especially since they are so much more personalized than anything currently on the market.

I didn't need much money to start, but Marcus insisted on investing nonetheless, so I didn't have to take out a small business loan. I have to admit, having a wealthy boyfriend who wants to use his money to improve the lives of people around him instead of showing off to them makes all the difference.

"I think we make a pretty good team."

"Me too."

He reaches around me, holding tight to my back so I don't fall as he grabs the marshmallow sticks. With me still cozy on his lap, he holds both sticks together, roasting our treats as much as he can.

When they are a perfect golden, he pulls them be-tween us, and we each pinch the hot gooey dessert from the stick. He blows on mine before I shove the whole thing in my mouth, grinning at him with sticky lips.

He does the same, chewing until he can swallow, then kisses me again. He bites into my lip, and I feel his tongue trail along some sticky residue. Pulling back, he says, "It's absurd to me that I never made time for this before."

"You didn't have me before. And you're stuck with me now, so get used to it."

"Stuck with you or stuck to you?" he asks, gripping my hand in his and licking the rest of the marshmallow off of it.

"Both, if you'd like." I grin, grinding into him again. This time he gives in.

Epilogue
Brooke

"I think I'm coming around to this whole dating rich thing," I tell Marcus, linking my fingers with his and leaning into his side as I take in the interior of the private plane. It's insane to see the difference between people who spend their money just to prove they have it versus spending it to help dreams come true for those they love.

"Is that so?" he looks down at me with a smirk before kissing the top of my head. "Wait until you see the bedroom."

My eyes go wide. "There's a bed? On a plane?" I've seen it in movies, but that's totally different than experiencing it in real life. "I guess we should probably let Maci and Dean have it since it's their wedding, huh?"

He gives me a pointed look. "I'm a giving man. I chartered this plane for them. But, I know for a fact those two have already joined the mile high club. So, this room is ours for the next seventeen hours."

I slap his chest. "We can't stay in there for a whole day."

"Says who?"

"What are you going to do? Handcuff me to the bed?"

He raises a suggestive brow at me. "If you want me to."

I grin. I love this man and everything in life we've explored over the past six months together. It's been mostly work, but Marcus has been so much better about taking time to enjoy other things. True to his word, we've taken a monthly off-the-grid camping trip, and he has a few resorts booked for the start of the year when it'll be too cold. Plus, whenever he can afford a full night off work, he pays a driver to take us to Portland or Vancouver. We've been slowly making our way through the list of breweries, wineries and local restaurants. He's only half the workaholic he was before. And some of his work includes helping me since my business has been killing it the past few months. Once we get back from Australia, Maci and Dean are moving out, and we're turning their room into my office.

As we walk through the aisle of the plane, everyone else is getting situated. We were the last to board as Marcus chatted with the pilot. Dean is hanging everyone's wedding clothes in the closet at the front of the plane. Maci and Avery are sitting next to each other in two massive tan leather seats with their book club book on their lap as they look out the window. Lexy is straddling Troy in a seat across the aisle, whispering what I'm sure are sweet nothings in his ear. Typical. I chuckle, squeezing Marcus' hand, and he kisses my head again. Troy's best friend, Cooper, sits at the window seat in the next row back with Dean's sister, Sophie, lying in his lap, her Kindle held above her face as he runs his fingers through her hair.

Maci and Dean's parents, Marcus' family, along with Avery's husband, their kid, and a few other friends are flying down in a couple of days. The rest of us are going early to celebrate like a joint bachelor and bachelorette.

I do not envy those two planning their guest list. I know Dean's dilemma with whether or not to invite his dad would be similar to one I'd have with my mom. She called about two months after we got home from New York to tell me that Beau was under investigation for disbarment. Of course I already knew that. Marcus' lawyer felt obligated to file a grievance once they found hard proof that he was illegally winning cases. My mom attempted to disguise her holier-than-thou attitude as love and care for me, but I see right through it. She went on about how it's a good thing I didn't end up with him, and that if I was happy without money and felt safe, that's what matters. I chose to keep a few facts about Marcus to myself because she doesn't deserve to know. And she proved me right by dropping all communication with me since–assuming there's no point in her maintaining a relationship that doesn't benefit her. I've felt plenty of love from Marcus' family, though, and Dad has visited twice already. It's more than enough for me now, and I'm so thankful I've let go of my need for my mom's approval.

Marcus leads me to the bedroom in the back, opens the door and guides me through with his hand on my lower back. Looking behind me, I catch Lexy shooting me a wink before we disappear into the room. Marcus closes the door, then backs me up against the queen bed covered in a fluffy white comforter. I fall backward on it, letting it consume me like a cloud. Glancing back to Marcus, I eye him, standing at the end of the bed, staring down at me.

"What?" I grin.

"A glimmer," he says, his elbow propped on his hand across his chest as he runs his thumb across his bottom lip.

"A private jet bed?"

"You." Without giving me time to respond he kicks off his shoes and crawls until he's hovering over me. "You spark joy every time I see you. Think about you. Remember that you exist."

I smile as he brushes his thumb across my cheek, then rolls to his side, not taking advantage of me yet. I turn toward him, my hand landing on the hem of his jeans where his black tee rides up a bit.

He kisses me softly, pulling me closer. "These past six months with you make me angry that I didn't find you sooner."

"I know," I tell him, running my hand up his back and down his side until it's resting on his hip again. "But it's better this way. Everything has fallen into place, you know? I don't think that would have happened if we weren't ready for it–if we hadn't experienced life and lessons the way we did before we met."

"You're right. I'll just have to appreciate all the time in the rest of our lives."

I pause, not concerned about the conversation I've been wanting to have but not exactly jumping to have it. Though, a wedding seems like the perfect excuse to bring it up. "Do you remember what you said to my mom? That day you met her–at lunch."

His thoughts drift back in time before he quickly snaps back to the present with recognition. "About marriage."

I nod.

"What about it?" he asks slowly.

"Do you mean it? That you don't want to get married. That you want to wake up next to someone because you *want* to, not because you're *supposed* to."

He searches my face like he's afraid to give the wrong answer. "I do. How do you feel about that?"

"I think that was part of the reason I left Beau. I'm not afraid to commit to someone. The right someone." I pause, deciding to take a leap. "To you. It's just . . . what you said really resonated with me."

"I meant it. It's something I've thought about a lot since I first heard it. I would reconsider if it's something you wanted, though."

I smile at the consideration and him holding true to no kids being his only non-negotiable when it comes to me. "I'm so happy Maci and Dean are taking this step. I think it was almost," I search for the right word, "necessary? Because he didn't commit to her for so long, you know?"

He nods in agreement.

"And Lexy and Troy. Marriage is everything they didn't think they'd ever have. Now that they get to see it in a new light–that it can be something healthy–I think it means so much that they get to live happily ever after that way. But me? When I was supposed to marry Beau, it was a contract. I was signing up to act a certain way, be a certain way. I know it wouldn't be like that with you. But I don't feel pulled to try it any other way. I like how we are now."

"I love how we are. I'd marry you in a heartbeat, love. But I don't need to sign a piece of paper to stick around.

I want to continue to grow with you, learn new things, *try new things*." He wiggles his eyebrows at that. "Be whoever we want to be with trial and error until we find versions of ourselves we love in whatever season of life we're in. We don't need a couple of rings to walk that path."

"Or a prenup." I make a face.

"I would never make you sign a prenup."

"I thought you were a smart businessman," I tease. "I would make me sign one."

"Well it's a good thing we aren't getting married then, isn't it? Plus, you're not doing too bad yourself." He grins, proud.

Last month, I secured a deal with the cancer wing of the hospital. Through donations, family members can fill out the forms for their sick loved ones. One company downtown hired me to make boxes for over one hundred of their employees, loving the idea that they can show they aren't just another corporation that treats all their workers as replaceable and the same. It's better than I ever dreamed when I initially had the idea to make my first boxes for Emma and Charlotte.

"I couldn't have done it without you."

"Yes, you could have. But I'm so damn glad I get to do it with you. Best investment I've ever made."

"Because your stake in my company is paid out in sex?" I ask, teasing him. Of course he's a true share-holder.

He chuckles. "I hope you don't give the bonus you give me to any of your other investors."

"Lucky for me, my boyfriend is rich." My playful grin widens. "I don't need any other investors."

He goes serious. "You know, even if I didn't earn another penny, I'd still be rich. I'll always be rich as long as I have you."

I roll my eyes even though I love his cheesy lines. "I love you."

He leans in, pressing his lips to mine, then only pulling back marginally. "I love you."

"Good." I grin. "Now let's join that mile high club you were talking about."

More by Tisa Matthews

If you loved this story, check out the **Finding Home** series on Kindle Unlimited.

And Then There's You is book one, following Maci's love triangle with Mack and Dean.

I Love You, So What? is book two, following Lexy and Troy's story.

Can We Just Be Happy Now? is book three, following the story of Dean's sister Sophie, and Troy's best friend Cooper.

Tied Up In Riches is book four, following the story of Brooke and Marcus.

While books three and four can be read as stand-alones, books one and two of the series should be read in order for the best experience.

Home is an extended epilogue featuring a POV chapter from each main character in the series! It's meant to be read after you've finished the series!

Unhitched is a standalone, modern day romance jam packed with 2000s nostalgia and swirled around with the turning 30 identity crisis. It's written by a millennial for millennials.

Acknowledgements

This story was never supposed to be written.

In book one, *And Then There's You*, Dean needed a friend. He needed someone who would always be in his corner during the battle of a love triangle. I racked my brain for a vision I could create, but for some reason, the same image kept coming to mind. The only character initially based on a real person in my life, Marcus was inspired by my favorite friend of anyone I ever "dated." He was the guy you were immediately comfortable with, even if the guy you were seeing left the room. He's the guy who will have *real* conversations with you, is loyal to a fault, the one you can't help but love, a loss that hits as hard as an inevitable college breakup. And apparently, he's the guy who makes for killer book character inspiration. So, my first and most important acknowledgment for this book is Madison. Thank you for being the guy you had absolutely no clue I needed a decade ago and for still being my friend now. For inspiring a character who not only is a likable and favorite side character but who was loved so much that I was pressured into writing him an entire story of his own. While the Marcus in this book has become his own person, he wouldn't exist if it wasn't for you.

I'll start this next part with a PSA: NEVER, I mean NEVER, name a character after a best friend. Because as I learned not once, but TWICE from this story ... sometimes side characters become main characters, and it's completely out of your control, and then you will regret it every single day. Especially when you have to make them fall in love and have sex and all you can picture is said friend for the first like four drafts. Hahah. Brooke, we gave Brooke her name on a whim–as a joke when I needed a name for a girl who was only supposed to play a small role in Maci's self-discovery journey. Eventually, she turned into someone so much bigger–in Maci's story and in the Finding Home family. But I guess that's how it kind of worked out with us, isn't it? You were a girl I met on the internet, and while we clicked quickly, there was no way of knowing our friendship would turn into what it is now. I'm so thankful for you always being the first set of eyes on my book and the first pair of ears in my life. I love you.

Despite my initial struggles of name/personality as-sociation with Marcus and Brooke, this story was so much easier for me to write than any of the previous three. Their journey came to me so effortlessly that I questioned the lack of edits compared to my other books. But I just knew what I wanted their story to look like from the moment I decided they deserved their own. Still, this book wouldn't have come together the way it did without a few other people too.

Arianna, you're always there to hype me up, to sup-port me as an author, to create the most beautiful flay-lays–but those aren't even the *best* things about you. You're always up at 3 a.m. to let me run an idea by you. You listen without judgment and hop in the car to delulu land with me. Our paths crossed because you met and love Cooper, and how much you love him is not even a sliver of how much I love you.

Meesha, no one lives in delusion about my characters being real as much as you do, and it's everything to me. The way you send me pictures of Dean and Maci's house, randomly text me to tell me you're thinking about a specific person and daydream with me about what they are doing with their lives, it's everything. The same words always seem to hit us equally hard, and each time it gives me that real feeling of someone understanding me. I'm so thankful for that.

To all my other friends who took precious time out of their busy lives to read early drafts, pre-edited copies, forgave me for ridiculous typos and mistakes where I knew better, THANK YOU. Your commitment to helping me when you have a hundred other priorities and a million other things you could have been doing means everything to me.

Specifically:

Heather (@heathergarvinbooks) and Bri (@author_b_izzo), my published friends, for pausing their own editing schedules to help me with mine.

Caitlin (@caitsbooknook) for helping me make sure my lawyer-y pieces made sense.

Stephanie (@the.bookish.dogmom) for verifying my childfree by choice conversations/actions felt authentic to real life.

Jason for being my Objectiveness.

Kortney (@kortcomebooks) for catching all my missing letters amongst editing your debut novel.

Kristen for making sure my characters felt in alignment with their personalities.

Katelyn for helping me secondhand with "research." This comes out weird, but she knows what I mean.

Katie (@nose.stuck.in.abook) for being one of my very first bookstagram friends two years ago, when I was still nervous to dive into this space and share part of my soul.

Maeghen (@maeghenmarie_reads) and Amanda (@amanda.readsbooks) for helping with a final proofread!

All of you, and so many others who gave their opinion on artwork details and scene specifics, had mini brainstorming sessions with me, shared posts, hyped me up, love my characters the way I do–you make this journey worth it.

You all are my glimmers every single day, and this book–my life–is so much more beautiful because of you.

PLAYLIST

Just Friends - Why Don't We
She Ain't Takin Your Call - Chase Wright
Home - Good Neighbours
Let's Go Home - Jake Miller
Vegas - Johnny Orlando
Keeping Score - Dan + Shay, Kelly Clarkson
Tomorrow - Fly By Midnight
Stargazing - Myles Smith
State of Grace (Taylor's Version) - Taylor Swift
Infinitely Falling - Fly By Midnight
Before You - Benson Boone
Onto Something - Jamie Miller
Your Bones - Chelsea Cutler
past life - elijah woods
Don't You Worry - Mark Ambor
Heartworks - Wingtip

About the Author

Tisa Matthews is an open-door contemporary romance author. She shares the same wanderlust as so many of her characters, moving states every few years for new surroundings, inspiration and stories—for life and writing. She is currently located in Vancouver, Washington where she loves exploring the Portland/Vancouver craft beer and food scene.

<u>CONNECT ONLINE:</u>
@tisa.matthews.books

www.ingramcontent.com/pod-product-compliance
Lightning Source LLC
Chambersburg PA
CBHW020238010826
48973CB00006B/1570